Tainted 3:

The Finale

T0178975

Tainted 3:
The Finale

Blacc Topp

www.urbanbooks.net

Urban Books, LLC
300 Farmingdale Road, N.Y.-Route 109
Farmingdale, NY 11735

Tainted 3: The Finale Copyright © 2024 Blacc Topp

ISBN 13: 978-1-64556-665-6

First Trade Paperback Printing November 2024
Printed in the United States of America

10 9 8 7 6 5 4 3 2 1

Distributed by Kensington Publishing Corp.
Submit Orders to:
Customer Service
400 Hahn Road
Westminster, MD 21157-4627
Phone: 1-800-733-3000
Fax: 1-800-659-2436

Chapter 1

Money Talks

Kochese lay perfectly still in the wooden coffin. He was being transported across the Mexican border by one of Manny's men under the guise of a dead man. Francisco Alvarez had been born in Forney, Texas, to parents who had been nationalized years earlier. They'd moved back to Mexico after they'd saved enough money to give them a leg up in their home country, but Francisco had opted to stay in the United States and had subsequently joined the US Navy. He'd served in the navy and, unfortunately, met his untimely demise while doing routine naval maneuvers off the coast of Yemen. His parents had insisted that his remains be shipped back to his homeland to be buried among his ancestors rather than being interred in the naval cemetery. But Francisco's parents didn't give a shit where Francisco was buried after Manny offered the family $50,000 US to use Frankie's identity long enough to get King Kochese into Mexico.

Kochese could hear the sound of voices growing closer. At first, the Spanish was muffled, but it grew louder as they approached the van. The rusty hinges of the van's door creaked loudly as his transporter opened it. "*Estoy transportando el cadaver. El es un hero de guerra,*" the transporter said.

Kochese didn't speak Spanish—only a few curse words—but he wasn't an idiot either. He recognized the words "transport," "cadaver," and "hero." The transporter was probably explaining to the border patrol that he was transporting the dead body of a war hero. Kochese stared up through the perforated cross on the lid of the casket, waiting to see the hand of the young Mexican man who had been entrusted to help him gain safe passage into Mexico. When he saw his hand, it would be his signal to draw a deep breath, hold it, and appear dead, but the signal never came.

No, instead, he heard the grizzled voice of the border patrolman whisper, "*No voy a molestar a los muertos,*" then, just as quickly, he heard the doors slam. Minutes later, they were on the road again.

"Señor King, we will be clear in approximately ten minutes if you wish to climb out of that box," Chico said.

"All right, cool. So what was all of that chatter about back there, mane?" Kochese asked, lifting the lid of the coffin.

"The *policia* was a curious old man, but here in Mexico, there is a profound respect for *los muertos,* or the dead. I simply explained to him that I was transporting your dead body and that you were a war hero, to which he replied that he would not disturb the dead."

Kochese climbed out of the casket and into the front seat, pondering the fate of Jasmine and his children. They sped down the road, leaving a cloud of dust behind them. The deserted road stretched ahead, flanked by endless desert on both sides. Kochese stared straight ahead, trying mentally to formulate a plan to reunite his family. Jasmine would have the twins soon, and he would not let his children grow up in the system. He'd put a few plans into motion but would have to reach Costa Rica safely before they could be executed. "Yo, did Manny give you the things I asked for, Chico?" Kochese asked.

"Sí, Señor. If you look in the bag beneath your feet, you'll see all your requested documentation."

Kochese slowly unzipped the bag. Inside was a passport, an ID card, $50,000, and a CURP card. The Clave Unica de Registro de Poblacion was Mexico's equivalent of the United States's Social Security card. The plan was simple. He'd be smuggled into Mexico with his fake paperwork and hop a plane bound for Costa Rica. There were very few countries where the United States didn't have extradition treaties, and Costa Rica was no different. Manny had connections in the third-world country, though, and with the sheer amount of wealth that Kochese had at his disposal, going into the country and amassing a strong presence, complete with protection from the government, wouldn't be a problem.

They pulled into a ramshackle town not even twenty miles from the border they'd just crossed. Children chased chickens through the streets, trying desperately to poke them with the sticks that they carried. Mothers bounced whining babies on their knees, attempting to comfort them from the sweltering heat. Ahead of him in the distance, a vehicle sped toward them. Kochese couldn't determine the type of vehicle it was because the heat waves distorted his view. An elderly Mexican man walked slowly, herding his team of goats through the streets, oblivious to the speeding vehicle headed in his direction. As the Jeep approached them, Kochese noticed it said *Policia* on the side. Panic set in, and Kochese fidgeted in his seat uncomfortably. He contemplated shooting first and asking questions later, but he was in a foreign country. Maybe he could pay his way out of his police troubles. In the US, the agents lived their holier-than-thou lifestyles, often refusing to take payouts for fear of reprisals. The United States had convinced many agents that honor was worth more than the almighty dollar—fools! Money talked, and bullshit ran a marathon. Kochese had seen enough and done enough to know that honor didn't pay the bills.

The green Jeep pulled alongside them and came to a stop. Chico and the two officers exchanged rapid words, then Chico turned to Kochese. "Señor King, this is where we part ways. These men will escort you to the airport. It was a pleasure making your acquaintance, sir, and I will see you in Costa Rica," Chico said.

Kochese didn't speak. He nodded in Chico's direction, grabbed his bag, and climbed into the Jeep with the police.

As they drove, Kochese thought about Jasmine, his sweet Jasmine, the mother of his unborn children. It had started as a game with him, using her as a pawn to get back at her snitching-ass sister, Monica. But after getting to know her, *seeing* the real her, feeling her, hearing her, he fell in love. She accepted him for who he was, and he, in turn, did the same. She was different—*they* were different from other people. It was almost as if they were telepathic in the way that they could read each other, something Kochese had never felt before, even when he thought he loved Monica. Monica had played him, making him look stupid to the underworld in Dallas. Not only had she been a federal agent, but she had also infiltrated his circle and, consequently, infiltrated his bed. Special Agent Monica Dietrich had taken Kochese's heart and his empire. Bird, Drak, and Monica had all betrayed him and left him for dead, but Jasmine had been his savior, and as much as he wanted to burn down the city of Dallas to get her back, he had to be smart. The Feds were crawling all over Dallas after Jasmine's capture, and his face had been plastered all over the news. Everywhere he turned, someone was staring or whispering into their cellphones. Kochese was public enemy number one, and he knew it. The only way to escape the death penalty and have any shot at getting back to Jasmine and his kids was to disappear.

They pulled into the small General Lucio Blanco International Airport. It mostly held tiny single-engine Cessna planes. Kochese would be able to inconspicuously board the plane and be in Costa Rica in a little under three hours. His destination was the coastal town of Limon, Costa Rica. There, he could ingratiate himself with the townspeople. What they likely considered real money, he considered pennies, and he knew it.

"Money talks. I don't give a fuck what language it's speaking," Kochese said aloud.

Chapter 2

Stone-Cold Bitch

"Jasmine, you have to talk to me. Where did Kochese go? I'm sure he told you. You're still protecting him, but he left you for dead," Monica screamed.

Jasmine only stared at her. She didn't have any conversation for Monica. Her twins were due any day, and she was handcuffed to a hospital bed. A single tear ran down her cheek, not from sadness but anger. If she could free herself, she'd strangle the life from Monica. Her sister treated her as if she were just one of her suspects. They were blood, though, and if Monica knew what Jasmine knew, she'd distance herself from the situation. Her only concern now was not losing her children. Kochese had promised they'd all be together, and she trusted his word implicitly. "Kochese is going to kill you, Moni. He's going to split you open and paint the streets of Dallas with your entrails if you don't let me go," Jasmine said calmly.

"Jasmine, you're blinded by love right now. Kochese took all of his money and disappeared. He's not coming back, Jasmine. He never loved you. He only used you to get to me. Why can't you see that?"

"Get the fuck out of my room. Nurse . . . Nurse!" Jasmine screamed.

Almost immediately, a nurse appeared. "I'm going to have to ask you to leave, ma'am. Miss Deitrich is in a delicate state right now, and I can't have you upsetting her," she said.

"Miss Deitrich is not only my sister but also a federal prisoner."

"She may be a federal prisoner, but right now, she's my patient, and the safety of her and these children are my only priority. So again, I'm going to have to ask you to leave, please," the nurse said more firmly.

Monica turned on her heels and walked away in a huff. She stopped and looked over her shoulder as she exited Jasmine's hospital room. Her baby sister, her Jazzy Bell, was staring at the ceiling. Her hair was wild and dull. No longer did it hold its healthy luster. Tears stained Jasmine's cheeks as she shot Monica a brief, pain-filled but hate-driven glance. It was in that solitary moment in time that Monica knew without a doubt that she'd lost Jasmine forever. She was worth saving, and she was more than worth believing in, but there was nothing Monica could do. She needed to find Kochese, though. It was imperative because, knowing King Kochese the way that she did, he wouldn't rest until he destroyed her.

It was no longer about right and wrong or good versus evil. It was about self-preservation. Between Jasmine's brain and Kochese's unlimited resources, they'd carved out a niche in American folklore as murderous masterminds. The story of the gruesome murders that they'd committed had been plastered on every front page and aired on every news outlet until it had essentially made the duo famous. It subsequently propelled Monica into a position she didn't particularly care for. Depending on who was asked, Monica Deitrich was either a media darling or a social pariah. Some looked upon her as the agent who put the nation's safety above her personal feelings for her sister, and they loved her for it. Others saw her as a traitor to family values and couldn't be trusted. She hadn't forced Jasmine—or Kochese, for that matter—into the life they'd chosen . . . or had she?

She'd pondered as much on the nationally syndicated *Nancy Grace Show,* and to the general viewing audience, she appeared torn and contrite. Her superiors had even admonished her because she'd hired attorney Richard "Racehorse" Haynes to defend Jasmine. *TIME* magazine named him one of the top six criminal defense attorneys in America, and although Monica didn't believe that Jasmine would ever walk free again, it was worth a shot.

Monica zipped up her coat and shoved her hands deep into her pockets. Winter had fallen upon Texas with her full fury, and as she exited the hospital, the cold, crisp wind whistled and whipped about her body, causing her to shudder from the rigid temperatures. She tried desperately to bury herself deeper into her red London Fog hooded trench coat but to no avail. The cold stabbed at her, piercing her frame, invading and setting up shop in her already frigid bones.

Monica sprinted to the parking garage across the street from the hospital, careful not to slip on the faint iciness that had begun to settle on the spaghetti bowl of roads and streets that wound through Dallas. The cold dulled her usually astute senses, and she was oblivious to her surroundings. She never noticed the two hooded figures that followed closely behind her, shadowing her every move.

Chapter 3

Realer than Fiction

Kochese nestled into the thick comforter that lined the king-sized bed. A light, muffled snore escaped the pit of his stomach, and he stirred but did not wake. Somewhere from beyond his dream state, he called to Jasmine, and she answered him. The sound of her voice startled Kochese. She sounded distressed, a hollow and desperate cry for help, beckoning to him from somewhere far away.

Then he saw her. She was in the middle of the ocean and appeared to be drowning as Kochese watched helplessly from the shore. He tried to go to her, but his feet were mired in muck. His body felt heavy, and the more he tried to move, the heavier he felt. Her head disappeared underneath the water and then reappeared moments later. Behind her and just out of her reach, Kochese saw a canoe drifting further out to sea. Only now, he was no longer standing on the banks but floating above the water, suspended between Jasmine and the canoe. As the canoe drifted further out into the ocean, he could make out the faces of two small children, a boy and a girl, who appeared to be no older than 4, maybe 5 years old. They looked neither bothered nor concerned about being separated from their mother. They stared up at Kochese, reaching for him. The piercing shade of turquoise that their tender eyes held was an exact mixture of Kochese's ocean-blue eyes and Jasmine's jade-green peepers.

"Kochese," Jasmine cried. But he didn't answer. Again, she screamed, "Kochese!" This time, he turned briefly from the children to give Jasmine his attention. "Baby, please save the twins, my love; save Angel and Apache." Kochese was torn. He reached for Jasmine, his hand barely grazing hers before she sank beneath the murky waters. He turned to the twins that Jasmine had affectionately called Angel and Apache. In the place where they had once sat were only skeletal remains, and sitting directly behind them and rowing the canoe away from Kochese was Monica. Fog rolled in from all directions, and then they were gone. Only the sinister glow of Monica's green eyes remained as they disappeared into the hazy fog. Kochese opened his mouth to scream, and his body dropped beneath the water.

He awoke with a start, bolting straight up in bed, and looked around. His pajamas were soaked with sweat, and he was short of breath. When reality set in, it made his heart ache. The realness of the dream had lulled him into a state of false tranquility. The dream had been so vivid, so lifelike, that Kochese had woken up crying. He reached to wipe the tears from his eyes, but there were no tears . . . only bandages. He looked around the plush room and nearly panicked until he realized what had happened.

Soon after he'd arrived in Costa Rica, he'd purchased the beautiful villa overlooking the ocean. It was nothing short of an awe-inspiring compound. He had a full staff of maids, butlers, and security personnel. What it would typically take to pay two people in the US and keep them happy was more than enough to keep his staff of ten satisfied and gainfully employed. With the average income in Costa Rica being under $1,500 a month, Kochese's employees earned $3,000 a month and were beyond grateful. The locals were clamoring to work for the gringo with no history and limitless dinero. He'd hired Manny and Chico as his heads of security, even commissioning them to find loyal soldiers who needed money and, more importantly, had a desire to kill if necessary.

Kochese had opted to have his reconstructive surgery at home for fear that the local Ticos would have him kidnapped in hopes of getting their hands on his money. His favorite of all of his staff was his chief maid, Lucinda. She had to be in her early sixties and was the gentlest soul he'd ever met. She barely spoke English, enough to get her point across but not enough to be annoying.

The room of Kochese's villa sat facing the Caribbean, and there were no walls, only large, thick panes of glass that gave Kochese an almost 270-degree view of his surroundings. He took the remote from the nightstand and clicked a button. Seconds later, the glass panes began to retract, opening the room to the outside world. He stood at the edge of his bedroom where the glass had once been and where the infinity pool began, looking out over the ocean. He'd come a long way from the "dirty little half-breed," as his mother had called him on so many occasions. He could own Costa Rica if he wanted, and he would, but that was the furthest thing from his mind.

"*¿Disculpe,* Señor King?" Lucinda said.

"Yes?" King said without turning around.

"You shouldn't be out of bed, sir. You need your rest."

"I feel fine, Lucinda. You worry too much. How many hours did I sleep? Oddly enough, I feel well-rested," King said.

Lucinda chuckled a little and walked to Kochese. "My dear Mr. King, you've been asleep almost four days."

King Kochese couldn't believe what he was hearing. He felt refreshed but weak. He'd lied to Lucinda, hoping she'd just let it go and not launch into one of her many speeches about King taking care of himself.

"Lucinda, I need for you to summon Manny and Chico. Also, I need you to send the doctor in as well. That'll be all," Kochese said as he walked out onto the expansive backyard. He sat at a poolside table dressed in white linen pajama bottoms and slippers. It was still winter in most parts of the US, but the weather was extremely tropical in Costa Rica. The sun's rays bathed Kochese with sultry warmth. He welcomed the heat and basked in its radiant glow. He had no idea what time it was, but judging from the sun's position, Kochese surmised it was noon or thereabouts.

"Hey, El Rey, you wanted to see us?" Manny asked.

"Yeah, but before we get started, I need for this fucking doctor to hurry up. Yo, you told him to leave the scar, right?"

"Yes, we made sure he understood to leave the scar," Chico said.

"Good—" Kochese started.

But his sentence was cut short by the appearance of his cosmetic surgeon. The elderly Spanish man came scurrying in Kochese's direction. He clutched his doctor's bag close to his chest and had a fretful look on his face. Kochese was sure that Manny had spread rumors—*true* rumors, mind you—of King Kochese's ruthlessness so he could totally understand where the man's apprehension came from. Kochese snickered. He wasn't exactly the boogeyman. He just happened to deal with bullshit on an entirely different level than most. King Kochese stood as the elderly man approached. He appeared to be on the verge of pissing himself as he looked nervously from Kochese to his henchmen and back to Kochese.

"Dr. Delgado, please have a seat," King ordered, pointing to an empty seat across from him, then continued. "Doctor, I need for you to cut these bandages from my face, and then I need for you to forget that you ever heard of me. Do you think that you can handle that? Before you answer, let me show you something," Kochese said. With his eyes still trained on the doctor, he snapped his fingers, and Chico produced a manila envelope.

Kochese tossed it onto the table between the two of them. Pictures spilled from the envelope. There was a confused look on the doctor's face as his eyes frantically searched the flicks. In one picture, the physician posed lovingly with his wife, Amelda. In another, he doted over his then-pregnant daughter Alicia and her husband, Roberto. The following few pictures were of his pride and joy, his young grandson, Julian Delgado. In another picture, Dr. Delgado is shown at a symposium accepting an award for his missionary work in war-torn Uganda. The following pictures showed him being mounted and violated by his West African lover, Kwasi. The photographs showed the old man in various stages of homosexual deviation. In one picture, Dr. Delgado was handcuffed to the headboard of a seedy hotel room bed with a red ball gag in his mouth. Kwasi was performing fellatio on the old man's semi-erect penis, and the doctor's eyes rolled back in his skull as if he had found the fountain of youth, ecstasy clearly written across his geriatric features.

"Don't look so alarmed, Dr. Delgado. Your sexual preference is your business, and as long as you keep your mouth closed about your procedural practices, then you have nothing to worry about. Your beautiful wife, daughter, and handsome grandson don't need to know that you're a shit packer, sir. Just in case that wasn't enough motivation, understand me when I tell you that if you cross me, I have no compunction about splitting each one of them from their eyelids to their assholes. I will dissect them and make you watch me do it. *Entiendes?*" Kochese asked.

With tears welling in his eyes, Dr. Julio Delgado slowly nodded his understanding of King Kochese's threats.

"Good. I'm glad we understand each other. Now, cut this shit off of my face. Let's see what the face that's going to torture Monica Deitrich looks like," Kochese said. A low, guttural groan escaped from somewhere deep within his bowels. A sinister muttering followed and then laughter . . . unshakable, unstoppable laughter.

Dr. Delgado made his way toward Kochese with shaking hands. In his mind, he could only think, *Este hombre es el diablo.*

He had no idea how right he was. King Kochese Mills was indeed the devil—the devil reincarnated.

Chapter 4

Lonely Is the Throne

"I've been keeping an eye on her just like you asked, my nigga. They have her on lock, but I'm working my jelly."

"A'ight, bet. Yo, did you handle that other thing for me?" Kochese asked.

Nae smiled. She knew that her old boss would be pleased with her. She didn't give two shits about men— any man, for that matter—but King Kochese was different. He'd helped her in more ways than she could count, and her loyalty to him was insurmountable. He'd never judged her, and even when everyone else around them told Kochese that he couldn't trust the lesbian, he'd taken a chance on her. So there was nothing Kochese could ask of her that she wouldn't do. If there was one thing that Nae knew better than anything else, it was how to seduce and manipulate women, so when Kochese commissioned her to kidnap his and Jasmine's twins, she was all for it. He'd gone as far as to tell her that if she merely set it up, he'd pay her $250,000, but if she actively participated, he'd give her an additional $250,000.

For weeks, Nae had watched the neonatal unit at Parkland Hospital until she'd found what she was looking for. She'd virtually stalked the young nurse's aide who worked the graveyard shift in the neonatal unit. She watched Koshi Blake, and the young girl most definitely had eyes for other females. Whether she'd taken the lesbian plunge was a different story, but Nae would most certainly try her hand. Koshi had the same regimented schedule every night: arrive at work by 7:00 p.m., make her rounds, check the babies, break at 11:00 p.m., sit in the hospital cafeteria having coffee until midnight, disappear into a hospital break room until around 4:00 a.m., and then clock out at 7:00 a.m.

Nae had stepped to Koshi as she sat alone in the cafeteria, having her nightly coffee and scrolling through her smartphone. She looked bored and fed up with the idea of working the nocturnal schedule. Nae knew from experience that when a person had had enough of any job, when they were at their wit's end, that's when they were the most vulnerable and the most susceptible to suggestions concerning money.

"Excuse me, may I join you?" Nae asked.

Koshi looked up from her phone and eyed the girl curiously. "It's a free country."

Nae sat and watched patiently as the girl continued playing with her phone. "Are you having fun?" Nae asked.

"Not really."

"I can tell," Nae said wistfully.

"And how is that?"

"It's written all over your face. It seems like you'd rather be doing me—I mean, doing something else," Nae teased. She noticed the flustered look that washed over Koshi's face and smiled.

"What makes you think I like girls?"

"I'm pretty good at those types of things. You feel me? Am I wrong, though?"

"I mean, I haven't tried being with another woman, but it has crossed my mind."

"So you're bisexual?" Nae asked.

"I'm neither. I'm a virgin," she said.

"Really? Yummy, yummy," Nae said, licking her lascivious lips. Those were the types of women she loved, the ones who'd never been penetrated by the male species and who'd never been touched by the female tongue. They were the easiest to turn out, and Nae relished the opportunity. "So, what if I told you I wanted to make you my girlfriend?" Nae asked.

"What if I told you I was hoping we would have this conversation from the moment you sat down?"

"That's good to know . . . very good to know," Nae said with a sly grin.

It was as easy as pie, and with Koshi as her inside person, she'd all but solidified a surefire plan. She explained all of this to Kochese, and he still had questions. For as long as she'd known him, he'd always been cautious *and* thorough, so his questions came as no surprise.

"How do we know that we can trust her, Nae?" Kochese asked.

"Because I'm spreading that quarter around, Chief. I only offered her twenty-five stacks, which she hastily took because she's in love with a bitch. Plus, her ass owes Uncle Sam like fifteen for some bullshit nursing program. Yo, remember ol' soft-ass, tricking-ass Junior from the Grove? Well, since you've been gone, that fuck nigga is on his ass from tricking with them bitches, so I offered him twenty-five, and he's with it. He'll be looking out when shit goes down. Altogether, I hired six people, but nobody knows *who* the babies are. They just know it's a job."

"A'ight, I trust you, my nigga. Just make damn sure everything is tight. Have you seen any Feds or police around the hospital since they admitted her?" Kochese asked.

"Just a couple of city cops rotating shifts. No Feds, though. That bitch Moni's ratchet ass is up here on the regular, though. I got a couple of people keeping their eyes on her."

"I'm willing to bet my life that that bitch Monica has Feds planted throughout the hospital. You can believe that," he scoffed.

"Yeah, probably so, but dig these blues, playboy. Two of the cats that I hired are hitters, so if shit gets out of hand, we're straight because they'll handle that. They don't give a fuck who they pop, you feel me?"

"Fa sho'. A'ight, Nae, I'll check in with you in a week or so. If something jumps off before I get in your ear, hit me up," Kochese said before disconnecting the call.

"Is everything okay, papi?" Manny asked.

"Yes, everything is lovely. What could be better? I'm a wealthy man, I'm about to welcome a gorgeous set of twins into the world, and I'm in an exotic land where the people see me as a god," Kochese bragged. He stood and opened his arms, gesturing toward the sparkling blue water for emphasis.

"You got that right, baba. The way you've been spreading money around and putting people to work virtually makes you untouchable in Costa Rica."

"Yeah, not to mention the US doesn't have an extradition treaty with Costa Rica, so I ain't worried about shit," Kochese exclaimed.

"Yes, they do, papi. Don't buy that shit. But you're one of the wealthiest men here, so as long as you keep a low profile, you'll never be touched."

"And how exactly does a man with more than a billion dollars keep a low profile, Manny?" Kochese asked.

"I don't know, baba, but we need to keep you out of the public's eye. There are haters everywhere, papi, you feel me?"

Chico sat mute to the conversation. He had known Manny for years and was loyal to him to a certain extent, but he *knew* Manny. Manny liked money, and the more money, the better. Since Chico had met Kochese, he'd watched him closely, and one of the things that he liked most about the man was that he was extremely loyal—to a fault almost. He gave genuinely and never asked for anything in return. Chico wasn't stupid. Of course, he knew that Kochese was a killer, but he gathered that Kochese was a killer out of necessity. Manny's conversations with Chico concerning Kochese were always conflicting. At times, his words bordered on adoration, and at other times, Manny allowed his envy to show through clearly, and it teetered on the verge of hatred. In Kochese's face, Manny was always *extra* helpful and *extra* attentive, just . . . *extra.*

"So, Chico, what do you think that I should do? You think I should keep a low profile?" Kochese asked.

"Honestly, El Rey, I think with the amount of money that you have and the love that you're getting from the Ticos here, you should do whatever the fuck you want to do. Even if the US came for you, the locals won't let them get within 100 yards of you without you knowing about it. No, *vato*, I think that you should do what you said from the beginning. I think that you can and should own this fucking town."

King Kochese looked at Chico for a long while, then at Manny, and then back at Chico. Although he was Mexican, Chico reminded him of Bird—not the double-crossing Bird, but the Bird that he'd grown to love over the course of their dealings. They had the same athletic build and angular face, and Chico couldn't have been much older than Bird would have been. Bird was only a kid when he and Kochese met, and he was desperate to get into the game. Kochese had tried to caution him against it, but he wanted in, and Kochese relented.

"Once you in, you in, little nigga," he had told Bird.

"I'm a loyal-ass dude, bruh. I'm just trying to get money."

And Bird had lived up to his word. He got money, and he was loyal. Well, he was loyal until he wanted to get out of the game. But there was no getting out of the game with Kochese unless you paid the toll with your life, a fact that he had preached to Bird on more than one occasion. So, for his insolence, Kochese sliced his ebony face. In turn, Bird had introduced him to Monica, the DEA agent. Chico's loyalty was all action, and he never spoke of "trust." He was secretive but not sneaky.

Manny, on the other hand, was the opposite. He tried too hard to convince Kochese of his loyalty. He was a chronic name-dropper, and it annoyed Kochese. Oh, by his account, he was good friends with Óscar Arias, Costa Rica's president. He would also brag about his alleged affair with Debi Nova. She was a gorgeous Costa Rican actress, and Manny couldn't stop talking about her. Kochese was nobody's fool, though. He knew that Manny was using him, and he'd made up his mind that if Manny so much as breathed wrong in his presence, he'd person-ally rip his heart out and roast it in a sautéed mushroom sauce in front of his corpse.

At that moment, King Kochese Mills felt like Jesus Christ himself. He knew the betrayal was coming, but he didn't know whether it would come from Chico, Manny, or both. Only time would tell.

Chapter 5

Two Souls, One Mind

"Push, Jasmine! You've got to push, sweetheart," the nurse screamed.

"I *am* pushing! Ughhhh, it hurts," Jasmine cried.

With every contraction, Jasmine's body felt as if the hands of God were crushing all of her bones at once. She screamed and thrashed about the hospital bed, pushing in the process.

"That's it, baby girl, you're doing fine. Oh my God, I see the head, Jasmine," the nurse gushed.

Jasmine pushed repeatedly for what seemed like forever until finally, she heard the soft, faint whimpering of her twins. Then Jasmine seemed to drift in and out of consciousness. Her body felt ravaged and weak. It wasn't until the head nurse placed her children in her arms that she seemed to gather a level of strength. "What are they?" Jasmine asked weakly.

"One is a boy, and one is a girl. They are gorgeous, Jasmine," the nurse said.

Jasmine looked down at her precious babies and felt the warm sensation of tears streaming down her flustered cheeks. She gazed from child to child and smiled. They were perfect in every way.

"We'll give you some time with your babies, Jasmine, before we take them to the nursery to run some tests. From the looks of it, dear heart, they are perfectly healthy.

Your son weighs six pounds nine ounces, and your baby girl weighs six pounds two ounces," the head nurse said.

They exited the room en route to their next delivery, but one of the nurses did not leave. Koshi stood in a corner, watching Jasmine interact with her children. After she was confident the other nurses were well away from Jasmine's room, she pulled up a chair and sat beside Jasmine's bed.

"I bet you're glad that's over, huh?" she asked.

But Jasmine didn't respond. Again, Koshi attempted to start a conversation with her, but Jasmine remained mute, staring at her perfect creations.

Koshi pulled out her cell phone and snapped a picture of Jasmine and the twins. Moments later, she exited the room on her way out, passing Nae dressed in scrubs. Nae took Koshi's seat and looked at Jasmine. Even after she'd just given birth, she was still beautiful. Her jade-green eyes beamed love as she cooed at her babies.

"They're gorgeous. They look like both of you guys," Nae said. Upon hearing the phrase "both of you guys," Nae now had Jasmine's attention. "King Kochese sends his regards, Jasmine," Nae said.

"How do you know my husband?"

"I used to work for him back in the day. He contacted me about getting you and the children to safety. He also told me to tell you he dreamed about y'all," Nae said.

"Really? Awww, I miss him so much. What was the dream about?"

"He didn't say. He only said that there was a boy and a girl and that their names were Angel and Apache."

"Angel and Apache . . . I like that," Jasmine said. She looked down at the twins. "Angel, Apache, Daddy said that's your name. Y'all like it? Huh? Yeah, Mommy's babies like their names," Jasmine said in her softest baby voice.

"We're going to try everything in our power to free you along with the twins, Jasmine, but I'm sure you know they have your room watched. I don't know if you've been able to see the news, but you and King are on every news channel. They're calling y'all Monopoly killers and shit. We been sliding around the hospital, doing a little recon too. There's only one guard outside your door, and they rotate every four hours, with a five-minute clear window between that rotation. Junior will come up to get you and escort you to the loading dock, where I'll be waiting with the twins. It's 2:15 now, so you have ten minutes until Junior arrives."

"Don't worry about me. Just get the twins to safety. If I get to you quickly, cool; if not, don't wait for me. Make sure that you tell Kochese that I said, 'Heaven don't want us, and hell can't hold us.' He'll know what it means. By the way, you never told me your name," Jasmine said.

"My name is Natrinelle, but everyone calls me Nae."

"Okay, Nae. I will trust you with my precious babies, but you have to make me a promise," Jasmine whispered.

"Name it. Kochese is family, so that makes you family."

"Take care of my babies, please. Don't let anything happen to them. And by no means don't wait for me if I'm not right behind you."

"You have my word that I will guard Angel and Apache with my life, Jasmine. I'll die before I let something happen to these babies. See you on the other side, baby girl," Nae said, slipping a handcuff key from beneath her tongue. She wiped the key on her scrubs and handed it to Jasmine as she rose to leave the room. When she reached the door and looked back at Jasmine, she winked at her, shot her a sly grin, and exited the room.

Koshi entered Jasmine's room and placed the twins in their neonatal crib. They snoozed peacefully as she wheeled them out of the hospital room.

Jasmine lay in her bed immobile, staring at the ceiling with tears running down her cheeks. She was happy that Kochese had sent reinforcements for them, but at the same time, she was filled with overwhelming sadness. What kind of life did she and Kochese bring their children into? There could be no happy endings because even if they were successful in their escape attempt, they would forever be fugitives. Although she had given the twins to the nurse freely, she felt as if they'd been ripped away from her. She had no idea when she might see them again, which frightened her. Jasmine felt helpless, like a small, fragile child stripped of all security. She felt much like she had during her first few days at the Buckner Home for Youth, lost and alone. She turned onto her side, away from the door, and unlocked the handcuff. She stared out the window and softly sobbed as she watched the frost melt slowly, becoming beads of saturation, rolling down the tempered glass. The pewter-gray clouds hung low in the sky, and Jasmine's mood matched them perfectly.

Hatred brewed in her gut, festering and boiling there like hot lava, and she felt like she might erupt any second. Monica had torn her family apart for the sake of furthering her career. In Jasmine's fragile mind, she hadn't associated what she and King did as wrong or evil. They were simply righting wrongs, and the people that they'd killed had been killed for a purpose. She and King weren't like other people, other killers that only killed for thrills. She promised herself that if she ever walked the streets again, Monica would die a horrible death. She would torture her until her sister begged for death to come and take her. Finally, Jasmine wiped the tears from her face and sat up in bed. She swung her legs from the side of the bed and tried to stand, but her knees felt unsteady, and she was exhausted. Blood had stained the front of her hospital gown, and as much as she would have loved to shower, there was no time. She rummaged through the backpack that Koshi had left there and found a pair of jeans, a hoodie, and a pair of sneakers. Then Jasmine climbed back beneath the covers and waited.

Chapter 6

Dallas, Texas

Minerva Patterson couldn't believe her luck. Well, she didn't really believe in luck. When she was growing up in the projects, her grandparents told her there was no such thing as luck. No, according to her grandparents, the Lord doled out blessings to those deserving and worthy, so her good fortune couldn't be luck. It had to be the Lord thy God shining His mercy and grace down on her.

At 30 years old, Minerva Patterson was among the few chosen to make it into the FBI's HRT squad. It was the FBI's Hostage Response Team, and they were the crème de la crème, all piss and vinegar. Minerva couldn't have been happier because not only would she receive a pay increase, but she'd also be a member of an elite group of specially trained men and women.

She'd been her grandparents' pride and joy, and as much as everyone else had counted her out, she'd overcome and exceeded their expectations. Minerva had never known her father and had had the displeasure of having an on-again, off-again relationship with her drug-addicted mother. She'd witnessed her grandparents nearly lose everything in their attempt to help her mother kick her habit. Sleepless, worry-filled nights and countless interventions followed until one day, she'd simply stopped coming around. Minerva's grandfather had always expected the worst, but her grandmother's optimism never wavered.

She'd tell Minerva, "She gonna come home, baby, and we gonna be a family again."

Her grandfather would counter with, "That there is my baby girl, my only girl, and I'm telling you, Melba, something bad done happened to my baby girl."

Those conversations had gone on for days and then weeks . . . until the police had shown up on their doorstep in the middle of the night. The entire family had been roused from their peaceful slumber on the eve of Minerva's sixteenth birthday. She stood timidly behind her grandparents, trying desperately to wipe the crusty sleep from her eyes, peeking between them as the officers delivered the news that Marvetta Patterson had been found dead behind Seoul Bazaar. Apparently, Marvetta had been raped, strangled, stabbed, and nearly decapitated. Her murder would go unsolved for years like the other murders of addicts and streetwalkers in Dallas, Texas. With the police force being so inundated with gang violence, somehow, the death of a crackhead prostitute didn't seem so important.

It was the loss of her mother that caused those closest to Minerva to assume that she would become a statistic. Some said that she'd fall victim to drugs, get pregnant, or drop out of school. Some assumed that it would be a variation of the three. Instead of letting her mother's death become her curse, it actually served to fuel a fire deep within her. Her grandparents encouraged her to grieve, but instead, she studied. They encouraged her to get out and be social, but instead, she studied. She studied so much that she was number two in her class by the time she graduated from Lincoln High School. College had been a breeze, and so had the training exercises for both the FBI and the HRT.

Minerva stared at the confirmation letter stating that she'd made the squad and felt overwhelmed with joy—a bittersweet joy, actually because as she held the letter that held her future, she sat between the tombstones of her grandparents.

"Well, Paw Paw, Nana, I made it, and before you get started, yes, I remembered to thank the Lord. Listen, I may be going away for a while, so I won't be coming to visit as often, but I wanted to say thank you," Minerva said. She took a swig from the open bottle of Crown Royal and continued. "Paw Paw, every time I wanted to quit, I could hear your voice say, 'Minerva, now, now, you gots to put your all into it. If you ain't gonna do it right, ain't no sense in doing it at all.'" She mimicked him in a deep southern voice.

"Yep," she said, taking another sip of her devil's nectar before pouring some onto her grandmother's grave. "I know Nana doesn't drink, Paw Paw, but we're celebrating, right?" Minerva stood up and twirled as if dancing with some imaginary suitor. The night had begun to fall over Dallas, but that didn't bother Minerva Patterson. She had no qualms about being in the cemetery after dark. To her, it was as easy as visiting her grandparents at home. She twirled and laughed as if she were involved in some sort of pagan ritual. "I guess God looked out for me, huh? Paw Paw, you were right. If you do good, then good comes back to you."

Between the twirling and the effects of the potent liquor, she felt dizzy. Minerva lay down in the plush cemetery grass between her grandparents' burial plots and gazed into the night sky. The stars shone brightly against the backdrop of the new moon, but even in the stars' brilliance, the blackness in the sky seemed to go on for eternity. A mere sliver of iridescent light escaped the throes of the nearly-eclipsed moon. Minerva seemed to lose herself in the darkness until it was no longer visible.

Suddenly, her clear view of the night sky had been blocked by a lone figure. A tall silhouette of a man spoke as Minerva tried desperately to focus. She wasn't sure whether he was an apparition or real, but whoever he was, he caused the hair on the back of her neck to stand up.

"Did I startle you?" he asked as Minerva scrambled to her feet, still reeling, feeling the effects of the liquor.

"Yeah, kinda," she said. Her hand instinctively felt for her agency-issued 9-mm pistol, but she didn't have it. It was tucked away neatly and safely in the center console of her Land Rover. She'd left it as she did on so many other occasions when she'd come to visit her grandparents' graves. After all, there were thousands of gravesites in the cemetery. *Maybe the man is here to visit a lost loved one,* she reasoned. Something about the man's look and demeanor belied Minerva's sense of logic. His ice-blue eyes were cold, callous, and filled with despair, and the scar on his cheek that ran from his temple to the corner of his crooked smile terrified her.

"Sorry to startle you, but I overheard you talking. Is that what you believe, honestly?" the stranger asked.

"Is what-what I believe honestly?"

"That if you do good, that good comes back to you," he said blankly.

"If you're a good person, put God first, and put out positive vibes, and good things happen to you? Yeah, I guess I do believe that," she said nervously.

"Can I share something with you?"

"Sure, why not?" Minerva said sarcastically. She wasn't about to debate her beliefs with a man she didn't know, no matter how handsome he was.

"God isn't here tonight, you see," he said as he removed a black pistol from his waistband. "God only hears the pleas of the wicked. He listens to them and pokes fun at them as they squirm in their own torment and agony. People like you, Minerva, you're sheep to him. He knows that you'll comply and follow His laws, so He ignores you. And even when you're in trouble, like right now, you're so far off His radar that by the time your number is called and He finally gets to you, you're already at the pearly gates waiting to see Him," he said.

Minerva's words caught in her throat. She recognized her belt holster at his feet, and her heart sank. He must have broken into her vehicle and stolen her gun. "Who are you? What do you want?" she asked nervously.

Deep, dark laughter bellowed throughout the hallowed grounds of the cemetery. "My dear Miss Patterson, I want the world to know I've arrived. I am a king among peasants and a wolf among sheep," he said before he pulled the trigger.

The first round struck her in the shoulder, and she stumbled backward, catching herself on her grandfather's tombstone.

"Oh my, I must be getting rusty," the killer said. He took aim, leveling the firearm in the direction of Minerva's head this time.

She wanted to turn and run, but fear had gripped her legs and refused to let go. Before her second thought registered, she felt the unfamiliar pressure of a bullet piercing the hard bone of her skull and then the welcomed pleasure of nothingness. Her body slid down the cold hardness of the headstone and came to rest in a crumpled heap between the burial plots of her grandparents.

Minerva's blue-eyed killer dropped to his knees above her body and stared at her. He straightened out her body and put her arms out as if she were about to be nailed to the cross. Finally, he straightened her head. Her lifeless eyes stared into the abyss, unfocused on one single point in the universe. He stood and surveyed his handiwork, but something was wrong.

"That's it," he shouted, snapping his fingers.

He kneeled again, this time removing a large hunting knife with serrated edges from the sheath attached to his belt. He slowly and meticulously cut the clothes from her supine, positioned body. After she was completely naked, he took his hunting knife and etched into the fleshiness of her stomach. Minerva's crimson blood appeared even darker against the mulatto hue of her skin.

"You know, you have nice titties for a dead girl," he said. He was still staring at her when headlights flooded the darkness, highlighting his depraved action.

"Hey, what are you doing? What's going on over there?" the caretaker asked.

But the murderer didn't say a word. He was still looking at Minerva's corpse, admiring the creative masterpiece that he'd carved into her bowels. He marveled at the jagged letters that he'd engraved into her flesh. He smiled with sadistic satisfaction as he turned toward the rotund and disheveled-looking caretaker. He met the man in the brightness of his headlights, not at all trying to conceal his identity.

"What are you-you-you, doing out here, mister?" the caretaker stuttered nervously, attempting to look past the bloody man's shoulders. He clearly saw what appeared to be a naked woman lying between two graves. "Is she okay, mister?" he asked.

"Does she look okay? Since you like to ask questions, let me ask you one of my own. Are you afraid to die, fat man?"

"I-I-I never really thought about it, I guess," he stammered.

"Well, think about it while I'm leaving. And Mr. Caretaker?"

"Yes, sir?" the caretaker said as he backed away.

"If I were you, I'd call the police and tell them that you met Satan tonight. Tell them of the horror you've witnessed and share the wonders of meeting evil face-to-face with them. Tell them that I am a king among peasants and a wolf among sheep," he said as he disappeared into the darkness of the wood line that surrounded the graveyard.

Chapter 7

Texarkana, Texas

Darkness had yet to extract itself from the city streets of Texarkana, and the late wintery chill whipped and whistled through the window of the lurker's black Buick LeSabre. It was either keep warm and toasty behind the tinted windows or brave the cold to smoke his beloved Pall Mall nonfiltered cigarettes. He'd chosen the latter, and judging from the pile of cigarette butts beneath the door of the vehicle, he'd been there for quite some time. He watched himself in his rearview mirror, transfixed on the glow of the orange, ash-tinged tip of his seventeenth cigarette. He'd been out of prison for forty-seven days and had no plans of returning. He stared at his icy blue eyes and laughed. *If Gabby DeRossi could see me now,* he thought. He let his index finger trace the newly acquired scar that stretched from his temple to his upper lip. He caught a sight from the corner of his eye that pulled him from his self-loving revelry.

A hearty figure of a man appeared at the front entrance of Krispy Kreme the stalker had tracked him to. The big man fumbled with the keys while balancing a cup of coffee and a jelly donut. The fat man put the donut into his mouth and red jelly oozed out onto his pale blue button-down shirt and his cheap tie and came to rest on the badge hanging from his neck. The assassin took

aim with his concealable rucksack sniper rifle and then
purposely blew his horn. The chubby agent whipped
around, spilling the hot coffee onto himself, cursing in
the process. When he opened his mouth to curse, his jelly
donut dropped from his mouth, and he cursed harder.
The killer already had the donut man in the scope of his
rifle, fingering his trigger patiently, waiting for just the
right moment.

The first shot pinged off the concrete, obliterating the
jelly donut at the fat man's feet. He wasn't a bad shot. He
did it to toy with the man. The second was high and to
the right, obliterating the donut shop window. It wasn't
until the agent heard the scream from inside that he
realized there was an active shooter. He removed his
sidearm and looked around, searching for a place to
take cover. The next shot caught him just above his belly
button, and the hefty man squealed in pain. He grabbed
his gut and looked at the blood in the palm of his hand,
confused. He tried to run, but blood was pouring from
his stomach, and he felt like his guts were on fire. He
dropped his pistol, and when he bent down to pick it up,
he fell to his knees. Another shot ricocheted from the
asphalt and struck him in the shoulder. The agent tried
to shimmy underneath a car for safety, but his stomach
was too big, and he cursed his laziness. He could hear
sirens somewhere in the distance and silently thanked
God.

The killer walked to him, kneeled over his body, and
watched as the fat man struggled to breathe. His eyes
blinked rapidly, trying to expel the pain, but it was no use.
The killer went to the window of the donut shop in full
view of all its patrons and smiled, intentionally letting
them see his face. When he was sure that he had their
full attention, he walked back to the agent and shot him
in his throat. He was halfway through the block when

he saw the first police car in his rearview mirror turning into the plaza.

As the first break of day crept up over the horizon of Texarkana's great pseudo metropolis, the killer aimed at his second victim. He zeroed his scope in on a young mother as she vacuumed her Chrysler minivan in the parking lot of an Exxon gas station. Her infant son watched from his car seat, mesmerized by the mobile hanging above his head. She would stop vacuuming frequently to chat playfully with the baby, and for a split second, the assassin felt a pang of guilt for what he was about to do—not because he cared for the lady or her child but because his mother hadn't really been a mother at all. His earliest recollections were hazy and spaced out chronologically. One thing was certain, though: He had never had any type of maternal connection to his mother. He felt like an alien, like his time on earth had started at no particular time, and it bothered him. He would get flashes of a past, but he could never quite pinpoint whether it was real or his imagination.

He massaged the trigger gently and tried to focus on his target. Tears had begun to well up in his eyes, stinging slightly, threatening his mission. He took the tip of his fingernails and dug into the fleshy softness of his neck, barely wincing from the pain until he felt the liquid satisfaction of his own blood. He didn't want memories; he didn't want recollections. He wanted to do as he'd been told, as he'd been paid to do. The thoughts wouldn't stop, though, the thoughts of him as a young boy holding the faceless man's hand as he led him into the abandoned warehouse. The harder he thought about it, the harder it was to concentrate, and then he heard it. It was the familiar voice he often heard, especially when he needed to make hard decisions.

Let's go, goddammit! We don't have all day while you try to piece together your miserable, piece-of-shit life. Snuff that bitch, and let's move on, the voice said.

"Shut up, just shut up! I'm gonna do it. Don't rush me," he screamed.

Maybe I need to do it, you little pussy. I always come to your rescue anyway, don't I?

"Yes, but—" he started.

But the voice interrupted him again. *But nothing. You're a coward. I know it, and you know it. I can feel your tiny bladder quivering right now. If you're a good little bitch and blow her head off, I'll unlock a few more memories. Now, pull the fucking trigger.*

His hand shook uncontrollably. "I don't want the memories. Keep them. They are torturous punishments, not rewards," he cried.

Boo-fucking-hoo. Cowboy the fuck up. We have work to do. Who's going to respect you if you're always whining and sniveling? This is a golden opportunity, so don't blow it. I won't let you ruin this for us.

Again, the killer tried to focus, but when he looked through his scope, he only saw the silhouette of the faceless man, the man who called himself Mr. Hinkle. He'd recognized the man from the small corner store at the end of the long dirt road across the railroad tracks from his house.

The killer blinked rapidly, trying to expel the horrid memory from his mind. "Make it stop, please! I'll do it, I'll do it. No more memories, please," he screamed.

Okay, no more memories if you just pull the fucking trigger, the voice said.

He wiped his tears with the back of his hand and squinted. He could see his target clearly as she replaced the vacuum nozzle. Just as she turned to go to the driver's side, he let his sniper rifle whistle. The slug ripped through the nape of her neck just above her shoulder blades and exited through her throat. The bullet fragment shattered the passenger-side window as her body slumped instantly. She never knew what hit her. All the while, her infant son continued playing with the mobile above his head.

Kill him too. Kill the baby, the voice screamed.

"I'm not killing a baby. He's innocent; he's just a child. I won't do it!"

Give me the gun. I'll do it, the voice countered.

"We were given instructions to follow. No children. We were told not to hurt the children!" the killer shrieked.

He gazed at the stopwatch glued to his Buick's dashboard. He had ten hours and fifty-three minutes to complete his mission. He was behind schedule and would have to move quickly if his task was to be completed by his 6:17 p.m. deadline. He was no fool, though. He'd disobeyed the voice, and there would be hell to pay.

Chapter 8

Trick-Ass Junior

Nae slid into an empty hospital room with the diaper bag that Koshi had left for her. She poured the contents out onto the bed and began to undress. She stuffed the clothes she'd taken off into the diaper bag and placed it onto the wheelchair. Now, Nae stood naked, examining the contents spread out on the bed. "This nigga better be glad I love his ass," she said to no one in particular.

Nae picked up the .25-caliber semiautomatic pistol from the bed and cursed loudly. "Goddamn, Junior, I know I said send me something small, but shit. Oh well, hopefully, I won't need to use this little bitty-ass pistol," she said out loud. Nae checked the clip in the toy-sized gun and chuckled at how petite the gun seemed. She turned quickly with the .25 and aimed it at the door as Koshi entered.

"Damn, you gonna shoot me, baby?" Koshi asked.

"Nah, you just scared a bitch. Knock next time, damn."

"My bad. You almost ready? The head neonatal nurse is leaving," Koshi said.

Nae lay back on the bed seductively and opened her legs, exposing the fleshy wetness that hid deep inside. "That means we have time for a quickie."

Koshi walked to her and inserted her middle finger deep inside Nae, who moaned and giggled with delight.

"Mmmm, maybe later. We don't have enough time. Let's get this shit done, and then we can play," Koshi said in a businesslike tone.

"Awww, shit. Now, let me find out my baby 'bout that life. Okay, okay, business now, play later. Got it." Nae removed Koshi's finger from her pussy and guided it to her mouth, tasting her own juices. "Damn, I taste good. You wanna taste?" she asked playfully.

Koshi snatched her hand from Nae's grasp. "Get dressed, Nae. We don't have time for this shit," she teased, tossing the hospital gown in Nae's direction.

"I'm going to get the twins. Be dressed when I get back," Koshi said.

Nae stood and dressed quickly. She wrapped the handgun in a towel and placed it on the seat of the wheelchair. Moments later, Koshi returned with the twins in her arms. They were fully dressed: Apache in baby blue and Angel in soft pink. Koshi placed the twins in Nae's arms, and Nae put her pistol in the folds of Apache's blanket. Koshi wheeled her out of the room and whispered in her ear, "Junior is downstairs waiting. Once you and the twins are clear, I'll let him know so he can get Jasmine. He told me to tell you that he has hitters on this floor and in the lobby on the first floor just in case shit goes sour," Koshi said.

Nae nodded but didn't look up. She was preoccupied with the two small lives she held in her arms. As Koshi wheeled her to the elevator, she scanned the floor for the people Junior had in place, but instead of seeing hitters, she saw people who looked out of place. Maybe she was just being paranoid, but there was a painter who wasn't painting, a contractor on a ladder with no tools in his tool belt, and a doctor who seemed shifty, like he was nervous about something. Maybe the painter and the contractor were working for Junior, but the fake doctor looked and behaved like a cop. His eyes darted toward both ends of the hallway, and Nae could've sworn that he nodded at her as Koshi wheeled her backward into the elevator. Just as the doors were closing, the fake doctor's hand appeared and tripped the sensor of the elevator doors, causing them to slide open again. He walked into the elevator and smiled at Nae.

"Those are beautiful babies. What are their names?" he asked with his slanted smile.

"The boy's name is Nunnayo, and the girl's name is Muh'fuckin' Business. Mind your business, playboy," Nae snapped incredulously.

"Whoa. No need to be so mean, young lady. I'm just trying to make conversation," he said.

"Well, I'm in no mood to hear you flap your clit lickers, man. Get the fuck on, fool," Nae spat.

The stranger's easy smile had now been replaced with a menacing scowl. All light drained from his face, and his eyes beamed terror. He removed his hand from the pocket of his doctor's coat and revealed a shiny chrome pistol. Nae wanted to reach for the .25 wrapped in Apache's blanket, but she wouldn't be able to get to it before he shot her and possibly hit one of the twins. If that happened, she wouldn't have to worry about the doctor killing her. King Kochese would beat him to it. The doctor glanced back, but his gun was still trained on Nae when he pressed the emergency stop button on the elevator.

"I told you that there was no need to be ugly. Now, let's try this again, shall we?" he said.

But Nae was silent. Her eyes, however, told an entirely different story. Her smoldering dark eyes brooded, and if left to her, she would have made him pay for pulling his gun on her. She wouldn't jeopardize the lives of Kochese's children, though, so for now, he had a pass. But they would have their time. She would make sure of it.

"Do you hear me talking to you?" he asked, inching toward Nae with his gun aimed at her head.

Nae nodded. "Yeah, I hear you, playboy."

"Good. Now that we have *that* cleared up . . . I'm here to help you, not hurt you," he said, putting his pistoled hand back into his pocket.

"Help me? Help me how?"

"King knows that you have Junior helping you, but he wanted a little extra protection, a sort of 'guarantee,' if you get my meaning," he said.

"Extra protection from what? I told him that I had it handled. And your goofy ass should've led with the fact that King sent you."

"Maybe I should have. And your goofy ass shouldn't be hiding a pistol in a baby blanket, so that makes us even. Now, King isn't concerned with whether you can handle it. He's more concerned with the fact that he knows people do desperate things when money is involved, and Junior has been down on his luck for a while now, wouldn't you agree?" His smile had returned, and it made Nae feel uneasy. His straight white teeth beamed and twinkled from the bright overhead lights in the elevator, but his eyes were still cold, murderous.

Nae stared at him. He was almost too perfect. His voice was a low booming tenor, and he spoke and looked like he was acting. He reminded her of an actor from a toothpaste commercial.

"Yeah, but that nigga Junior would never cross King, man. He knows better."

"That may be the case, and if it is, then good. Everybody still gets paid, so it's no biggie, but if anything should happen to these twins, we both know that this thing won't end pretty. So accept the help, get paid, and live happily ever after," he said, restarting the elevator. It clumped and whirred and continued its journey downward.

Nae looked over her shoulder at Koshi, who hadn't uttered a word throughout the entire conversation. She looked at Nae as if to say that as long as she got her money, she didn't give a damn about anything else. Nae looked from Koshi to the Hollywood dentist. "Okay, playboy, I'm with you. I can see King doing some shit like this. That's why I'm not even questioning you. I've heard of dotting the i's and crossing the t's, but this muh'fucka here, boy . . ." Nae said, shaking her head.

"Good girl. Now, instead of going through the front door, I have a car waiting on the emergency room side," he said.

"All right, Koshi, when we get off the elevator, get Junior up to Monica. Then I want you to go your own way. Call me later, and we'll settle up," Nae said.

"Okay. Damn, I know what to do. Make sure you call me because I still owe you a play date," Koshi said, rubbing Nae's neck playfully.

The elevator dinged, the doors slid open, and they all stepped out, except the doctor was now pushing Nae and the twins toward the emergency room. Koshi gave one last look in Nae's direction, then disappeared down the corridor leading to the lobby of Parkland Memorial Hospital.

Junior scrolled through his pictures until he reached the photo of a slender, naked, tanned blonde adorned only with a pair of pompoms. He had met this young white girl named Heaven coming out of the mall and almost tripped over his own feet when she passed, and he saw her ass. He was used to seeing white girls with asses, especially since every Tina, Tit, and Mary were getting BBLs, but Heaven's shit was natural. He could tell by the bounce.

"Godddd daaaamn. Hold up. Lemme holla at you right quick." He spit some other mack daddy, wannabe bullshit, and she ate it up. It wasn't heavy or deep, not even funny. It was mostly the two bulges in his pocket: one a wad of money, the other a wad of dick. "How old are you, snow kitty? What's your name?"

"Snow kitty? That's new," she giggled. "My name is Heaven, and I'm 18."

Junior loved them young—not go-to-jail young, but young enough to appreciate his rep. Besides, they loved drugs, and as soon as Nae gave him his bread, he was going straight to Heaven—literally. She was 18 and had the body of a 25-year-old tennis player. Junior's mouth watered, just thinking about getting into her young pants. He'd already gotten a quarter of Smurfberry Kush, a dozen mollies, and a new drug that had hit the streets called Bright Eyes. It was supposed to be the equivalent of popping an X pill while riding a unicorn and snorting sunshine—well, at least that's how the crafty dealer had pitched it to him.

Junior was a trick, and he knew it. He loved women, and women loved him . . . for the most part. He'd never thought about trying to settle down. He had convinced himself that he'd be a playboy until the day he died, and the more women, the merrier. In front of him was a slender, white, curvy police officer, and he felt the familiar stirrings of his whore gene trying to manifest. He massaged his crotch, moved to the back of his car, and leaned against the trunk. He reached into his pocket and removed a half-crumpled box of Newport. "Excuse me, Miss Officer. Do you have a light?" he asked.

She assessed Junior with his flashy jewelry and sagging jeans, rolled her eyes, and then snorted. "I don't smoke, and you need to do that at least fifty feet from the entrance of this hospital," she said, pointing to a sign.

Junior's eyes followed the antenna of the walkie-talkie that she used as a pointer. "Damn, baby, you don't have to act like that," he said.

"I'm not your baby, and judging by the pile of cigarette butts beneath your door, I think you already have a light."

"You trippin', shawty. Yeah, I'll move if you gimme your phone number. Let me show you Junior ain't all bad," he said, trying to be cute.

"Okay, Junior, do you have ID?"

"ID? Yeah, I got ID, but I ain't did shit for you to need my ID, though."

"You can either give me your ID, or I can arrest you."

"Man, fuck all of that. I ain't did shit. You said move, so that's what I'ma do."

"Stop fucking moving. Turn around and put your hands behind your back," she ordered.

The officer put one hand on her gun and removed the walkie-talkie attached to her shoulder strap with the other. "I need backup, code 10, code 32, code 10-31. I repeat, I need backup," she said.

"Yo, ma'am, I just asked for a damn light, and you're doing all of this? My lighter burnt out, that's all. Now, I gotta go to jail because I didn't see the fucking sign? This is bullshit. I need to stop fucking smoking if a light is that serious," Junior said nervously. If she checked him, she would find drugs on him, and he couldn't afford another case. Her backup came quickly, almost too quickly, and Junior began to fidget, shifting from one foot to the other.

Monica parked her Impala and walked toward the front of the hospital. She chuckled to herself at the heated exchange happening at the front entrance. She couldn't make out the faces but could see one suspect and at least four cops. She could hear the suspect screaming at the top of his lungs that he hadn't done shit. *Yeah, that's what they all say, asshole,* Monica thought. As she got closer, his face became clear. She knew him, but she couldn't place him. She stopped and stared at him for a long while, trying to remember where she knew him from. He looked up and noticed Monica and the blood drained from his face instantly, like he'd seen a ghost. He dropped his head, trying to shield his face.

And then it dawned on her how she knew him. It was trick-ass Junior, the midlevel, drug-dealing, self-proclaimed Casanova from King's organization who loved drugs and women. King's organization? Was it a coincidence that Jasmine was here giving birth to King's children, and one of his flunkies was standing outside being detained by the police? It was possible, but Monica doubted it very seriously. Her heart sank, and she changed her casual gait to a quicker pace. Before she knew it, she'd broken into an all-out trot toward the front door. She was moving so fast that she didn't notice the young nurse rounding the corner, and they collided, sending them both tumbling to the ground.

"Damn, bitch. You need to watch where the fuck you're going," Koshi spat.

"I'm so sorry, and no need for the name-calling." Monica stood and straightened her clothes, letting the girl see the FBI badge and gun holster on her waist.

"You're right. Have a nice day," Koshi said as she sprang to her feet and headed for the front door. Her stomach was in knots. She wasn't sure if the FBI was there because of the twins, but she wouldn't stick around to find out. The quicker she got this shit over with and got her money, the better.

Monica reached the elevators and pushed the button frantically, watching the neon numbers on the glass panel change as if watching them would somehow convince them to hurry. She cursed under her breath and ran to the stairwell, taking the stairs two at a time until she reached the third floor. It was where Jasmine had given birth. She doubled over to catch her breath, then stood and looked around to gather her bearings. She walked directly to Jasmine's room and peeked inside. Jasmine was curled into a semiball, with her back turned to the door. Monica had never had a baby, but she was sure that giving birth was an arduous task, so she assumed that Jasmine was undoubtedly exhausted.

Monica quietly backed out of the hospital room and faced the nurse's station. She put her hands on her hips and looked around. *Junior being here is no coincidence. My gut never lies,* she thought. Monica made her way to the nursery, but as she drew closer, a frantic nurse rushed past her, heading in the same direction. She didn't know what was happening, but she followed closely behind the nurse, matching her speed.

"What's the big hurry?" Monica asked while showing the lady her badge.

"Two babies missing! A set of twins," she screamed.

"What?"

"Yeah, this entire hospital will be locked down in a second."

"Fuck!" Monica shouted.

She had no idea that she was too late. She had no way of knowing that her nephew and niece, Apache and Angel, were already onboard a private plane bound for the sandy shores of Costa Rica.

Chapter 9

Jesus Wept

He'd wandered home, bleeding and barely coherent. He could hear the music blaring before he reached the front steps, a sound that was all too familiar. He also noticed that his mother tied the red bandana to the banister outside their house. If he saw that bandana, he was supposed to stay away until it was removed because it meant that she was busy entertaining "friends."

That night was different, though. He needed his mother, and he couldn't wait. He tried his best to gather his senses. He tried to rehearse an excuse, something feasible that he could present to his mother because she would be infuriated by his intrusion. He mumbled until he'd finally come up with something he thought she'd believe. He took a deep breath and stumbled into the dark living room of their small, wood-framed house. By candlelight, he noticed his mother on the couch with a stranger whose face he could not see. Her leg was draped across the lap of her lover seductively, and she still hadn't noticed that he'd entered the house. He brazenly flicked on the wall switch, flooding the sparse living room with ambient light.

"Mommy, I'm hurt. I need your help," he screamed.

"Go in the bathroom and put some alcohol on it. Where have you been?" she asked, not even bothering to look up from her guest.

"I don't think alcohol is going to help, Mom."

She turned slowly to face her son and gasped in horror. "Oh my God, you little bastard! What have you gone and gotten yourself into? You're dripping blood all over my carpet," she yelled in a high-pitched, southern drawl.

The young boy collapsed under the trauma of his wound. When he finally came to, his mother was standing over him, incensed with rage. Through blurred vision, he saw his mother reaching for him, not in a maternal, caring way, but grabbing at him violently, as if his collapsing on her dirty, dime-store carpet would somehow taint their already squalid dwelling. Behind his mother, still sitting on their tattered and beer-stained couch, was his mother's lover de jour. It was the couch he'd dragged from the trash heap that the plumber, Mr. Jacobs, had placed there. He'd virtually furnished their whole house by digging in the trash and was proud of it. Before he'd found the furniture, there wasn't any furniture, only things his mother found on the side of the road that could be used as furniture: a large cable spool that had served as their table, milk crates that they'd found, and turned into chairs, and old fruit crates spread around the house, stacked at different heights and used as shelves. Compared to that, the things that he'd found were lavish.

The man stood and walked to the boy's mother's side, and his identity became clear. It was Mr. Hinkle, the man who had raped him and left him for dead. He heard his mother mumbling something about Mr. Hinkle becoming his new stepfather, and he fainted again. When he finally regained consciousness, he'd been moved to that same piss and beer-stained couch where his mother bedded her johns. His mother and Mr. Hinkle stood over him, glowering, albeit for different reasons. His mother because he'd disturbed her raunchy fit of debauchery, and Mr. Hinkle for fear that he'd expose the depraved and sadistic acts he'd subjected the boy to.

But there was no fear in the boy because he knew his mother would defend him. "Mommy, this is the man that hurt me! He did this to me," he whined.

"There you go again, boy. Every time I'm happy, you hafta tryin'a ruin it somehow. He told me he has to get on to you sometimes 'bout not mining when you're at that store you been working at. Says even when he looks after you, you give him sass, and I can believe it. He's going to be good to us. Why can't you just be happy for me?"

"He tried to kill me," he said.

"Oh, nobody is trying to kill you. It's just your imagination. I'm going to get you some help, but don't you go to spewing those lies when the ambulance comes. If you make me lose my sweet Jimmy, I'll never forgive you," she threatened.

His mother disappeared into the kitchen where the phone was and dialed 911. He never understood why they only had one phone or why his mother had chosen to put it in the kitchen, but those thoughts were interrupted by the stench of stale beer and cigarettes as Mr. Hinkle leaned close to his face. His hot, harsh breath sliced through his nostrils like a hot knife through butter. It not only smelled of liquor and smoke but also the putrid, ripe odor of recently expelled vomit. He breathed deep and heavy, not six inches from the boy's face.

"When they get here, you'd better tell them that it was anyone but me, or so help me God, I will skin your mother alive before I ever see the inside of a jail cell. You liked our time together, and we're all going to be one big family," Mr. Hinkle whispered. Spit dripped from his drunken lips as he kissed the jaw of the frightened boy.

He was trembling as he looked toward the kitchen. His mother stood with her back to the pair, still on the phone, undoubtedly trying to explain how her 8-year-old son could have possibly gotten a stab wound.

By the time the kid came out of the hospital, his mother had married James Hinkle Jr. He'd given the EMTs and the police a bullshit story about a Black man molesting and robbing him as he made his way home from school, even taking them back to the crime scene where Mr. Hinkle had performed his perverted acts. He'd given them a hurried description. It wasn't until he found out that Mr. Tuttle, the middle-aged Black janitor who worked at his school, had been arrested that he realized he'd inadvertently given them a description of him, maybe because he thought all Black people looked alike, or maybe because Mr. Tuttle was the only Black man that he knew. At any rate, the police released the boy into the custody of his mother and Mr. Hinkle.

After dinner the night of his release from the hospital, he crawled into the sleeping bag with his back to the door, and a steak knife clutched in his hands. He would no longer be a victim, and if Mr. Hinkle came to his room tonight, he would die. Soon, he heard the faint creaking of the rusty hinges of his bedroom door. A thin sliver of light pierced the darkness as Mr. Hinkle slipped into his bedroom, clad only in a pair of dingy white boxer shorts.

"You asleep, boy?" he asked.

He did not answer. Instead, he gripped the steak knife tighter.

"Wake up, son," he said.

The boy turned and met the man's gaze. "I'm not your son and don't want to do this. Please, just leave me alone."

"Whaddaya mean leave you alone? We're family now, right?" Mr. Hinkle grabbed a handful of the boy's *sandy-blond hair and guided his face toward his crotch. The musty odor of sweaty balls and expired sex had trapped itself in his tangled nest of bushy pubic hair, and the boy's sparse dinner threatened to expel itself from his quivering bowels. Tears streaked his dirty, white, youthful face. He grabbed the pervert's penis.*

"That's right, that's right," Mr. Hinkle said lustfully.

The boy jammed the steak knife into the fleshy muscle between the base of his abuser's scrotum and his asshole.

The man shrieked in pain, cursing and reaching for the boy as he fell to his knees, but the boy skipped backward out of reach. He ran to the kitchen and grabbed another steak knife from the drawer. He didn't remember much after that, but according to the police, he'd stabbed Mr. Hinkle forty-seven times and had driven a meat cleaver into the skull of his mother while she slept off her Jack Daniels-induced coma. He'd obviously blacked out because when he came to, he was in an all-white room strapped to a gurney.

After a while, the voice came to him, comforting him when he needed him most. They had forged an unbreakable bond that had been tested and that he hoped could be repaired.

In his lifetime, he'd killed a total of thirty-seven times, and most of those had provoked no emotions.

I guess you think you've done something? I'm not going to forget that you disobeyed me. You should've killed that baby, the voice boomed repeatedly in his head, threatening to unravel the last little bit of sanity that he had.

Chapter 10

Know Your Place

King Kochese stood in the upstairs office of Club Mil Cincuenta and stared at himself in the mirror. If the deal that Chico and Manny had put into place worked out, he'd be the proud owner of one of the hottest nightclubs in Costa Rica. He fell in love with the plush, three-story club the minute he stepped foot inside. He paced back and forth, never taking his eyes off the mirror. He hadn't thought it was possible, but he'd done it—well, the doctor had actually been responsible for it, but he was amazed, nevertheless.

Kochese rubbed his smooth, chocolaty skin and smiled. The doctor slowly darkened his skin tone by injecting concentrated melanocytes into him until Kochese was satisfied with the hue of his skin. Even after his plastic surgery, he still felt like he looked the same, and that frightened him. He needed to become someone totally different; the only way for him to do that was to change completely. It had been an easy transition when he'd transformed himself into Khalil Cross because he was already fair-skinned. The melanocytes had fused to his skin cells and deepened his melanin, giving him a rich Idris Elba-ish tone. He still held his rugged features and ice-blue eyes, but they were just darker. The combination of dark skin and light-colored eyes made Kochese look evil, which he liked.

Kochese looked toward the door and paced nervously. "Man, this muh'fucka wanna get this cake or what? How the fuck are you going to be late to a meeting that *you* set up? That's that bullshit that I don't like," he said.

"Calm down, baba. He'll be here," Manny said.

Kochese didn't argue with him, but he let his eyes slice through the rotund Spaniard. Manny was getting on his last nerve. He'd fumbled the ball on more than one occasion where Kochese was concerned, and it was getting old. If he didn't need Manny, he would've murdered him after the first couple of offenses like he had done in the old days. "Why don't you go to the bar and get me a drink, Manny?" King asked, his irritation showing clearly.

"Why don't you send Chico, baba?"

"Because I didn't fucking ask Chico, Manny. I asked you. Is that a problem?" Kochese asked.

"No, sir, boss. I'll get right on that. Do you need anything else?" Manny asked sarcastically.

"Yeah, Manny," Kochese said, removing the gold-plated Desert Eagle from his waistband and placing it on the large, raw oak desk. "I need for you to lose the attitude and remember who the fuck you're talking to. My skin tone changed, but not my attitude. Don't get it twisted, bruh," he said calmly.

Manny was frozen. He wasn't sure how to take what had just happened. He and Kochese had been friends for years and had never had a problem. Manny had a choice. He could either do as he was asked, or he could confront Kochese and risk dying. His pride told him to save face in front of Chico, but his common sense told him to let it go. Manny reluctantly decided to follow common sense.

He shuffled his mammoth frame toward the door leading to the bar with his head low. Kochese had broken his spirit because he'd exposed the facade he'd created for Chico. He had made it seem like he and Kochese were much closer than they were.

As he exited, Chico dropped his head and fumed silently. His jaw was tight, and he was ashamed that he had called this man his mentor. He hated a liar, and since he'd worked for Manny, he'd caught him in so many lies that it was irritating.

"What's really good, Chico? What's that look about?" Kochese asked curiously.

"I've worked for Manny for many years, and it's hard to speak against him. I just don't like what I'm seeing, King."

"Dead that shit. You work for me now, entiendes? So you can say whatever you want. What's the business?" Kochese asked.

"He exaggerates and lies, so I never know what to believe. It makes me distrust him, which bothers me because I've known him since I was very young."

"What kind of lies, Chico? I hate a fucking liar," Kochese barked.

Chico opened his mouth to answer Kochese's question, but Manny entered the office with Rubio Contreras in tow before he could. Both men were hefty, and Kochese chuckled, thinking of what would have happened had both men tried to enter the office simultaneously. It would have truly been comical to see them wedged in the door, stuck. It would be like trying to squeeze two raw biscuits through a keyhole.

"El Rey, please forgive me for my tardiness. I was—"

Kochese put up his hand to stop the man from talking. "I don't care about your private affairs or excuses, Mr. Contreras. I don't like wasting my time, especially when I intend to make you a rich man. I actually take it as a form of disrespect, but I will give you a pass this time. Now, Chico, show Mr. Contreras his money."

"Kochese, Señor Contreras was in a meeting with the minister of defense," Manny chimed in.

Kochese ignored his comment and opened the two small suitcases that Chico had placed on the desk. Both cases held rows of neatly stacked one-hundred-dollar bills.

"As requested, Mr. Contreras, $2 million American for the club. Now, there's just a matter of the paperwork," Kochese said.

Rubio Contreras walked to the briefcase, removed a stack of the new money, and thumbed through the crisp bills. He was nearly drooling at the prospect of spending his newfound wealth. Without turning away from the money, he reached into his inside jacket pocket and removed the deed and the bill of sale for the building. Kochese snatched them quickly and examined the papers.

"Looks like everything is in order, Mr. Contreras. Chico will escort you to your vehicle. If these Ticos see you leave here with those two cases, they're bound to put two and two together and blow your head off before you can trick off some of that money, playboy." Kochese laughed.

Moments later, Chico and Costa Rica's newest millionaire disappeared into the club, and Kochese slammed the door and turned on Manny. "Take a seat, Manny. We need to talk, pimp."

Manny did as instructed, sitting on the outdated but comfortable leather couch. He knew that it wasn't a request. It was an order that he obeyed with no hesitation. Kochese took a seat on the desk and stared at Manny. Who gave this fat piece of sweaty shit the authority to speak out of turn, or better yet, what made Manny think that Kochese was the kind of man that would allow him to disrespect him? He loved Michael Ross, and he had put a bullet into his head. He loved Bird, and he'd murdered him. For that matter, he'd grown to love the loyalty that Drak lied about, and he had tortured him. Manny? Kochese didn't give a fat rat's ass about Manny. He would only need him for a bit longer, and when the time came, he would gut the fat man and make him watch his own intestines ooze from his body.

Chapter 11

Mama's Baby, Daddy's Crazy

Monica jogged slowly through the park, pushing Millicent's stroller. Noisy Boy trotted beside her, giving her a cursory glance occasionally. Through his rehabilitation at the kennel, he'd gotten stronger every day. Monica had babied him for a while, but he had become lazy and lethargic. She wasn't sure whether dogs suffered from depression or not, but if they did, Noisy Boy was a prime candidate for doggy Prozac. He'd limped and whimpered around the house and refused to let Monica walk or bathe him. He barely ate and had dropped from his healthy, lean fifty pounds to a thin thirty-five pounds. His ribs weren't showing, but he looked smaller, weaker. She understood him, though. Noisy Boy felt like he had let her down, not to mention he had nearly killed the man who had raised him. Her baby, her boy, her puppy was an emotional wreck.

Monica didn't think like most people. Most people looked at dogs as dumb animals whose sole purpose was to keep them entertained, but Monica saw Noisy Boy as something else. He functioned more like a temperamental child, whining when he didn't get his way, even going so far as to trot off when being scolded, much like teens might when they've been grounded. He finally walked when Monica put her foot down and talked to Noisy Boy more like a human being than a dog.

"You've been moping around this house for months, and it's getting on my nerves. You stink, little boy. Okay, so what because you had to bite your daddy that you're going to be a little bitch about it? Come on, man, you're stronger than this. You're lying there on that pad like Noisy Girl instead of my Noisy Boy. Do I need to take you to the vet and have your balls snipped? I might as well because you're acting like a little bitch right now. If somebody came up in here right now to harm me or Millie, you wouldn't even be able to protect us. You want to be the man around here, barking and calling shots and shit? Then you need to get up and act like it," Monica screamed. She was saying those things to taunt him, hoping, praying that it would spark a fight. She didn't know if he would ever be the same, but she loved her dog.

Monica peered over her shoulder as she walked away from him to check on Millie. She fixed her meanest mug and whispered, "Bitch," in Noisy Boy's direction. As she turned, she heard Noisy Boy let out a loud yelp. She heard the familiar *click-clack* of his nails sliding across the terrazzo tile floor. Noisy Boy scurried past her and stood in front of her with his tail wagging ferociously. A muffled but resounding growl emanated from his gut, and a sharp but authoritative bark followed.

"What?" Monica said, kneeling.

Again, he barked.

"You mad because I called you a bitch?" she asked.

Again, he barked.

"Okay, I'm sorry I called you a bitch. You happy now?" Monica asked.

Noisy Boy sat back on his haunches, hoisted his leg into the air, licked his own balls, looked up at Monica, and then barked again.

"Ohhhh, okay, I'm sorry for threatening to have your little balls snipped," she laughed.

Noisy Boy didn't bark. He did, however, limp to Millicent's crib and lay in front of it as if to quell Monica's worries about his inability to protect them.

Now, watching him outside, active and happy, made her happy, but there was still the matter of Kochese and Jasmine's twins being kidnapped. She wasn't sure whether she could rightly call it kidnapping because she was sure that Kochese was responsible for it. Her attempt to speak with Junior had ended uneventful and unfruitful. Kochese still had a hold on the young man, and Monica didn't understand it, but she'd tried her hand anyway.

"Junior, you're looking at a lot of time for those drugs, not to mention kidnapping," she said.

"Kidnapping? Man, I ain't kidnapped no-muh'fucking-body."

"Yeah, maybe not, but by the time I'm finished padding charges against your bitch ass, you'll be washing Boogie Fat's boxers in Lexington Federal Prison. Now, where are the fucking kids?" she said.

"Bitch, don't come in here threatening me with that bullshit. You already crossed my homeboy, and now you come at me like I'm some snitch-ass nigga? Like your little fuck boys, Bird and Drak? Fuck you, trick. Send me back to my cell, ho. Get ya paperwork together, and let's crank it up. I ain't new to this shit; I'm *true* to this shit. Long live the King, bitch. He's a king among peasants and a wolf among sheep," Junior screamed, spitting on the thick bulletproof partition that separated them. He banged the receiver of the phone against the glass and screamed inaudible curses in her direction.

"Yeah, whatever," Monica said before standing to leave.

She had to shake thoughts of Junior, Kochese, Jasmine, their twins, the agency, all of it, because today was supposed to be about her relaxing with her babies. Monica stopped and sat on a park bench to rest and check on Millie, who cooed and giggled as Monica lifted the sunshade of her stroller. "Well, hey, pretty girl, hiiii. You hungry?" Monica removed a baby bottle from the diaper bag and Millie from the stroller. "Okay, now, little chunky. I may need to get you some diet Similac, giiiirl."

Millicent giggled as if she got the joke. "You know, you and Noisy Boy are my only sources of joy? I really mean it. As much as I hate to admit it, I can feel Jasmine's pain with being away from her children because I can't imagine being away from you. No, I can't," she said softly to the smiling baby. Formula puddled and dribbled from the corners of her tiny mouth. "Okay, young lady, no smiling with your mouth full." Monica took a small baby blanket from the bag and wiped the corners of Millicent's mouth. When Millicent finished her lunch, Monica put her against her chest and gently tapped until she heard the deep, rumbling belch of satisfaction escape from the baby. She kissed her and placed her back in the stroller.

Then Monica stood, stretched, and took a long swig from her water bottle. The water went down cold and refreshing, pooling at the bottom of her stomach. She had only had a banana and an English muffin with peanut butter earlier, and she had burned that off on the first leg of her jog this morning. It was a ten-minute trek back to her car if she cut across the park and the edge of the golf course. She was still mentally planning her route when her phone rang. She reached into the small purse attached to Millie's stroller, removed her cell phone, and glanced at the screen. "Shit," she cursed before answering. "Hello?"

"Agent Deitrich, we need to see you as soon as possible. We have a problem. Have you watched the news this morning?"

"Actually, no. What's the problem?" she asked.

Agent D'Angelo was silent on the other end of the phone. Monica had known him since her days in the academy and had fallen in love with him instantly—not the type of love that made women salivate and stare in dreamy-eyed euphoria. Her love for Antonio D'Angelo was respect for a man who had overcome many obstacles to become the youngest director in FBI history. He was perhaps the most beautiful man that she'd ever met. He wasn't what Hollywood thought beautiful. As a matter of fact, he wasn't most women's idea of beauty, either.

But Monica wasn't like most women. She liked the fact that he wasn't a gym rat like most of the other agents. He had a nice body and worked out to stay toned, but nothing extensive. He was built up nicely, but when she looked at him, she could see that it wasn't all washboard and ripples. That was fine with Monica because what he lacked in six-pack abs, he more than made up for in personality. His deep dark chocolate skin complimented his six-foot, 230-pound frame perfectly. Agent D'Angelo would walk into a room, and his smile would light up whatever space he occupied. He exuded strength and confidence, and she melted every time his velvety baritone filled their class.

He was her tactical procedures instructor and, consequently, her lover for a while. She'd learned so much from the young agent, and he'd helped her immensely during her transition from DEA to FBI, not to mention he'd filled a void in her when Kochese had killed himself—well, when she'd *thought* that he'd killed himself. They'd started fooling around shortly before Jasmine and Kochese had gone on their Monopoly game-charged killing spree, but it was just that—*fooling around*. Noisy Boy had made certain that no man could get close to Monica, so she stopped seeing Antonio because the few times he'd come around, Noisy Boy had barked and growled at the agent relentlessly. He'd called often, merely wanting an explanation for their sudden *breakup,* as he'd called it.

"Agent Deitrich, are you there?" Agent D'Angelo asked.

"Yes, I'm here."

"How soon can you be here?"

Monica was surprisingly curt with Antonio. He'd disturbed her revelry, and she wasn't particularly happy about it. "How soon do you want me there, Antonio?"

"Let's not do this on the phone, Monica. This is a grave matter, and I need you right now. Just get here . . . soon," he said and then disconnected the call.

Whatever it was had to be serious because Antonio D'Angelo never turned down an opportunity to talk about their *relationship.* Monica turned the stroller around and jogged back toward her black, unmarked Dodge Charger.

Chapter 12

Darkness Falls

"Hello?" Monica said into her cell phone.

"Hello, Monica."

"Who is this?" she asked.

"After all we've been through, you still don't recognize my voice?"

"Kochese?"

"Yeah, bitch. Kochese. As a matter of fact, that's *King* Kochese to you," he said maliciously.

"Why don't you show yourself? Let's talk and iron this thing out."

"Why don't you go fuck yourself? Better yet, why don't you kill yourself and save me the trouble?" Kochese said sarcastically.

"Listen, little man, I don't have time for your games. What do you want?"

"Little man, huh? I wasn't little man when I had your snitch ass dick drunk."

"You weren't a serial killer then, either. Where are the babies, Kochese? Where are my nephew and niece?" she asked.

"Don't worry about my children. You need to be concerned about freeing your sister."

"And why would I do that, Mr. Badass?" she asked sarcastically.

"Don't get slick, bitch. And you would do that to keep me from burning down your fucking life."

Monica didn't speak. Kochese was trying to bait her, and she knew it.

"How many bodies did Jasmine and I have? Like sixty and some change? There are 365 days in a year, and I'm going to drop a body every fucking day until you release my wife. You think your shaky-ass career can withstand a 365-victim body count? I don't. So, whatever you have to do to free Jasmine, you'd better do it. I've already started, so you're behind. The longer you wait, the more bodies I dump," Kochese said.

"Free her? How am I supposed to do that, Kochese? I don't have that kind of clearance."

"Man, I'm not trying to hear that bullshit. Just fucking do it. And, Monica?" Kochese said softly.

"Yeah, man, what?"

"I'm surgical with my shit, so you already know there's a method to my madness and a design to my method, bitch. I'm going to save you, that bastard baby, and that disloyal-ass mutt for last. I'm a king among peasants and a wolf among sheep," he said, then disconnected the call.

Monica looked at her phone, bewildered. She didn't understand Kochese's last statement. *A king among peasants and a wolf among sheep?* What did that mean? Junior had made the same statement. Kochese loved to play mind games, but one thing was sure about the maniacal killer: he always made good on a promise. He'd told Monica that he would drop a body every day until she secured Jasmine's release, and she knew that he meant every word of it.

She'd met her young nanny, Porscha, at home and dropped off Millicent and Noisy Boy. She liked Porscha because she didn't mind coming to Monica's house to babysit, and Noisy Boy seemed to love her. Plus, Monica had surveillance cameras installed throughout the house, so it was easier to have an in-house sitter. Porscha was also a recent high school graduate who went above and beyond when it came to Millie and Noisy Boy. She took excellent care of Millie and was a godsend with Noisy Boy. She bathed, walked, and often spent her money to have him groomed by the mobile groomer. Monica would try to reimburse her, but she would never accept it, so Monica would always include it in her check. She bathed Millie and fed her, and whenever Millie went to sleep, Porscha made a point to clean Monica's home. She couldn't ask for a better caregiver for Millie and Noisy Boy.

But Kochese had spooked her. She hastily dialed Porscha's number and prayed that she would answer. Her phone went to voicemail, and Monica panicked, but Porscha called her back before she could hit the redial button.

"Hey, Miss Deitrich, I didn't hear the phone. I was changing the baby," she said out of breath.

"That's fine. Listen to me closely, Porscha. I know you have a regimen with the baby and the puppy, but I need you not to leave the house. It's imperative. No walks, no park, nothing. Lock all the doors and windows. If you have the blinds open, I need for you to close those as well."

"You're scaring me, Miss Deitrich. Is everything okay?" she asked.

"No, Porscha, everything is *not* okay. I need you to promise me that you'll do as I ask. I'll contact you as soon as I can give you more details. Promise me."

"I promise, Miss Deitrich," the young girl said in a shaky voice.

Monica disconnected the call and turned her sirens on. She sped through the streets of Dallas en route to the

FBI building. Kochese's statement that he had already begun his new game would explain why Antonio sounded so shaken. Kochese Mills, or Khalil Cross, or whatever name he was going by nowadays, was one of the most ruthless men she knew, and he would stop at nothing to get his way. She honked her horn furiously. "Come on, get the fuck out of the road," she screamed.

Honk, hoooonk!
Honk, hoooonk!

"Oh my God, doesn't anyone work in this goddamn city?" she screamed.

Monica saw an opening and switched lanes quickly. She looked to her right to mean mug the person who had been in front of her moments earlier and found herself even angrier when she saw the old lady behind the wheel. She was driving a car much too big for her tiny frame, and all Monica could see of the lady was her grayish blue hair and white knuckles. She had half a mind to pull the lady over for not yielding to an emergency vehicle, but she doubted the old woman could even hear the sirens. She muttered inaudible curses about how old people should stay off the road and how they needed to be retested after reaching a certain age. She chuckled to herself because if Pop Pop were still alive, he'd be one of those old people on the road with nowhere to go. She'd often teased him about driving too slowly, saying he'd be standing still if he drove any slower.

His response was always the same. First, he would laugh in his booming baritone, then say, "If I have to speed where I'm going, dear heart, then that means I should have left earlier."

Whenever she thought of her grandfather, she naturally thought of Jasmine. Her grandfather had died of natural causes, true, but whenever someone asked how he died, she always told them that he died from a broken heart. He'd gone to his grave believing that Jasmine would come home soon. Even after leaving their weekly visits with Jasmine at the Buckner Home for Youth, Pop Pop would remark that Jasmine was just *puttin' on*. He said she was the smartest girl he knew next to Monica, and she wasn't talking because she didn't feel like the world was ready for what she had to say.

"Jazzy Bell got mo' floatin' around in that head of hers than most people out here walking the street, and until those doctors come to her on her level, she won't utter one word. She'll come around when she gets good and ready . . . You watch," he'd said.

And now that Monica thought back on it, he'd been right. Jasmine was far more intelligent than Monica had believed. Monopoly had been their childhood game, and Jasmine had been calculative enough to weave an intricate murder scheme out of it. Sure, Kochese helped her, but Jasmine was the mastermind and author. She was sure of it. It saddened her that she and her sister had taken such different paths. Monica loved her sister. Even through the murders and psychotic episodes, she still saw Jasmine as her baby sister. The little girl she used to eat cereal with in front of the television, watching Saturday morning cartoons. The little sister who used to look up to her and follow her around. No one knew Monica's struggle; no one knew about her sleepless nights, her pain. No one would ever know how many times she considered just wheeling Jasmine out of Parkland Hospital and helping her to disappear. But she couldn't. She had taken an oath to uphold the law, and she took it seriously. Monica sighed heavily. The world was bearing down on her shoulders, and she knew the floodgates of tears were approaching. She tried to shake it off, but a dense black cloud was hanging over her head.

She pulled into the parking lot across from the Federal Building and parked. Monica beat the steering wheel until she could no longer hold her tears. "Goddamn you, Jazzy, for making me choose between you and my job," Monica cried. The guilt was eating her alive for what she'd done to her sister.

When the higher-ups had debriefed her, it was she who'd suggested that as soon as Jasmine gave birth, she be moved to a more secure location. The deputy director had agreed, and Jasmine had been sent to Shadowville State Hospital to await trial.

Monica gripped the steering wheel until she felt her knuckles go numb. She rocked back and forth violently, forcing her agony to show itself. Monica stared into the rearview mirror and watched herself cry. It was a habit she'd picked up as a child, and whenever she did it, it seemed to calm her pain. She laughed at how ugly she cried. She didn't have the beautiful Hollywood cry that was plastered on silver screens across the world. No, there was nothing attractive about streaked eyeliner and runny foundation.

Monica composed herself and made her way across the street. As she moved, she looked at the asphalt beneath her feet, a ritual that she'd started after Muldoon's death. For months after his murder, she'd watched the bloodstains dissipate until, finally, there were no more remnants of his grisly demise.

Chapter 13

A Real Purpose

Kochese was in love. His son and daughter had arrived safely, and they were even more beautiful than he could have imagined. He sat on the edge of the couch, staring into the dual silk-lined bassinets he'd had specially made for them. Apache watched his every move with the same intensely turquoise eyes that Kochese had seen in his dream. He wondered if the newborn knew who he was, but he dismissed it. How could he know who he was? Whatever the case, he was watching, and Kochese was afraid. He couldn't remember the last time he'd been scared, but with the children, he was afraid. He was terrified of failing them. After all, he was a fugitive from justice. The Feds could come bursting in at any given moment with guns blazing, and the thought of that alone terrified him. He held these two precious lives in the palms of his hands, and they were depending on him. He was afraid he couldn't be the father they needed, the kind of father he'd been denied as a child.

He watched the tiny heaves in their fragile chests, relishing the magnificence of their innocence. Kochese lifted his son and brought him close to his face, breathing in his essence. He gazed into the eyes of the child that would carry his legacy. Sure, he had a daughter, but she would eventually become a woman, take a husband, and carry *his* last name. But Apache Mills would forever carry the Mills name.

The tiny child was barely the size of a loaf of bread and smelled of purity and baby lotion. The smell was foreign to Kochese. He hadn't been around many babies in his lifetime, but he welcomed the scent. In his brief encounter with his son, a plethora of emotions ran rampant in his head. He questioned his entire being. He questioned his life's plan—a plan he'd set into motion and intended to carry out for Jasmine's sake. Things were different now, though. Holding Apache in his arms made him want to change.

He took his son to the king-sized bed and laid him gently on his back. Then he went back to the bassinet and picked up Angel. She cooed softly and shivered ever so slightly, and Kochese cuddled her close to him. She took a deep breath, and when she exhaled, he heard the faint whisper of her mother's voice. It was soft and high-pitched. It struck Kochese as surreal. He sat on the edge of his bed and placed her on his lap.

"I have no idea what I'm doing, Angel, but I love you and your brother very much. I promise always to be here. I promise always to hold you down, and no matter what happens, just remember that you and your brother were conceived with the highest form of love possible. I know you don't understand. You probably don't even hear me. But I just needed you to know these things," Kochese said softly.

Angel's eyes fluttered open. She was identical to her brother, even more so with her eyes open. He placed his baby girl on the mattress next to her brother and got down on his knees. He put his hands on each of their stomachs and bowed his head.

"God, it's me, Kochese. Listen, mane, if the things people say about you are true, you know my heart. I know I'm a bad person, and I know that you probably wrote me off a long time ago, but my kids are innocent. My childhood was messed up, but I'm sure you already know that. I never gave a damn about anything in my whole life, but I'm asking you, God, please protect my babies. Protect their mother, God. She's just as lost as I am, but if she feels half the love for these two as I do, then I know she's hurting. Help me show them that they don't have to live the way that we lived. Maybe I don't deserve a favor. Maybe you're not even listening. But just in case you are, God, I'm begging you, please take care of my children," he prayed.

Kochese had never been spiritual, let alone a praying man, but he needed to believe. He needed to believe that there was something greater than himself, something powerful enough to protect his family. He'd lived his entire life by the barrel of a gun, and if, by chance, that fate might befall his children, he would never forgive himself.

Kochese scrambled to his feet with a new resolve. He felt the world had been lifted from his shoulders, and an enigmatic calmness had come over him. Kochese wiped his tears and called for his maid.

"Ojé, Lucinda, come take the twins to the nursery. Tell Manny I said I want two armed guards outside their door and one on the terrace 24/7. Also, have Chico meet me in my office. Gracias," Kochese said.

"As you wish, Señor King." She produced a small bell from her apron pocket, rang it, and seconds later, a younger, prettier version of Lucinda appeared.

After they left with the twins, Kochese made his way to his office. The hallway leading to his private office seemed so long. The deep ridges of the bleached oak walls seemed to flow effortlessly into the gray and white marble floor. He opened the large double doors to his office and was greeted by the smell of money and polished mahogany. He sat behind his uncommonly large desk and lit a blunt. Kochese inhaled deeply and held it. He hadn't smoked any green since arriving in Costa Rica, but he needed it. He had an unsettling queasiness in his stomach, a sense of dread he couldn't put his finger on. The milky-white smoke filled his lungs, rushing his senses and giving Kochese instant satisfaction. He leaned back in his high-backed leather king's throne and took another hit. He held it just a tad bit too long and burst into a maniacal coughing fit. Kochese was still coughing when he heard a light tap on his office door.

Chico timidly peeked through the door. "Is everything okay, King?" he asked.

Kochese waved his hand to signal to Chico that all was well. "Have a seat, Chico," Kochese said through watery eyes and bated breath. "I know that Manny made the arrangements for my papers, but how possible is it for you to get them for my new identity?" Kochese asked.

"I suppose it would depend on what type of papers and what they would be used for."

Kochese rose to his feet and placed his palms flat on the desk. He leaned over and beckoned for Chico to come closer. "Do you see how black my skin is? I want to infiltrate the institution where they keep my girl," Kochese said.

"Give me a few days. I have a few contacts of my own, El Rey. This man can work wonders. How much time do I have?"

"I won't give you a time frame, but I need this done as soon as possible. If you need anything, let me know," Kochese said.

Chico nodded and made his way to the door. As he reached for the doorknob, he felt Kochese's hand on his shoulder.

"Chico, I don't want anybody up on this game. Nobody, dawg, you feel me? Not even Manny's fat ass," Kochese said.

Chapter 14

You Mad?

The front desk guard nodded a cordial but somewhat distant greeting in Monica's direction. He never really made eye contact, but it was quick and cold when he did. He'd also never once held a conversation with Monica. She didn't mind that the guard refused to talk. If there was one thing she didn't need, it was another Mr. Chadwick. Kochese had killed the sweet, elderly man for nothing more than to gain access to the Federal Building. Less-than-eager federal employees milled about in the lobby en route to their respective offices to eke out their meager earnings. They talked among themselves in humdrum tones, complaining of the woes of working-class life. Monica smiled to herself. People amused her. They found fault in everything when, in all actuality, they should have been glad to have a job.

She entered the elevator and drummed her fingers along the outer seam of her navy-blue slacks. The elevator ride took forever, and she didn't feel like thinking. She looked at herself in the mirror and winced. She looked like a church usher in her blue business suit, white button-down blouse, close-toed pumps, and pearls. Monica exited the elevator and headed toward Agent D'Angelo's office, but before she made it, he came from an adjoining conference room and motioned for her to join him there.

"Come in, Agent Deitrich. Have a seat," he said.

Five different agents were present, not including Monica or Agent D'Angelo, and everyone had their eyes glued on Monica.

"Agent Deitrich, I am going to ask you a few questions, and I need you to be as forthcoming as possible," Agent D'Angelo said.

To Monica, his tone sounded strange, like a veiled threat. She wasn't sure where he was going with his questioning, but she would play along. After the call she'd received from Kochese, the quicker she brought their conversation to light, the better. "Okay, D'Angelo, go ahead. I'm listening."

He opened a file before her and slid it across the table. She perused the pictures inside the file, and her stomach sank. The pictures were of several gruesome murders, but the murders weren't what made her stomach drop. It was a group of time-lapsed photos of King Kochese as he pulled the trigger of an automatic pistol, blowing a man's brains out. She stumbled and nearly fell, but she caught herself.

"Agent Deitrich?" D'Angelo said.

But Monica didn't answer. She was still lost in the photos, still trying to calm her acrobatic stomach.

"Agent Deitrich, we need to get down to business," he said more firmly, letting his hand rest on her.

He'd managed to pull her from her trauma-induced trance, but her gut still ached. "O-o-okay."

"When was the last time you had contact with your sister?" D'Angelo asked, pulling out a small notepad. He knew Monica Deitrich intimately, but he'd never had the opportunity to know her as a person. According to the agency, she could do nothing wrong. She was a government darling, and whenever the higher-ups spoke of her, they used flowery terms like "asset," "trooper," "straight arrow," etc. D'Angelo knew better because everyone had secrets. Everyone had skeletons in their closet, and every man, woman, and child on earth had a breaking point. There would always be that one incident that caused people to make not-so-wise decisions.

"I saw my sister a few days ago at the hospital just before she gave birth to this bastard's children," Monica said. She had nothing to hide but knew better than to start volunteering information.

"Have you had any contact with Kochese Mills, a.k.a. King?"

"Actually, he called me about ten minutes after I talked to you. He told me that if I didn't have Jasmine released, he would kill someone every day, and from the looks of it, he's living up to his word," she said.

"So, you expect us to release your sister? The United States doesn't negotiate with terrorists, Miss Deitrich."

"First of all, that's Special Agent in Charge Deitrich to you. Second, save the corny-ass clichés. Did I say that I expected you to do anything, Agent D'Angelo? No, I didn't, so miss me with this bullshit. My sister is damaged and dangerous. I know this. But I also know Kochese Mills well enough to know he will keep his word. Trust me," Monica said.

D'Angelo stared at Monica. He loved the fire and her passion for her job, but Monica Deitrich was a handful. He had to maintain his rugged exterior lest she realize his attitude was only a hollow shell. He ached for her, and she left him with no hope or explanation.

"Yes, ma'am, Special Agent in Charge Deitrich," he said softly but sarcastically. "If you'll have a seat, there's more," he said.

D'Angelo motioned to the middle-aged agent nearest the light switch. A dulling hush, thick with tension and uncertainty, filled the room. D'Angelo and Monica's minor tiff seemed more like a lover's quarrel than a debate over procedure. Each man in the room recognized it but remained quiet for fear of receiving a tongue-lashing from Special Agent in Charge Monica Deitrich.

Agent D'Angelo fumbled with the keys on his laptop. He pressed play, and the screen of the 42-inch wall-mounted television sprang to life. On the screen, Kochese was smearing the brains of the unsuspecting agent all over the cold concrete. There was only one problem.

"Oh my God!" Monica screamed as she leaped to her feet.

"Is there a problem, Agent Deitrich? Don't tell me you're squeamish," an elderly agent teased.

Monica looked at the man and burned holes into his flesh with her eyes. "Yes, there's a problem, and it has nothing to do with being squeamish. I don't think that's Kochese Mills."

"What do you mean that's not Kochese?" D'Angelo asked.

"I could be wrong, but the smile is all wrong, and his stride is forced, like there's a hitch in his step," Monica said.

"Would you bet your career on that, Monica? Maybe we have a copycat on our hands, Agent?"

"Copycat maybe, but I seriously doubt it," she said, still looking at the screen, then added, "would you bet your career that it is that son of a bitch Kochese?"

There had been too many *coincidences* lately for this to be anything other than a ploy by King Kochese Mills. She knew it and would prove it—even if it cost her her life.

Chapter 15

You Got It, Flaunt It

King hadn't had the opportunity to dive into the night life of Costa Rica. Manny was under the impression that Kochese needed to stay hidden, but the king had a plan. He and Manny were two different types of people. Manny was the type of man who was satisfied with his family and whatever fortune he'd been able to amass. Kochese was one of the wealthiest men in Costa Rica, but he wanted more. He wasn't satisfied with only being one of the richest. He wanted to be the most powerful too. The underworld of Costa Rica was just about as powerful as the political structure there, and Kochese wanted to own them both. He didn't *need* the money, and he didn't *need* the exposure, but he did *need* the political pull and insulation that came with wealth. After so many years of being the man in Dallas, he couldn't see himself just laying it down and being a square.

Kochese entered his club through a side door with four of his closest soldiers in tow. Tonight, he would lay out his plan to all involved. Some would agree, some wouldn't, but he wasn't concerned. If they disagreed with the new structure, then they would be murdered—no arguments, no disagreements—just elimination. The club was dimly lit, and no patrons had started to arrive yet, so Kochese would have plenty of time for his meeting before the club got slammed.

"Ojé, King, everyone is waiting for you in the conference room," Chico said.

The bodyguards entered the room first, followed closely by Kochese and Chico. Two soldiers took up position at the door while the other two went to the opposite end of the room. Manny was seated at the head of the table, and his most trusted soldier, Lolly, sat next to him. The other seats were occupied by thoroughbred street dudes that Chico had handpicked himself at Kochese's behest. Kochese directed Chico to sit at the head of the table on the end closest to the door. If Manny were trying to make a statement, Kochese would make a bigger one.

"I'm glad all of you cats decided to take this meeting. Since I've been in Costa, I've noticed that crime is massive here. I don't mean that in a disrespectful way. I simply mean that there is opportunity lurking around every corner. I want to build an organization with you Ticos. I want everyone to eat, and I want to own this entire fucking country. If you're not with an American coming in and making you rich, just say the word, and we can kill this deal right now," Kochese said. He watched each man in the room intensely. There seemed to be no opposition, so he continued. "I've handpicked each of you for a specific area of interest. Victor, you and your boys control most of the cocaine that comes into the country. Ernesto, you and your boys are doing well with that Russian pill connect. Mauricio, you just about control all of the skin trade here. And, Diego, your international chop shop ring is priceless. I want to help expand these fields so that everybody gets more paper. No longer will each crew operate independently of one another. Instead, we'll move as a unit. One team, one vision. I'll grease the proper officials to ensure we go untouched," Kochese said.

He'd purposely not mentioned Manny, Lolly, or Chico. He could tell that the omission had gotten under Manny's skin, and he liked it. To drive his point home, he walked over and placed his hand on Chico's shoulder.

"From now on, if anyone needs me for anything, money for more product, protection from the *policia*, whatever, you make sure that you go through Chico. Manny, you and Lolly will run the club," he said.

Manny and Lolly whispered among themselves, almost silently debating until it was too much for Lolly to take.

"Nah, papi, fuck that. This *pinché chongo* comes down here and thinks he can do this shit to us? You ain't gotta say shit. *I'll* say something," Lolly screamed.

"What seems to be the problem, Lolly?" Kochese asked.

"The problem is that we've been moving in these streets of Costa Rica just fine, and then you come in and make us some fucking barmaids? Nah, papi, I don't think so. I have my own squad, and I'll get my own fucking money. Half of these *maricones* in this room have worked for me and Manny at some point, and now you want us to answer to these pricks? I don't think so. You can go fuck yourself."

"Yo, check this shit out. First of all, if you disrespect me again, we will have a major muh'fuckin' problem. Second, listen, nobody is saying that you have to get down with my program, but you won't move so much as an Alka-Seltzer in this bitch unless you're on my team. This shit is nonnegotiable, mane, so choose wisely," Kochese grinned.

"Yeah? Well, fuck you, fuck your team, and fuck anybody that doesn't like it. I'm Lolly. My fucking reputation in this shithole country is solid." Lolly stood up to leave, and Manny grabbed his wrist, but Lolly snatched his arm away. "You can stay here and be his flunky if you want to,

Manny, but not me. Can't you see that he's trying to play us?" Lolly said.

He was about to continue with more of his tirade, but before he could utter another word, Kochese crossed the room and planted his hands firmly around Lolly's throat. He applied constant pressure until he felt Lolly's body go limp, and then, just before he lost consciousness, he released his grip and slapped him to bring him back to reality. Without hesitation, Chico stood and was on top of Lolly before he could compose himself. He whipped out his chrome .380 and beat Lolly's face mercilessly. He pistol-whipped him until crimson-red blood gushed from his open wounds. Chico held Lolly's ponytail with a death grip, and as he opened his mouth to protest, Chico sent the butt of his gun crashing into his mouth, causing an explosion of blood, teeth, and gums. He turned to Kochese, who had a look of satisfaction and excitement written across his ebony features.

Kochese let his eyes roam from Lolly to Manny, so Chico moved in on Manny. He cocked his pistol and held it to Manny's cheek. Manny held his hands up in a submissive manner. He was nobody's fool. Chico was obviously making a play for second in command, and if he contested, he would surely meet the same fate as Lolly.

"Whoa, Chico, *calmate wey*. Calm down. I'm on board. If King wants me to run the club, I'm cool with that," Manny said nervously.

"Anybody disrespects El Rey, they will answer to me. None of us have seen the type of money he is willing to expose us to, so I think we owe him our respect and loyalty. Entiendes?" Chico said.

Slowly, each man nodded his understanding. The thing that each man present knew but that Kochese hadn't learned yet was that Chico was a killer. Everyone except for Kochese knew what Chico was capable of, and they had an equal measure of fear and admiration for the man.

"Now that that's out of the way let's get back to business. This organization will work like this: whatever you've been investing in your business, I am going to double that," Kochese said.

A murmur of excitement filled the room, and Kochese held up his hands to silence them. "I know that with more work comes more responsibility, but you'll also make more money. I'm going to devote as much money as it takes to not only own this country but also to knock the US off of its pivot. If you have family in the US, tell them let's get this paper. We are going to flood the streets with a billion dollars' worth of dope, if that's what it takes. They'll be outgunned, outfinanced, and outmanned. This is the beginning of a hostile takeover, my niggas," Kochese said triumphantly.

"Excuse me, papi, but how will we run our organizations over here *and* do a hostile takeover over there? Don't get me wrong. I like money just as much as the next man, but my concern is finding enough manpower to take over the US streets effectively," Victor said.

"I assure you, Victor, by the time I'm done, we'll have people lined up *begging* to fill out an application to ride this money train. Just like I handpicked you cats, I expect you to help me handpick the best and the brightest that the underworld has to offer," Kochese said. He walked to the head of the table where Manny still sat and tapped him on his shoulder. "Since you're running the club now, why don't you go to the bar and get us a bottle to toast with? Take Lolly with you," Kochese sneered.

It wasn't a request, and everyone knew it. Slowly, Manny rose to his feet. He didn't understand why Kochese had turned on him the way he had, but he'd rather be a barmaid than dead. Manny helped Lolly to his feet, and they disappeared into the club. Kochese didn't trust them, nor did he like them. The adage, "Keep your friends close and your enemies closer," rang true in more ways than one.

"Okay, gentlemen, now that Manny and his little rat are out of the room, I want you Ticos to know that I have tremendous faith in you. The only reason that Manny is still alive is because he's helped me in the past in my time of need. That other muh'fucka, Lolly? I don't know him and don't care to know him. I want every one of you rich like me. Ballin' like me. We can all eat; we can all get this money. If you niggas hold me down and stay loyal, I give you my word that the world is ours, and I'll make each one of you rich beyond your comprehension," Kochese promised.

Manny entered the room on cue with a drink tray in hand as if he'd been at the door listening. Lolly followed close behind with his head held low. He looked like a sad puppy, scampering with his tail between his legs. Manny put a shot glass of Louie XIII in front of each man, keeping one for himself. Kochese raised his glass and looked around the table, but he stopped before making his toast.

"Manny, trade glasses with Lolly," he said.

Manny did as he was told, and then Kochese traded glasses with Manny. If Manny had tampered with his drink in any way, Lolly would know about it and hesitate to drink it. Again, Kochese lifted his glass. "Here's to a bright future. I want you to go home tonight and fuck your wives. I want you to wake up in the morning after a good night's sleep and fuck them again. I want you to take them shopping tomorrow, and then I want you to tell them that you are about to conquer the world because tomorrow begins the rest of your lives, mane. Salud," he said.

"Salud!" the men yelled in unison.

"There is only one thing that I require. Can anyone guess what that is?" Kochese asked. Before any of them could answer, Kochese walked to the wall and removed a large hunting knife that hung there. "The only thing I require is complete and utter loyalty to this organization. Nah, scratch that, this *family*. I need to know and trust that it'll be freely given no matter what I ask. Entiendes? Diego, come here, mane."

The tall, dark-skinned Costa Rican man walked to Kochese with no fear registering in his eyes. He stood only three feet from King Kochese and looked into his eyes. "What's up, El Rey?" he asked.

"Will you die for me, my nigga?" Kochese asked.

"Gladly."

"Will you steal for me?"

"Without hesitation."

"Will you kill for me?" Kochese asked, watching him closely.

Diego hesitated briefly, but that moment of hesitation told Kochese everything he needed to know. He plunged the hunting knife deep into Diego's chest and forced him to the ground. A gasp of horror and surprise filled the plush office. The lanky Spaniard struggled against Kochese's weight, but it was futile, and the more he resisted, the deeper the knife sank into his heart.

Diego gurgled and choked on the pink, foamy mixture of blood and saliva that oozed from his mouth. King stared deep into his eyes as Diego slipped into the afterlife as if he'd drawn some kind of magical life force from the dying man. He withdrew the knife from his chest cavity with one swift, squishy motion. Then Kochese stood and smiled at his newfound soldiers.

"See, my niggas? There's no room for hesitation. Diego was a bitch nigga. What kind of real man would die for a muh'fucka but won't kill for him?" he said, wiping the blood off the blade onto Manny's shirt. Kochese handed Manny the knife. "Kill ya boy, Manny. Kill Lolly, or so help me God, I will filet and soufflé your big bitch ass, mane!" Kochese barked.

Lolly tried to back away, tried to find a means of escape, but Victor pushed him toward Manny. His legs went limp, and his body felt weighted. He wanted to cry out; he wanted to plead for his life, but he wasn't a coward.

Manny spun him around in one smooth and rhythmic motion so that Lolly's back was pinned to his massive stomach. He hugged him tight with one arm and slit his throat with his free hand. Lolly had just enough time to look around the table at the men gathered there. He wasn't sure whether he was fading away and hallucinating or whether their faces were really those of demons. They smiled at him, tormenting and taunting him, beckoning for him to follow them to somewhere beyond the darkness. He reached for one of them, but the imp was too far away, and suddenly, he was gone. Lolly stumbled toward his childhood friend Ernesto and pulled him close.

"Why, mi amigo?" he asked.

"Because you've always been a *rata,* and as you know, ratas don't last long in the jungle, *puto*," Ernesto said.

He shoved Lolly back toward Manny, and Manny let the blade of the knife sink into the base of Lolly's skull. Lolly smiled at Ernesto and dropped to his knees. He blinked rapidly, trying to expel the long nap he knew he was destined to take, but it was useless. He slipped into a dark place where the demons waited. They were there to take him home, where rats were welcomed, and angels dared not tread.

Chapter 16

Little Rock, Arkansas

The dilapidated house sat inconspicuously at the bottom of a hill just off Market Street near downtown Little Rock. It was ideal for what the killer had in mind. He'd rented a sparse room in the basement of the house from an elderly white woman named Mrs. Slidell. She hadn't done a background check or asked for a driver's license, which was perfect because he never carried identification anyway. It had taken Mrs. Slidell ten whole minutes to go down the stairs to show him the apartment.

She was decrepit and wore a dingy, tattered housecoat with furry slippers that had seen better days. The fur on the house shoes and housecoat matched with its matted and dirty cheetah print. As she unlocked the door at the bottom of the stairs, he heard her mutter that rent was due on the first of the month, and she made no exceptions. She eyed him curiously as he strode through the small one-room dwelling. Whoever had lived there previously had smoked in the apartment because the stench of mold and stale cigarettes had a stranglehold on his nostrils. He pulled the string to an overhead light, but nothing happened.

"You have to screw the lightbulb in. I don't know why my grandson Jessup did it that way, but that's what you have to do," she said.

He twisted the bulb, and a dim but revealing light filled the room, partially flickering on and off intermittently. He didn't understand how she could call it an apartment. It was more like a storage room. In the far corner were Christmas decorations stacked haphazardly around the water heater. An empty gift set box that had undoubtedly housed her housecoat and slippers sat near the base of the mountain of moisture-stained boxes. The floor was a dull, cold concrete with no sheen to speak of, maybe because the water heater she'd covered with the boxes had leaked in the past. He could tell it was prone to leaks because the boxes had been water-stained at the bottom. In another corner were piles of old sheets and blankets, and he surmised that some time ago, perhaps many years ago, there was a baby or, at the very least, a small child living there because the pile smelled of urine. Had it not been for desperation, there was no way that he would have even considered living in such squalor, but then again, he wasn't exactly going to be *living* there. His objective was clear, and he would only be there for a week at the most.

The old lady reached into the pocket of her housecoat and removed a crumpled box of Benson & Hedges menthol 100 cigarettes. She lit the obvious reason for her frail and fragile body and deeply inhaled as she leaned against the railing of the stairs. Her frame had long since left her in retaliation for her love of nicotine. In between puffs, she coughed and hacked until the phlegm from deep within her lungs came in small bursts. She held the cigarette between her two brittle fingers, coughing and spraying her tepid clumps of green slime speckled with reddish orange blood. She used the slickened bottom of her shoe to smear it into the untreated cement.

"So, whaddaya think? Do you like it?" she asked.

He looked around nervously and then just as quickly stiffened. He could hear the voice from deep within his head surfacing, unlocking doors, and clearing cobwebs from the recesses of his psyche.

Kill this old broad. You owe me. You were supposed to kill the baby, but you didn't, did you? So, you owe me, the voice said.

He grabbed his head. "No!" he screamed.

"No? No what? Oh, you think you're too good for this here room? I'll have you know my grandson Jessup grew up right here in this room, and he works for the FBI. So iffin' he can grow up to be somebody, then there can't be nothing wrong with this room," she huffed.

"What? Oh, no, ma'am, I wasn't saying no to liking the place. I like it fine. It's cozy and quaint, almost secluded. I'll take it. How much do I owe you?"

"Well, at seventy-five dollars a week, that'll be $300 for the month, and I only take cash. I don't like to deal with the banks because the extra money'll mess up my Social Security." She coughed.

He pulled out a wad of crumpled twenty-dollar bills and handed them to the old woman.

"There must be $400 here. You've gave me too much," she said, rifling through the bills.

"It's okay; just take it. I'm grateful that you're letting me use the place. I'm a very private person, so I would like it if you didn't come down here without my permission, please."

"That door from the outside that we came through is the only way in or out. The door at the top of the stairs has been nailed shut for quite some time. I won't come down here as long as you promise not to have any wild parties," she teased.

He assured her she had nothing to worry about and bid her farewell so he could set up his house of horror.

As he dressed, he thought of the old woman who had rented him the space. To the average person, she may have been regarded as vile with her constant hacking, brittle hair, and weather-beaten skin. The ripe odor of mothballs and cigarette butts didn't help either, but he didn't see her that way. He saw a woman who had probably outlived all her friends and most of her loved ones. He saw a woman who cared for her family with hard work and sacrifice. He saw a loving, older woman who, for all intents and purposes, could have very well been his grandmother. He'd concocted an entire fantasy about how life would have been had she been his grandmother. The smell of freshly baked, soft cookies wafted through the air. Birds flitted upon the windowsill of her freshly washed panes, chirping and tweeting the sweet melodies of an approaching spring. He played cowboys and Indians with the neighborhood children in their backyard. As a reward for behaving, his grandmother brought them freshly baked chocolate chip cookies and a tall pitcher of ice-cold lemonade.

He closed his eyes and smiled. His fantasy was so real that he could feel the warmth of the sun and the tingle on his skin from the breeze. Something wasn't right, though. He could feel a presence creeping up on him. It was the voice. He was coming. He could always tell when he was coming because his head pounded, his pulse quickened, and everything looked black around the edges. He looked around the room, but he didn't see him. He looked in the faded and dusty mirror . . . and there he was. Through the oily fingerprints and hairline cracks of the antique cheval mirror, the voice stared at him, scowling as if he might jump out and end it all.

This is the type of shit I'm talking about. You don't even know that old-ass lady. For all you know, she could be on the phone with her grandson, the police officer, right now giving us up.

"She wouldn't do that. She likes me," he screamed.

Yeah, that's what you say now, but just wait. Nobody will ever be there for you like me. You're hardheaded and fragile. That's why you need me to keep you safe.

"Safe? Is that what you think? That you keep me *safe?*" he asked incredulously.

Remember Pee Wee from the youth home? Yeeeeah, I bet you do remember Pee Wee. Who helped you with that little problem?

"You did. But—"

But nothing. If it hadn't been for me, you would've been in that orphanage braiding his nappy-ass hair and washing his drawers.

"Don't. Please don't do this to me!" he screamed. But it was too late. The memories had come flooding his mind like a tidal wave.

Pee Wee was a 13-year-old man-child who had experienced far too much in his short time on earth. Sex, drugs, crime . . . He'd done it all, so much so that his mother had grown tired of his antics, and while the mischievous boy was in school, she'd simply moved. She moved an entire apartment in less time than it took him to complete a full day of school. He'd come home to find the door of their second-story apartment wide open. The only things that Pee Wee's mother had left in the apartment were the few tattered clothes that barely fit the boy and a note scribbled in her less-than-legible handwriting that read:

Pee Wee, I left you five dollars in the kitchen drawer. Don't try to find me. I think it's best if we just go our separate ways, boy. I've done everything that I possibly could for you, but you're a bad seed. You steal my weed, you're taking my pills, you steal my cigarettes and money. You even drink up my

*liquor and then put water in it. I'm tired of being
a mama, especially your mama. Anyway, don't
spend that money on no weed. Make sure you eat.
 Mommy*

*Pee Wee was 13 years old, but he was built and looked
more like he was 18, hence his experience with sex.*

*While in the youth center, he'd heard tales of Pee
Wee's legendary phallus. He'd also heard that Pee Wee
had a thing for young boys. One day, while he was in the
shower, Pee Wee came in and insisted that they share
the shower stall. Before he could object, Pee Wee was
naked and standing there with a fully erect penis. He
tried not to look, but the sheer size of it had him in a
stupor and terrified at the same time.*

"You like this dick, bitch?" Pee Wee snarled.

"No!" he said, looking away quickly.

"Why the fuck you looking at it then?"

"I wasn't," he said.

"I'm going to make *you like it. Tonight, when the nuns
go to sleep, I'ma take yo' booty," Pee Wee said.*

*He panicked. He didn't know what to do, so he sprang
from the shower with soap and suds still clinging to his
frail 10-year-old frame. He ran naked toward his room,
leaving a trail of wet, soapy footprints in his wake. As
he made it to the room that he shared with seven other
boys, all he could think about was Mr. Hinkle and the
savage things he had done to him. Pee Wee would never
have the opportunity to do the same.*

*The staff at the youth home must have known that
Pee Wee had an affinity for young boys because he
was isolated from the rest of the boys at night. He was
the only boy out of fifty allowed to have his own room.
While the rest of the boys chose to play basketball and
walk around the track, Pee Wee lifted weights daily in*

the small weight room of the youth home. So, besides being bigger than the other children, he was stronger and more muscular.

The night that Pee Wee was supposed to come into his room to take his booty, the boy had sat through dinner, petrified, as Pee Wee and his friends had stared at the frightened boy, laughing, taunting him, and daring him to tell. He crept away from the cafeteria and stole away to the gym. Once there, he put a two-pound weight into the pocket of his baggy jeans and returned to his room. He placed the weight underneath his pillow, sat on his bed, and waited. He tried to read his favorite X-men comic book again but couldn't concentrate. Time seemed to be moving slowly, so slowly that he went out into the TV room out of sheer curiosity.

Pee Wee was ridiculing him in the middle of the floor, reenacting for the other boys how he'd run from the bathroom crying. They were doubled over laughing— well, most of them were laughing. Some of the younger boys who had been Pee Wee's victims didn't find his show amusing in the least bit. He stood at the entrance of the TV room, silently fuming, trying to brush aside the harsh sting of the tears welling in his eyes.

See, man, he will have everybody laughing at you and picking on you. I'll take care of you, though, like I always do, the voice said.

He returned to his room, lay across his bed, and dozed off. He'd just settled into a somewhat peaceful slumber when the voice jostled him awake.

Wake up; it's almost time, the voice said.

"Bedtime, boys," one of the nuns yelled.

Moments later, the sound of light switches clicking off, mixed with the disappointed chatter of the young boys, could be heard echoing in the halls. Mother Grigsby was the meanest of them all, and it was best if you were

*asleep, or at least pretending to be, when she came by
to do her count. He lay awake on his stomach, his head
pressed into his pillow and his hand firmly gripping the
two-pound weight.*

   It's time, the voice said.

   *The boy sat in bed and tried to adjust his eyes to the
darkness. There were no night-lights, flashlights, or candles. There was no noise other than the faint snoring of
the youth home residents. The only light visible was the
moonlight shining through the stained-glass window of
the chapel at the end of the hall. He went to the opposite
end of the hall toward Pee Wee's room. If anyone caught
him out of bed, he would simply explain it away as him
going to the bathroom because it was on the same end of
the building as Pee Wee's bedroom. Before reaching the
man-child's room, he could hear the deep, nasally drone
of Pee Wee's snoring. It was loud and syncopated, very
arrhythmic in its pattern. He inched his way into Pee
Wee's room and stood over him, glowering, gripping the
weight tightly with his tiny hands.*

   *Not yet! We have to be smart. What if he screams?
We'll get caught. You can't let him scream.*

   *He kneeled quietly and picked up one of Pee Wee's
smelly tube socks that were thrown carelessly across
his Pro Wings gym shoes. He stood and felt a surge of
anger and adrenaline rush through his body. The threat
of being anally brutalized by the teenager, coupled with
his snoring, was driving him insane. With one swift
motion, he shoved the sock into Pee Wee's open mouth.
He kept pushing until he heard Pee Wee gag from the
sock at the back of his throat.*

   *Pee Wee's eyes popped open, and before he could get
his hands up to resist, the boy brought the two-pound
weight down on Pee Wee's head with all of his strength.
There was no struggle, only blood and silence. Pee Wee*

lay still, but the frightened preteen kept hitting him until he heard the sound of Pee Wee's hard skull bone crack. He beat him until his face was a mangled mess of blood and exposed flesh.

After he was sure that Pee Wee was dead, he made his way to the bathroom and washed the blood from his body into the sink. He took his bloody underwear and T-shirt off and dropped it into the laundry chute. He stood naked in the mirror, staring at his frail frame. The bones of his chest and ribs poked through his skin, giving him an unhealthy and sickly look. He slunk back to his room, grabbed underwear from his footlocker, and climbed into bed.

See how easy that was? I'll always take care of you. Tell the truth: it felt good, didn't it? the voice asked.

"What if we did that for nothing?" *he whispered.*

For nothing? He was going to hurt you, just like Mr. Hinkle.

"But what if he wasn't? What if he was just talking, you know, being a blowhard?" *he muttered softly.*

And what if he wasn't being a blowhard? Maybe next time I should stay in my place and see what happens. Maybe he'll fuck you, and maybe he won't. That's a lot of maybes. Do you really want to take that chance?

"No, but I—"

Suddenly, the room was flooded with light, and he felt the cold, familiar sting of Mother Grigsby's yardstick across the fleshiness of his back. "Who are you talking to, boy?" *she hissed.*

"Ouch!" *he screamed.* "I was praying. I was talking to God."

"And just what were you talking to our Lord and Savior about?" *she asked softly. She'd softened at the prospect of converting one of the young heathens entrusted to her care.*

"*I was asking God if He could bless each of us with a home with good parents, and I asked Him to bless the kids out there who are still being done the way I was. When you hit me, I was asking God to give you patience because I know that you get frustrated with us,*" he lied.

By the time he finished speaking, the old, grizzled nun had tears in her eyes. She couldn't believe that she'd actually gotten through to one of the hardheaded children. "*Praise the Lord. I'm sorry I hit you. Bless your heart. Get some sleep, and we'll pray together in the morning,*" she said as she rubbed the spot on his back that she'd struck with her yardstick.

That had been years earlier, and as much as he regretted it, the voice would have him kill her too not long after that fateful night.

Chapter 17

Welcome to Purgatory

Jasmine's head rested against the darkly tinted window of the black, unmarked federal van. They had her hands and feet shackled together and then shackled to the floor for added security. Her orange one-piece jumpsuit made her skin itch in places she couldn't reach, and she was irritated.

"Where are you guys taking me?" she asked. The federal agents who oversaw her transport to the airport treated her as if she'd been on the run for years versus a woman who had just given birth a month earlier.

A muscular agent with no facial expression looked in her direction but didn't speak. He looked to be in his early thirties, with sandy-brown hair and a thick mustache. Jasmine couldn't see his eyes because of the dark shades that he was wearing, but she was sure that he was judging her.

"Are you deaf and dumb or just dumb? I asked where I was being taken. I have a right to know," she muttered. Her question was rhetorical, but the agent answered it anyway.

"I am neither, but you're a threat and a flight risk, ma'am. Hence, the rabbit suit," he said, referring to her orange jumpsuit. "You will have your day in court, but until then, you will be housed in a secure, undisclosed facility." And as an afterthought added, "It's not every day that we're in the company of such a prolific serial killer. You should be proud; you and your wack-job boyfriend made it to the FBI's most wanted list."

His voice was deep and southern, but his dialect wasn't a Texas drawl. If Jasmine had to guess, he sounded more like he was from Alabama or Mississippi.

The agent shifted his bulk and adjusted the black flak jacket that he was wearing, emblazoned with FBI across the chest.

"Husband," Jasmine corrected.

"Excuse me?"

"You said my boyfriend, so I corrected you. He's my husband, not my boyfriend."

"Boyfriend, husband, serial killers, it makes no never mind to the government, and I could give a fat rat's ass either way. One thing is certain, though. You two will never see each other again. Now, sit back and shut the fuck up."

That's the same statement that Monica had made just before she turned her over to these dickheads, and as much as she hated to admit it, they were right. Likely, Jasmine would never see Kochese or her children again. She had been so close to escaping that, for a moment, she thought freedom was in her grasp. Jasmine had successfully slipped from her hospital room and eased into the stairwell. When she made it to the first floor, she waited, listening. She could hear talking, but the voices sounded far away. Jasmine eased the door open and slid into the corridor. A pudgy white nurse wobbled past her with a curly red Afro, rosy cheeks, and piercing blue eyes. Jasmine couldn't decide whether she looked more like Napoleon Dynamite or the little fat kid from *Bad Santa*. Jasmine had to fight the urge to get in her ear and say, "Are you fucking with me about those goddamn sandwiches?" The nurse would probably not have a clue that it was a line from a movie and go full Karen mode on her.

The nurse disappeared through automatic doors, and Jasmine headed to the exit. She felt weak, and some crimson fluid leaked through the jeans she wore. The heat from the midmorning sun was brutal, only adding to the sickness that had her stomach churning and knotted. Jasmine closed her eyes and leaned against the brick wall, trying to gather some strength. She heard the voice just before the rapidly approaching footsteps, and her eyes popped open. It was Monica's voice.

"Jasmine!"

This bitch, Jasmine thought.

"Jasmine, I need you to turn around and put your hands behind your back," Monica said, gun aimed in Jasmine's direction.

"You ain't gotta do this, Monica. I'll leave, and you'll never see me again."

"I can't do that, Jazzy. As much as I want to, I can't."

"Why not? It's just me and you out here. You don't have to do this. I'll disappear, I promise," Jasmine said, inching toward Monica.

"Stop fucking moving, Jazzy," Monica said as she backed away a few paces. She removed the walkie-talkie from her hip and spoke into it, her gun still pointed at Jasmine. "This is Agent Deitrich. I have the suspect in custody."

The talkie crackled, and then a voice said, "Ten-four. What's your location, Agent?"

Monica looked around, "I'm at the east exit facing the pharmacy."

"Ten-four. Be there directly; over." And with a hiss and a crackle, the conversation ended.

"So, you're going to let me go to prison for the rest of my life? What happened to 'No matter what happens, Jazzy, I'll be there'? What happened to 'We have to take care of each other'? You finally have a chance to do right by me, and you won't do it." Jasmine's voice had started to tremble, and she wanted to cry. "Oh well, I have never needed you, and I never will. I hope you have sleepless nights for the rest of your miserable life, knowing that you're taking a new mother away from her newborn children."

"No, Jasmine, *you* took yourself from your children. You fell in love with a murderer. You gave birth to a murderer's children, and you went on a killing spree with Kochese like some deranged Bonnie and Clyde shit. You did all those things, *not* me. This isn't on me. This is all you, baby girl."

"I have all the things that you wish you had. You wish you were married to Kochese, and you wish you had his children. You were jealous from the first time I met him, and once you found out it was King, you had to find a way to ruin it. How does it feel knowing that I married the man of *your* dreams? Knowing that your little sister took your man," Jasmine smirked.

"How does it feel knowing you will never see him again?"

"I swear if I ever get my hands on you, Monica, I will rip you to shreds." Jasmine sneered and spat a wad of spit in Monica's face, just above her left eye.

An FBI agent approached the duo with his gun drawn, aimed at Jasmine. "Turn around, put your hands behind your back, and don't move."

But she didn't turn around or put her hands behind her back. Instead, she held eye contact with Monica. She was used to being institutionalized, but that was before she was a mother. There was a hole growing in her soul, and she felt hollow. She longed for her children as if she'd been their mother for an eternity, and she pined for Kochese. From his sinuous muscles to his ice-blue eyes, she missed him, his comfort, his words. In his arms was the only place that she had ever felt safe. Jasmine feared never seeing her family again, and sadness choked her. She wanted to release the pain that she felt, but she wouldn't cry. She would not give Monica the satisfaction of bearing witness to her grief. Finally, she turned around and clasped her hands behind her back, and was taken into custody.

Now, as the van pulled to the curb of Love Field Airport, the media rushed to them as soon as they caught sight of Jasmine's haggard face. Her green eyes were puffy from crying, and her hair was a mess of wild, dry curls. Her jeans were stained from the liquid that had been leaking, her mouth was pasty and dry, and her lips felt tight. Four federal Marshals pushed past the ruthless reporters and took custody.

"Miss Deitrich, where are your children?" a reporter asked, trying to shove a microphone into her face.

"Where is your boyfriend, Miss Deitrich?" asked another.

"He's my husband," Jasmine corrected in a voice barely above a hoarse whisper. The Marshals proudly paraded her through the airport as if they'd captured the Unabomber. Travelers and spectators stopped and stared, pointing at the pretty prisoner and her procession of Marshals. They ushered her through security quickly and out onto the tarmac, where a plane from the Bureau of Federal Prisons waited. Had she known that they would use such lax security with her, she would have most certainly gotten word to Kochese to come for her.

You can wish for Kochese to save you on the one hand and shit in the other hand and see which one gets full the fastest, sweetie. They're sending your black ass to the nuthouse, Jasmine thought.

Chapter 18

Welcome to Shadowville

Shadowville State Hospital was hidden in a valley crater between four mountain peaks. Even on the sunniest of days, daylight never reached the prison. Shadowville was so deep in the Allegheny Mountains that it was called the New Alcatraz because there was no escape. There was no fencing or barbed razor wire, no guard tower or attack dogs . . . just miles and miles of thick forest and an overly eager staff willing to hunt you down and inflict pain—a lot of pain. Many of the prison staff were residents of the small town that sat at the mountain's base. It had been a booming coal mining town in the late 1800s and early 1900s but had devolved into a ramshackle enclave of old houses, abandoned businesses, and people either working at the prison or tied to the community by generational history. Some of the inhabitants hated the outside world because they felt forgotten and shitted on. That ill will and resentment showed in the demeanor of most, if not all, of the prison staff, and they routinely took their frustration to work. They may have called it a state hospital, but it was a prison, and the faculty never let the inmates forget it. Shadowville housed the throwaways who had offended America the most, the ones that the nation wanted the world to forget.

Jasmine sat with her back against the cold steel wall of her cell, sketching the parts of the prison she had visited in the six months since her arrival. She always took mental notes and snapshots, remembering as many details as possible while she sketched. She could weave intricate and detailed illustrations of her surroundings into her sketches. To the naked eye, they looked like busy sketches and doodles. But Jasmine had exit routes, potential allies, and faults within the hospital's security infrastructure, all obscurely embedded in her artwork, details only she would recognize. She hadn't met many inmates because every cell in Shadowville was isolated. The women only saw one another in the recreation yard, but Jasmine never talked to any of them. Most of them were either dazed zombies full of pills or were having better conversations with the voices in their heads. Jasmine liked being alone in her cell with no distractions, just her and her thoughts. Suddenly, the lock on Jasmine's cell popped, and she stood and placed the sketch pad beneath her pillow. When she turned, Ernest was standing in her doorway.

"Are you going to rec today, JD?" he asked.

Jasmine liked Ernest. He was the only guard she had come in contact with on the compound, and he treated her like a human being. He took time to talk to her and get to know her. Well, as much as she allowed him to know. She let him do most of the talking on the occasions that they conversed, and she found that he knew a wide array of subjects, especially where the prison was concerned.

"Yeah, E, let me grab my book. How you been? Haven't seen you in a couple of days. Is everything okay?" Jasmine asked. She grabbed her sketchbook, took her pencil, and stuck it in her hair behind her ear.

Ernest didn't answer. He was staring at the lopsided sketch of Barak Obama that hung on the wall over her bunk. In it, a cigarette dangled from his lips, and his right eye was only partially open while ringlets of smoke drifted past. He looked serious, as if in thought. "That's a new one, huh?" he said, nodding at the drawing.

"Yeah, I sketched that one last night. Could have done a little bit better on the shading, but I like it. Come here and look close," Jasmine said, pointing to the sketch. "Look into his open eye."

Ernest walked to the wall and leaned across her bunk until he was at eye level with the drawing. Barak's eyeball was a microsketch of the Monopoly mascot, "Rich Uncle" Pennybags.

"Damn, you be going deep, I see."

"That's all I can do . . . try to look deep and see shit other people can't see. I'm in constant introspect mode, thinking, rethinking, and overthinking. If it's thinking involved, I'm doing it, and that shit gets exhausting."

Ernest produced handcuffs and held them up, waiting for her to extend her wrists.

Jasmine eyed the handcuffs and smiled. She walked to her door and looked down the hallway in both directions. At the very end of the hall, an asshole guard named Sullivan escorted an overweight nurse as she wheeled a pill cart in the opposite direction and eventually disappeared around the corner. Jasmine turned and faced Ernest with her wrists extended.

"I'm probably really taking a chance by telling you this, but I trust you. I have to get out of here, and you're going to help me," she said.

A sly grin spread across Ernest's face. "Oh, really? And what makes you think I would agree to that?"

Jasmine shrugged her shoulders. He had a point. Who was she to make that assumption?

"I *must* get out of here, Ernest. The longer I stay here, the more I realize that I'll probably spend the rest of my life behind these walls unless they give me the death penalty, and that's not an option," she said.

Ernest put his hand on Jasmine's shoulder and nodded toward the hall. "Let's hit the rec yard and talk about it there. There are too many eyes and ears around here to be yakking recklessly."

Once in the rec yard, Ernest removed the cuffs from Jasmine's wrists, and she rubbed them, more from habit than discomfort. "So, what's up? You said we couldn't talk recklessly in there. That means you'll help me?" In the distance, she watched six women play a game of three-on-three volleyball. She didn't want to look at Ernest to make their conversation obvious.

"You see how green and lush these trees are? When I was in the military, I always felt more at home in the jungle. I always felt free. All my brothers thought that I was crazy, thought that I was off somehow because I liked to be in the wild. I joined as soon as I turned 18 and gave them ten years, only to be medically discharged because of a psyche eval. I answered their questions honestly and to the best of my ability, and they tried to make me out to be some kind of monster. But I was only being the monster that they created." Ernest looked sad like he'd lost something dear to him. "Look at the north mountain and tell me what you see."

Jasmine did as she was told, scanning the mountain until her neck was bent and her eyes were to the sky. The mountain was massive and seemed to go on forever.

"All I see are mountains and trees," she said, confused.

"Exactly. That's what everyone sees, just mountains and trees. But I live on that mountain, and that's your way out."

"Can I ask you an honest question, E?"

"Of course."

"Why are you helping me? I mean, I'm thankful, but why me?" Jasmine asked.

"My mother died in a place much like this, and I can only imagine how she must've felt being away from me. No mother should be forced to live without her children," he said, disappearing into the hallway.

Chapter 19

On Everything I Love

Ernest and Jasmine had been making plans during their clandestine meetings in the rec yard for weeks. Before he left home for work each day, he would light a candle and set it next to an open window facing the prison. As they talked, he would point out the candle daily until the location was burned into Jasmine's head. It was imperative that when she ran, she ran in that direction to aid in her escape. The day had finally come, and as Ernest reported for work, he stopped by the receptionist's desk and spoke with Mrs. Becky, the near-sighted, elderly corrections officer who could barely see the nose on her face.

"Hey, Mrs. Becky, is Tanner in today?" he asked.

"Yes, as far as I know, she's making her rounds on the west wing. How are you today, honey?"

"I'm fine. I need her to sign off on my vacation request, so if you see her, please tell her I'm looking for her," he said.

"I will, sweetheart. Have a wonderful day, Ernest."

He softly whistled as he made his way to Jasmine's cell, trying to appear calm, but inside, he was nervous and anxious. He'd stayed up most of the night perfecting his plan. Within the hour, Jasmine would be a free woman.

He slid his access card, and the red light beeped and turned green. The door of her cell popped open with a clunk. "Jasmine, are you busy?" Ernest asked, slipping into her room.

As always, when he came to visit, Jasmine was sitting on her bunk with her back against the wall, her head buried in her sketchbook. She trusted Ernest, true, but what if, just *what if* he was full of shit and had baited her? Even after her escape, she would need to find a way to contact Kochese, and her only connection was Nae. She wasn't sure whether the number would still be good or whether Monica had already gotten wise to Nae. What she did know was that she needed to get to her babies. She turned to face Ernest and tried to force a smile. "No, I'm not busy. What's up, E?"

"Are you ready to do this?" he asked.

"Now? Yeah, I mean . . ." Jasmine didn't know what to say. They had talked and rehearsed for weeks, and now that the time had come, she was nervous.

"I understand the apprehension, but if we do it as we discussed it, everything should go smoothly. I brought you a few things that you'll need to get out of here without incident," Ernest said. He opened his backpack and removed a roll of duct tape, a small blade, and a black prison guard's uniform. The entire hospital was color coded according to the wing that a guard was assigned to. The guards assigned to her wing wore khaki uniforms, but the guards that patrolled the rec yard wore black uniforms like the one Ernest had brought for her.

"Ernest, you brought these clothes like you expect me to just walk out of here with no worries," Jasmine said incredulously.

"That's exactly what I expect you to do. I know that you and Officer Tanner have had words with each other, but I also know that it hasn't been lost on you that you two favor each other a great deal."

"You're crazy. We look nothing alike," she protested.

"Maybe not to the trained eye, but you guys have the same wavy hair, slender build, and skin tone. There are enough similarities for you to waltz right out of here, Jasmine."

"And what will Miss Tanner do while I'm stealing her identity? Congratulating me as I stroll out of these gates?"

"That's what the duct tape is for. We'll tie her up and gag her until you're free. Once you're gone, someone will eventually find her," he said.

Jasmine had other plans for Officer Tanner. She would make damn sure that she never spoke to another person with the same disrespect with which she'd addressed her. Tanner was sitting on her bunk when she returned from medical one day, thumbing through her file.

"What are you doing in my room?" Jasmine asked.

Tanner didn't look up from the file when she spoke. "You're pathetic, you know that? You're a disgrace to women like me who wish that they could bear children but can't. It's always the ones that don't give a fuck about their kids that are blessed with them."

Of course, Jasmine had taken offense because, first off, the guard didn't know her situation, and second, she didn't have any right to go through her files.

"You don't even know me. You don't know shit about me because if you did, we wouldn't be having this conversation."

"I know all that I need to know. You're a murderer who cared more about some dick than you did your own children. How do you feel knowing that you'll rot in here and some hardworking woman like me will be raising your children?" she'd said as she spat on Jasmine's floor. "Clean that up when I leave, stupid," she added.

Officer Tanner had turned to leave, but not before burning a lasting memory into Jasmine's brain.

The sound of Ernest's voice pulled her from her sinister daydream. "Be ready in an hour. I'll ring this phone once and hang up when Tanner is close to your cell. It'll be in your hands after that. I'll sound the alarm once you pass me in the hall and make it to the rec yard. The entire complex is going to go into lockdown. That should buy you enough time to get into the trees and reach my place. When I make it there, we'll head down the other side of the mountain," he said.

Jasmine pulled Ernest to her and hugged him tightly. It was in her darkest times that a little bit of faith had been restored in men, and she appreciated him for that. "Even if this doesn't work, Ernest, I just want to say thank you."

Jasmine laid her black outfit across her bunk as a distraction because it would be the first thing she saw as soon as Tanner walked into her room. The element of surprise was always a good thing, and she would make it work to her advantage.

Jasmine heard the faint sound of the cell phone vibrating and buzzing on her bunk and then went silent. She made her way to the door leading to the hallway and opened it. Tanner was already two rooms past her own but still close enough for Jasmine to call out to her without drawing attention to herself.

"Excuse me, Officer Tanner, could I see you for a second?" Jasmine said in her sweetest tone.

"I'm making my rounds. I'll be back later after pill call."

"It's kind of important, though," she said.

Officer Tanner huffed and rolled her eyes. She didn't like Jasmine Deitrich. She didn't know why, but she didn't. Had she been honest with herself, perhaps she would have realized that Jasmine was everything she wasn't. Sure, she had a steady, paying job and a decent life, but according to Jasmine's file, she was beyond smart. She was a prodigy, a proverbial free spirit who could outthink the average person tenfold. She could also do something that Anicia Tanner would never be able to do: give birth.

She turned on her heels and walked the few grueling paces back to Jasmine's room. As she entered, her eyes were immediately drawn to the uniform laid carefully across the bunk. Next, her eyes were drawn to Jasmine's slender yet curvy body as she stood before her naked.

"I don't know what you call yourself doing, Miss Deitrich, but I don't swing that way," she said.

"Don't flatter yourself, bitch. I'm strictly dickly," Jasmine said, brandishing her blade.

Officer Tanner opened her mouth to scream, but before the sound escaped her lips, Jasmine punched her in the throat. She stumbled backward, catching herself on the edge of the stainless steel desk. Fear and confusion spread across her face as she tried to run past Jasmine to reach the door, but Jasmine grabbed her by her hair and slung her toward the bed. As she went down, her forehead caught the edge of the metal bed frame and rendered her unconscious. Jasmine stripped the officer naked and threw her clothes into the corner in a crumpled heap.

Then Jasmine went to the door, peered out into the hallway, and her heart sank. Standing at the receptionist's desk on the far end of the hall was Agent Monica Deitrich—her sister, her nemesis. She ducked her head back into the room and tried to pick up Tanner from the floor, but she was too heavy. *Think, Jasmine, think,* she thought. She knelt, turned the officer's back to the door, and extended her wrist. With one sweep of her blade, she slit Tanner's left wrist. Just as Jasmine stood up, she heard the familiar beep of an identification card, but the heavy steel was already ajar.

"Jazzy, we need to talk," Monica said as she opened the door. She entered and panicked. "Oh my God, Jasmine!" she said, dropping to her knees. She turned Officer Tanner over and gasped. Monica scrambled to her feet and was met with a right cross to her chin. She tried to shake off the dizziness from the sucker punch, but Jasmine caught her with an uppercut and another right cross.

"You little bitch. It's been a long time since I tapped that ass," Monica said, wiping the blood from her lip.

"Yeah, but we're not kids anymore, Monica, and I don't plan on taking any more ass whippings."

"I'm DEA-trained, little girl. You're gonna take this ass whipping and love it," Monica retorted.

"I'm Buckner Home-trained, trick. Fuck all this talking. Knuckle up, bitch."

Monica rushed Jasmine, who promptly sidestepped her older sister, punching her in the ribs in the process. Monica doubled over in pain, and Jasmine took the opportunity to grab her by her shirt and ram her head into the wall. She slid down the wall and lay there, trying to expel the cobwebs dancing in her head. *What the fuck just happened?* Monica thought. She used the wall as leverage as she struggled to stand. She took a defensive martial arts stand and beckoned Jasmine to bring it.

"That Kung Fu shit won't work today, slim," Jasmine taunted.

Without warning, Monica advanced toward Jasmine, rifling her with a barrage of kicks and slaps, finishing it off with a snap kick to Jasmine's chin. Jasmine stumbled backward over Tanner's body and felt the blade that she had used to slice the woman's wrist. What should have served to knock Jasmine out only made her angrier.

"If you kick me again, I'm going to cut your fucking leg off," Jasmine said, spitting blood. She stood slowly, her naked body heaving, anger and adrenaline oozing from her pores.

Monica advanced in Jasmine's direction, throwing a flurry of punches. Her fist connected with Jasmine's jaw and then her temple. Jasmine went down on one knee, searing pain coursing through her body. Just as Monica was about to finish her with a punch to the head, Jasmine buried the blade deep into Monica's thigh. She screamed, but it was cut short by Jasmine's fist being buried in her gut. Jasmine stood, grabbed Monica's head by her hair, and brought it down toward her knee with all her strength. Monica lay unconscious on the floor with her eyes rolled in the back of her head.

"I told you not to fuck with me, bitch. I should slit your fucking throat, but I'll save that for another day," Jasmine sneered.

She dressed quickly and looked in the mirror. She had a few scrapes and bruises, but she would be fine if she kept her head down. Jasmine ran the brush through her hair and tried to make herself more presentable. Before she left the room, she retrieved Tanner's prison identification. She would need it to access the rec yard.

Jasmine exited her cell and made her way toward the rec yard. She saw Ernest standing at the receptionist's desk, chatting with Mrs. Becky and effectively blocking her view of Jasmine as she made her way down the hall leading to the recreation yard. She swiped the ID across the reader, and the first door clicked open. The black combat boots she'd stolen from Officer Tanner squeaked against the cold, white, clinical tile floor as she hurried toward her freedom. The whole ordeal seemed eerily like her escape from the hospital, and the threat of being discovered loomed heavily. She reached the second door, swiped the ID, and again, the door clicked open.

Jasmine stopped briefly, threw her head into the air, and breathed deeply. She hugged herself, trying to escape the frigid temperatures of the cold West Virginia wind. Then she dropped her head and walked toward the wood line at a brisk pace. She had just reached the forest's edge when she heard the alarm sound.

Monica was dreaming about her days in elementary school. She was looking for Jasmine in the halls because the fire alarm was going off. Probably another stupid fire drill, or maybe this time, the school really was on fire. She tried to snuggle in her bed even deeper, but she wasn't in a bed at all. There were no covers and no soft mattress.

Her eyes flickered open slowly, and she realized that she'd been unconscious. She stumbled to her feet and staggered to the window, the knife still lodged deep within her thigh, burning, threatening to drive her insane. She squinted to focus, and that's when she saw her. Jasmine was making her way through the security gate. Her sister was a free woman—a fugitive on the run.

Chapter 20

Gotta Bring Ass to Get Ass

Monica stumbled out into the hallway, the blade still buried in her thigh. As far back as she could remember, she and Jasmine had never come to blows—maybe a little shoving here and there, but never an actual fistfight. Now, Jasmine had even gone so far as to stab Monica in the leg. She needed to get to the phone and quickly because she'd awakened to find her phone destroyed, floating in the blood from her leg. Monica's vision was blurry, and she could barely focus, not to mention the racket of the alarm blaring overhead, which caused her head to pound even more so than the ass whipping that she'd taken. Jasmine had really done her in. As mad as she was at her little sister, Monica managed a weak half smile through her aching jaw. She slowly walked to the receptionist's desk, where Mrs. Becky sat talking with Ernest.

"Oh my Lord, baby, what happened to you?" Mrs. Becky asked.

"Did you see a patient leave here? She may have worn an officer's uniform," Monica asked.

"No, I've been right here talking to Ernest. We haven't moved except to initiate the fire drill."

Monica turned to the man that the lady had referred to as Ernest. He looked uneasy and nervous, as if he might bolt at any second. Even in the frigid temperatures of the hospital, he'd begun to sweat, which made Monica suspicious. His eyes darted feverishly, not settling on any single point. He also shifted from foot to foot. Yeah, he most definitely had something to hide, and Monica meant to find out what it was.

"Who initiated the fire drill?" Monica asked.

"I initiated it. Why do you ask?" Ernest said nervously.

"I'm asking the questions, sir. Why now? Why initiate the fire drill now?"

"I didn't just decide to do it. I was going by the schedule," Ernest replied, handing her a copy of the agenda. "The hospital is trying to find a way to readjust the system because, as it stands now, the entire hospital goes into lockdown, which, according to the fire department, is a fire hazard," he added.

"I see. And you just so happened to test the fire alarm the same day that one of this hospital's most dangerous patients escaped, huh?"

"Ma'am, I don't know these patients' histories. I come here to do my job, no more and no less. As Mrs. Becky said, we were here talking the entire time, and the only person who walked by was one of the men fixing the alarm and Officer Tanner. I assumed she was leaving for the day because she works the eleven to seven shift, but she works overtime occasionally," he huffed.

Monica looked toward Jasmine's room and then back to the two employees. Could Jasmine have been that calculating and cold-blooded? Damn right, she could, and Monica knew it. She eyeballed the list that Ernest had given her.

Ernest's day was completely mapped out for him on paper. Monica found it odd, but if that's how the hospital ran their shifts, then so be it. She couldn't worry about something as trivial as a work schedule. She had to act fast if she was going to catch Jasmine. If Jasmine had contacted Kochese, Monica would never see her again. He had enough money to make her disappear just as he had himself.

"Do you have a phone I can use for a long-distance call?" Monica asked.

"Sure. You can use this one," Mrs. Becky said, handing her the phone, and then she added, "Ernest, will you please go to the director's office and let him know that we have an escapee on the loose?"

Monica watched Ernest disappear down the hall as she placed a call to Agent D'Angelo. He picked up on the first ring, catching Monica slightly off guard.

"Agent Deitrich, I'm glad you called. Where are you?" he asked.

"I'm in West Virginia. I came to visit my sister."

"We have a serial killer on the loose, and you're taking personal time to visit family members?"

"I use the term 'visit' loosely, D'Angelo. I came here hoping that she could help us capture King Kochese," Monica said.

"So, let me get this straight. Your sister and her lover went on a killing spree, bloodying the streets of the US, made two babies, then this same sister helped said lover escape and consequently evade capture and kidnap their own children. This is the sister you're visiting, and who you expect to help you with your case? Either you're delusional, or I'm missing something," Agent D'Angelo said sarcastically.

His tone irritated Monica because she knew he did it just to get on her nerves. D'Angelo was cocky, but he was good at what he did. He was good at *everything* that he did. If Monica had to guess, she would've bet money that D'Angelo's problem with her stemmed from his belief that his sexual prowess should've left her powerless against his charm. Monica, however, had never let a dick control her actions, and she wouldn't start now. Hell, for that matter, she had been in love with Kochese Mills. *His* sex game was phenomenal, and she'd been willing to send him to prison for life. So, she was certainly not going to bow down to Agent D'Angelo and his bomb-ass head. True, good head was hard to find, but it wouldn't make or break her.

"Listen, D'Angelo, I don't need your sarcasm right now. We have a real situation, so save the bullshit."

"Yes, you're absolutely right. We do have a problem right now, so I need you on a flight to Wichita ASAP," he said.

"I really think my time would best be served here."

"And why is that, Agent Deitrich?"

"Jasmine escaped today," Monica said.

"Wait, what? Okay, I'll call the US Marshals to get the ball rolling on locating your sister. Meanwhile, I need you en route to Yeager Airport. I'll have a plane waiting for you when you arrive," D'Angelo said, disconnecting the call.

She turned to Mrs. Becky. "I need you to get these doors opened right now. I have a plane to catch," she said.

"I understand that you have a plane to catch, baby, but if we don't dress that nasty wound on your leg, you'll be dead before that plane that you need to catch lands. Take a seat. I'll call the infirmary," Mrs. Becky said.

Chapter 21

Wichita, Kansas

Cyril Griffin stood before the mirror of his dank motel room. He used the cheap, rough motel towel to wipe the blood from his face and hands. He'd only intended to strangle the hooker who called herself Peaches, but she'd gotten on his nerves. She wasn't any better than the other six women he had stuffed in his motel closet. Cyril had happily explained that he couldn't perform unless they played dead while he was doing his business, and to get the money, they'd agreed. Two of them had stripped down and, immediately upon seeing his small, flaccid penis, had laughed at him and inadvertently sealed their own fate. Three of them had simply made a noise while he was trying to mount them, and he'd snapped because corpses didn't make noise. His sixth victim talked too much.

And then there was Peaches. She'd agreed to the price, and when he'd gotten naked, and she saw his little dick, she'd not only laughed but also demanded more money. She'd claimed that part of the reason that she was a whore—or *escort,* as she called it—was because she was a nympho, and part of her payment was her ability to get off from the act. She said with his cock being so small, there would be no way for her to get an orgasm, and, therefore, she would have to double her price. Cyril had tried to haggle with her over the price, saying that the customer was always right, but Peaches wasn't trying to hear it.

"Baby, look at that little thing. You probably won't make it past my clit. Don't you think I deserve more money, daddy?" she asked.

Reluctantly, Cyril added two more crumpled twenty-dollar bills to the two he'd pulled out to give her. As she reached for the money, Cyril struck her violently across the face, sending her crashing onto the bed.

"When I tell Pretty Lonnie that you put your hands on me, he's going to fuck you up!" she spat.

"Whore, the next time you see your pimp, he'll be pimping you out in hell for sips of cold water. Now, get on your fucking knees."

Peaches got onto her knees and looked up at Cyril warily.

"Open your mouth!" he ordered.

She opened her mouth, and Cyril's penis was so short that he had to press his pelvis against her face to fit it inside her mouth. She began to suck it, but there was no change.

"Just stop, stop!" he screamed. He lifted her to her feet by her hair and slammed her onto the bed.

Cyril Griffin straddled Peaches and wrapped his large hands around her neck, but there was something different about Peaches. She was a fighter, giving Cyril the full advantage of her feistiness.

Her tenacious manner was the reason why Cyril now stood in the motel mirror, cleaning her blood from his body. He didn't like fighters. He liked the submissive type that bowed to his life-altering power. So, rather than strangle her, he decided to stab her—repeatedly. Afterward, looking at her bloody, naked body had aroused him, and he'd made love to her bloody corpse.

Cyril sat naked at the small, rickety desk and scribbled something onto a piece of paper. He smeared the words *Albert Desalvo* onto the wooden desk with Peaches's blood. Cyril dressed slowly and gathered his things, and then he removed each of the bodies from the closet and placed them in different positions around the room to add to the theatrical effect. He opened the door to leave but stopped short to give his masterpiece a second look.

Just as he turned to leave, a short, stout Spanish woman with a thick neck and even thicker accent muttered, "Housekeeping," in his direction.

"It's a mess in there, ma'am," he said. And as an afterthought, he handed her a twenty-dollar bill and a note that read:

I am a king among peasants and a wolf among sheep.

Chapter 22

I'm Going Home

Jasmine was traversing the mountain just as she and Ernest had rehearsed, no matter the feeling go straight. *Climb until you reach a narrow dirt road. Stand up, keep the lights of the prison on your right side. Walk twenty steps, look left, and you will see the candle glowing.* Her hands were bleeding from the climb, and every muscle in her body ached. Her mouth was so dry that she could barely swallow, and her throat burned, but she couldn't stop. At least the slope of the mountain wasn't as steep as she had imagined. Instead, she tried to convince herself that she was just doing some much-needed exercise. The prison's alarm grew quieter as she climbed, and when she looked to see how far she had come, she was astonished at the distance. *Keep pushing, Jasmine.* She could see the tiny specks of light from flashlights searching the prison grounds for her, and she pushed forward, willing herself ahead, until finally, she felt the flat, muddy road at her fingertips. She stood in the center of the road and smiled. Then she turned to her right. Jasmine followed the instructions she had been given until she reached a small, nondescript wooden cabin that could have been mistaken as abandoned if not for the candle burning in the window.

As soon as she entered, she took the candle and ex-
plored the cabin. She searched each room, raising a
few windows in the event she needed a quick exit. She
reached the last room and tried to open the door, but it
was locked. From what Jasmine could see, Ernest lived
a minimalist lifestyle, and though his place was small,
it wasn't cramped and was very clean. His furnishings
were sparse, and everything was neatly placed. With
what Ernest had told her about his military training, she
understood his need for order. Jasmine leaned against
the door and sighed heavily. What if Ernest had gotten
caught? What if he didn't come? Shit, what if he's a serial
killer, and there are bodies in the locked room? That
thought alone made Jasmine giggle. *Wouldn't that be
some shit?* she thought.

Soon, Jasmine heard an engine and saw headlights.
She blew out the candle and waited. She searched her
cargo pants pocket for the knife, then remembered
that she had left it buried in the bitch Monica's leg. She
crouched low to the ground, and as soon as the headlights
went off, she scurried silently to the corner furthest from
the door and blended into the shadows.

Ernest stepped from his Jeep, moving fast but not
hurrying. He tapped lightly on the door.

"Did you make it, JD?" he whispered.

"Yep."

"I didn't want to just burst through the door and get
stabbed or anything."

"I don't have that knife you gave me, but I was going
to beat you with this," Jasmine said, holding up the
smartphone that he had given her.

"Bludgeon me to death with a Cricket phone? Got it."

"What happened after I left, E?" Jasmine asked.

"I didn't expect to leave this early, but the warden sent
me home after he heard your sister interrogating me

like she knew I helped you. She repeatedly asked me the same questions as if I would break. So I just kept playing dumb with her, but in my mind, I was on some military, name, rank, and serial number-type shit."

"Aw, shit, let me find out, E-Boogie got a little gangsta in him. Where is she now?" she asked, tapping E-Boogie in the chest.

"I don't really know. She said she wanted to talk to me, so stick around, but she was already gone after I returned from the warden's office. Look, we need to get the fuck out of here before the world comes crashing down. We can play twenty questions while we're on the road, but every second we waste here talking is a second we risk getting caught. The warden called the Federal Marshals, so it's only a matter of time before they catch your scent."

Jasmine was impressed. She knew Ernest was intelligent, but he had never displayed this level of strength and authority. She had always thought him to be meek from his tone, but tonight, he was a different man . . . a soldier.

Ernest pulled a pin light from his pocket and went to the room at the back that Jasmine had found locked earlier. He removed his wallet, removed a key from one of the pockets, and unlocked the door. The room was full of computers. Each of them had a different face, language, and country with corresponding time zones on them. In all, Jasmine counted seven separate computers.

"What's all of this, Ernest?" she asked.

Ernest moved expertly around the room, grabbing things, shoving them into a green army duffle bag, then handed it to Jasmine. He took the kerosene lamp on the hall table and dumped it on the computers. Then he struck a match and tossed it into the room, and a bright, orange fire erupted. Jasmine could feel the sudden surge of heat against her face, and she instinctively touched her eyebrows.

"Damn, Ernest."

"Car now, talk later," he grumbled.

They left the property through a trail at the back of Ernest's cabin. It was only wide enough for the Jeep, and it was pitch black ahead of them, except for the dull glow of the vehicle's headlights. Jasmine could feel the branches and leaves brush her face as Ernest navigated through the woods.

"Reach in the backseat and grab the black bag. That's yours," he said.

Jasmine reached back and felt around until she touched the bag, afraid to take her eyes off the headlights. She pulled it by its strap and set it in her lap. There was a prepaid Tracfone, a change of clothes, and ten one-hundred-dollar bills. At the bottom of the mountain, Ernest pulled into the center of a field of high grass and killed the headlights.

"You'll get reception here, but make it quick." Ernest reached across Jasmine, opened the glove compartment, and removed a pistol.

She took the phone from its packaging. "Do you still have that pin light, E?" she asked as she rolled up her sleeve.

He handed it to her. "I gotta take a piss."

She held the light on the dots she had crudely etched into her skin with her fingernail. She had arranged the dots to look random like she had a self-mutilation addiction, but it was braille and happened to be Nae's number. She quickly dialed the number.

"You've reached, Nae. I can't come to the phone right now, but if it's important, leave me a message. If not, hang up and let me nose-dive in this pussy again."
Beeeeppppp

Jasmine didn't leave a message. She did, however, disconnect and call Nae's phone right back.

"Hello!" Nae barked from the other end of the phone.

"Nae, it's Jasmine. I need your help," she said.

"Jasmine, who? I don't know no Jasmine."

"I know you're trying to be safe, but I don't have time for this shit right now. I'm on the run, and I need you to put me in touch with King," she screamed.

"How do I know it's you?"

"I don't know enough about you to quiz you, but I will say this: if King Kochese finds out that I'm on the streets, I contacted you, and you didn't help me, I don't have to tell you what he'll do to you," she said.

"Let me call him and have him call you. I'm not taking nobody to King unless he tells me to. I hope you understand my situation."

"Fair enough. Tell him time is of the essence," Jasmine said, disconnecting the call.

Ernest stood a few yards from the Jeep, looking over the field toward Russell Nunn's bootleg house. Russell called it a farm, but he definitely brewed bootleg whiskey, which was his business. *Everybody has their secrets,* he thought. He wasn't sure why he was doing what he was doing for Jasmine, but he felt compelled to help her. He'd watched his mother's mental state deteriorate until a nosy neighbor called DCF, and once the state got involved, they had her Baker Acted. He was 17 years old when his mother was taken away from him and placed in a mental institution. The fact that his eighteenth birthday was only days away had saved him, and the caseworker had personally taken him to the Army recruiters' office.

He walked back to the Jeep and climbed inside. "You good? Where we headed?"

"Not sure yet. Waiting on a callback. Question, Ernest. If you stay here, you realize they'll come for you, right?" she asked.

"Yeah, I do."

"You don't seem worried."

"I'm not."

"Why not?" Jasmine asked. This man was more of a mystery than she thought.

"Because what's done is done, and me sitting back worrying about the boogeyman coming isn't going to solve shit, so it is what it is," he shrugged.

"Do you think you could kill if it came down to it?"

"I suppose anyone can kill if it's necessary."

"I can take you with me when I leave, but I will warn you now. King is like a wolf that smells blood. If he senses weakness in you, he will not accept you in the pack," she said flatly.

"I didn't help you to gain anything in return. I helped you because I like you. I think you're a great woman who deserves to share that greatness with people who love her, not rot in a prison cell. I'm just happy to have had you as my friend," he said.

"So, will you tell your friend about those computers?"

"I can hack *anything*, Jasmine. I've hacked into government systems, medical facilities, and, my favorite, banks. I've bypassed some of the most intricate firewalls in the world."

Jasmine opened her mouth to agree with Ernest, but before she could, her phone rang. "Hold on, E. I need to take this. It may be our ticket out of here," she said, answering the phone. "Hello?"

"Jasmine, baby, is this really you?" Kochese said excitedly.

"Yes, my love. It's me."

"How did you get out? Where are you? Are you okay?" Kochese asked. He had so many questions for her, but he knew they were short on time. Nae had made that much perfectly clear.

"A guard from the prison helped me escape, baby. Right now, we're in the middle of a field waiting for your instructions."

"Say no more, baby. When I got the word from Nae, I jumped into action. My man Chico says there's a private plane waiting for you at a small airstrip just outside Snowshoe.

"Ernest, do you know where Snowshoe is? Is it close to here?" Jasmine asked.

"Yeah, I know it well. It's about an hour's drive if we stick to the back roads and push it."

"Baby, did you get that?" Jasmine asked.

"Yeah, I heard him. Go to hangar 13 and ask for a cat named Fuego. He'll bring you home. Ernest, homie, I don't know how to repay you, but I got you, bruh, trust."

"King, I'm going to bring Ernest with me because you know what they'll do if we leave him here," Jasmine said.

"Do what feels right, baby. I trust your judgment. We can't wait to see you."

"I can't wait to see you and hold my babies. I'm so excited. I love you, baby. I thought you forgot about me for a minute," she said sadly.

"You know better than that. I could never and would never dream of forgetting about you. See you soon," Kochese said.

"On my command, fellas. 1 . . . 2 . . . 3 . . . Let's go!" the commander yelled.

The US Marshals' tactical team burst through the doors of the cabin with guns drawn. There were six of them, spread into teams of two as they executed their search of the apartment.

"Team 1, clear, sir," one officer shouted.

"Team 2, clear, sir," yelled another.

"Looks like we just missed them, sir."

"How do you figure that, Sergeant?" the commander asked.

"Two sets of fresh footprints, sir."

"In fugitive time, that may as well be a week, son."

"Commander, you've got to see this," an officer yelled from Ernest's computer room.

As the commander entered the room, he stared perplexed, mouth open. In the center of the floor sat several computers, torched, still smoking. From the looks of it, the backs had been removed, and so had the hard drives. The computers left were mere shells of CPUs that may have once held pertinent information.

He heard another officer yell from the back of the cabin, "I got fresh tire tracks back here, Commander."

Chapter 23

Tick, Tick, Boom

Ernest drove fast on Route 303, but he didn't speed. The last thing that he or Jasmine needed was some overzealous, hillbilly cop pulling them over trying to meet his speeding ticket quota for the month. He glanced at Jasmine, who had reclined her seat and closed her eyes. She had become the little sister that he never had, and he would die before he let anything happen to her. He looked in the rearview mirror and saw headlights. They were far away, but they were gaining on them fast. "Jasmine, wake up. We got company."

Jasmine opened her eyes and looked around, confused, trying to shake off the grogginess. "What?" she asked, rubbing her eyes.

"Behind us. We have company," Ernest repeated as he pressed the gas pedal to the floor.

"Shit, how far away are we?"

"Maybe ten minutes. The airfield is just over that ridge. After we clear this hill, I will drive blind with the lights off so they can't track the taillights."

"How the hell are you gonna see in the dark, E?"

"You let me fuck this duck; you just hold his wings."

"That's the countriest shit I ever heard, E."

Ernest laughed. "Reach under your seat and hand me those goggles."

Jasmine gave Ernest the goggles, which he put on while driving with his knee, and when he made it to the top of the hill, he killed the lights. "Night vision, JD."

Ernest could see the jet near the end of the runway, but half the distance between them and the plane was a helicopter near the trees. He investigated the aircraft as they passed and saw a man and a woman inside, but they weren't moving. Ernest zoomed past it and pulled up to the side of the jet.

"Are you Fuego?" Jasmine asked.

"Indeed. King sent me to bring you home, baby girl. Who dis?"

"This is E. Look, we can get acquainted in the air, but we got people on our asses, probably ten or fifteen minutes behind," she said.

"Okay, no worries. How good of a shot are you, E?" Fuego asked.

"I can hold my own. What's up?"

"Look," Fuego said, handing Ernest a set of binoculars, "you see the helicopter? Now look underneath the pilot's seat."

"Oh shit," Ernest said.

"If you can hit that shit, that's enough explosives to light up the whole fucking valley."

"Who are those people in the helicopter?" Ernest asked.

"Corpses from my abuela's mortuary. Now, look underneath the helicopter. We rigged some guns and shit to draw their fire. Here," Fuego said, handing Ernest a sniper rifle. "I'm going to get this big bitch rolling. As soon as you take the shot, I'm going full throttle, got it?"

"Got it." Ernest aimed, waiting.

"Let's get it popping, primo," Fuego said as he hit the button on an iPad, and automatic gunfire erupted. "Take the shot, E."

Ernest lay in the doorway of the jet and inhaled deeply. He turned a knob near the scope to focus his aim. He exhaled and let his finger tap the trigger. The explosion rocked the small jet, and Fuego, true to his promise, hit the plane's throttle and accelerated down the darkened runway.

"Hoolllly shit, E, that was some good fucking shooting, bro. Oh my God, did you see that explosion? You must've hit that bitch right on the triggering mechanism," Fuego screamed over the roaring engine.

"Nah, I hit the gas tank. There wasn't a way to miss with this Mk 12 SPR, so I guess you can say I had a little help." Ernest smiled, pride dripping from his modesty.

"Y'all on some real bromance shit, Fuego. How long before we reach Kochese?"

"A little over four hours, señora."

Jasmine settled back into the leather seat and closed her eyes. Without opening them, she said, "Thanks for everything, E. I owe you my life."

"You don't owe me shit. Get some rest."

Chapter 24

Trophy Case

The FBI had completely emptied the El Rancho Motel just off of I-35 in Wichita, Kansas. Each occupant of the small, run-down motel was questioned and then released. Many complained about who would cover their relocation to other motels in the area. An old lady sat in the doorway of her room in her wheelchair and eyed Agent D'Angelo angrily.

"Y'all can't just come in here and put us out on the street. Where we s'posed to go?" she spat in his direction.

Agent D'Angelo was questioning a short, fat maid. He was already struggling to understand her pieced-together English, and now this. "Look, ma'am, there is an active murder investigation going on, not to mention the numerous violations that I count just looking at this place. The bureau will cover relocation costs, so don't worry."

"I like this one here. What if I don't wanna go nowhere?" she rebutted.

"Then you're more than welcome to stay here, but you won't have a room to sleep in. I don't have time for this shit." D'Angelo turned his back to the woman and continued his questions. "And then what happened, ma'am?"

"I knockayyyy on the door, and the white man withaaaayyy scarro open it and say, he *solo necesita toallas limpiaa.*"

"What?" D'Angelo asked.

"She said he only needed fresh towels," Monica replied as she walked up behind him.

"Where'd you come from?"

Monica pointed over her shoulder to the black, unmarked sedan parked behind her. She turned her attention to the maid. *"Hola, señora, ¿cree que podría describir a este hombre a un dibujante? Cualquier cosa que puedas recordar y que creas que podría ayudar será apreciada,"* Monica said, resting her hands on the woman's shoulders.

"Se, ¿Hay alguna recompensa?"

D'Angelo looked from woman to woman, confusion clearly showing on his face.

"I asked her if she could identify the suspect for a sketch artist, and she says yes, but she wants to know if there is a reward," Monica said, taking pity on his confusion.

"I'm sure we can scrounge up something. She should want to help on the strength that we don't call ICE, immi-gration, you comprendé that?" D'Angelo said, snidely.

"Noooo, noooo, no immigration, no no," the maid said, waving her hands wildly, dismissing them as she walked away.

"What's wrong with you? She might have been our only good lead."

But D'Angelo didn't answer. He just walked away. Monica wasn't sure what was going on, but the yellow tape, light from police cars, and police milling around collecting evidence was all too reminiscent of Drak's murder scene. Wichita, Kansas, was a bustling town, contrary to popular belief. The extent of Monica's knowledge regarding Kansas was that Dorothy from *The Wizard of Oz* and her dog, Toto, had been swept up in a tornado there. She also knew that Kansas was home to some of history's most notorious serial killers. To date, besides the gruesome murders that the BTK killer had committed in Kansas, the only other one that stood out to her was the Bloody Blenders, as they were called. Ma and Pa Blender, along with their son John and their daughter Kate, were personally responsible for eleven known murders. They would welcome travelers into their home who looked for a meal and a place to spend the night with open and inviting arms. Then during dinner that night, one of the Blenders would bash in the skulls of the unsuspecting houseguests with a hammer and then slit their throats. They'd then be robbed of their money and valuables, and their bodies shoved through a trapdoor into the cellar. When the townspeople became suspicious, the Blender family disappeared, never to be heard from again. The bodies of their victims were found buried in a vineyard behind their house. Inside the house, two bloodstained hammers and a bloody straight razor were found.

When Monica transferred from the DEA to the FBI and became a profiler, that case was one of the first she studied. The case was easy to remember because it always reminded her of *The Texas Chainsaw Massacre* movie—not so much the method of killing, but rather, the aspect of the family working in tandem. She wondered if Jasmine, King, and their children would become the Blenders.

She envied Jasmine for giving King not one but two children, something that her body had refused to do. During her work on the King Kochese case, she'd silently hoped she'd get pregnant by the young kingpin. She'd fantasized about helping King escape justice and disappear with him and their child. Each time her period had been late, Monica had eagerly taken a pregnancy test . . . only to have her hopes dashed when the test read negative. Her mind shifted to Millie, her baby, her precious pudding cake. She loved her as if she'd given birth to the baby herself. She would have to call the nanny and have her put Millie on the phone once she was settled into a hotel room and got a hot bath. She needed to hear her coos and gurgles. It was the only thing that would quell the sense of dread that was brewing in her gut.

"Agent Deitrich, Agent Deitrich? Are you okay?" a young agent asked.

"I'm fine. Why do you ask?"

"I've been standing here calling your name. Agent D'Angelo is waiting for you at the crime scene. It's in room 201, ma'am," he said.

Nothing could have prepared Monica for what lay ahead of her. When she stepped into the hotel room, D'Angelo stood in the midst of the FBI's forensic team. Cameras flashed rapidly, and the room was filled with unintelligible chatter. Monica fought past the other agents in the room to see what the fuss was about.

In the center of the bed lay the body of a young man, maybe twenty-five years old. Two women had been placed in the sitting position with their backs against the foot of the bed. Their knees had been brought up to their chests, and their arms were folded over their knees and bound with telephone cord. Their heads lay cradled in their arms, resembling small children upset about being placed in timeout. The other four victims had been posed on their knees beside the bed, two on one side and two on the other. The arms of the women had been folded into the praying position and again bound with telephone cord. It was a macabre sight.

D'Angelo stepped up next to Monica and put his hand on her shoulder. "Is this shit psycho or what? Look at this," he said, guiding Monica to the desk built into the motel wall. The name "Albert Desalvo" had been written on the desk in blood, and next to it was an FBI badge in a bifold and an identification that read, *Agent Ryan Quinn.*

Monica felt a cold chill rush through her body, and she shivered. "What the fuck?" she said in a hushed whisper.

"Yeah, my sentiments exactly. And that's not all." Agent D'Angelo handed Monica a plastic evidence baggie with a slip of paper in it.

Monica read it and her words caught in her throat. "*I am a king among peasants and a wolf among sheep.* D'Angelo, how can this be? Do you know what this means?" Monica asked.

"It means that your sister's psycho boyfriend is at it again. Walk with me, Deitrich." D'Angelo walked out onto the balcony of the motel and moved to the end of the runway, and Monica followed. "Monica, with these sightings and killings, there seems to be one common factor," D'Angelo said.

"What's that? I mean, they all have that one saying, I know."

"It's not only that, but also at each murder scene, a witness was left alive, and they all describe King Kochese when asked what the perp looks like, right down to the scar," D'Angelo said, baffled.

"And how can you be so sure? I mean, we're dealing with a man with unlimited resources."

"I can be so sure because no matter how much money he has, it's still physically impossible for him to be in two places simultaneously. These murders are taking place at the exact same time. While the murder was happening in Dallas, multiple killings were happening in Savannah. While these murders were happening here, there were multiple murders taking place in St. Louis. I haven't put this thing together yet, but there's a pattern here," D'Angelo said.

"Maybe you're right, but this doesn't fit King's MO."

"Look, it's six now. Why don't I have Agent Tolski drop you off at the hotel where we're staying, and I'll pick you up there at, let's say, eight? That'll give you time to get cleaned up and get some rest. I'll finish processing the evidence." D'Angelo said.

"Let's make it nine. That'll give me time to make phone calls and dig into these case files."

The hotel that the various FBI teams had checked into wasn't much better than the run-down motel where the murders had taken place. Monica wasn't bourgeoisie by a long shot, but the outside of the hotel left much to be desired. It reminded her of some of the less-than-savory spots she'd been in when she was undercover in King Kochese's organization.

When Monica walked into the hotel lobby, she was pleasantly surprised. It was clean and smelled like fresh fruit. Behind the check-in counter, a perky, young, white girl smiled her brightest smile as a man, whom Monica guessed was one of her agents by his attire, plowed her with some of his best lines.

She ignored the young agent and presented her credentials to check into her room. Not even two miles away, the FBI had set up a mobile base of operations, and Monica knew that it would be a long night. With that in mind, she wasn't in the mood to wait while the agent tried out his Mack Daddy lines. She thought of D'Angelo and sighed. He'd always been so cool, calm, and laid-back, never really allowing the agency's pressure to get to him, but Monica saw worry and dread written on his face when she'd spoken with him earlier.

"So, what's it like being in the FBI?" the young hostess asked.

"Excuse me?"

"Being an FBI agent, what's it like? Is it exciting?"

What's it like? Is she serious? She had to see that Monica was battered and bruised. She must have noticed that Monica's clothes were torn. She would have surely noticed the bloody slacks and pronounced limp, a limp from the wound inflicted by the tip of Jasmine's blade for which Monica had yet to seek medical attention beyond having Mrs. Becky clean and dress it. Monica purposely never openly discussed her cases with civilians because most of them wouldn't understand them anyway. Something about the giddiness in the girl's voice and the goofy smile plastered across her face irritated Monica. She'd probably asked the near-rookie agent the same question only minutes earlier because he looked butt hurt as if his answer had somehow not measured up to her expectations. She patiently waited for Monica's response, as if she were about to tell some sort of enchanting tale.

Monica leaned in close to her. "What's your name, sweetheart?" she asked.

"Heather."

"Well, Heather, being in the FBI, especially the unit that I'm in, is like letting society take a gigantic shit in your face. No matter how hard you scrub and wash, you always smell shit. We are out here investigating some of the most deranged killers known to man. So, you go to sleep at night worried that someone that you've put away has escaped or that a criminal that you're hunting will find you first and cut your fucking head off while you're asleep. And when utter exhaustion finally overtakes you and you do drift off to sleep, the nightmares begin— well, not really nightmares, but rather, *recollections*. Recollections of the dead bodies, of the decapitated corpses, of the severed body parts, of the blood, guts, and brains of not only adults but also of children who will never see their first day of school. As a matter of fact, there's a serial killer on the loose right here in little ol' Wichita," Monica said.

Slowly, over the course of Monica's conversation, Heather's once-wide smile had disappeared, and Monica saw what she was searching for: the look of fear and terror on the young girl's face. She gave Monica her room key with not so much as a "thank you and come again," which pleased Monica. Little Miss Sunshine needed to know that life wasn't all Disney, rainbows, and lollipops.

The elevator dinged open, and Monica stepped in, settling at the back, leaning her head against the mirror. She felt the gravity in the pit of her stomach as the elevator ascended to the third floor and shuddered. Before stepping out of the elevator, Monica poked her head out into the hallway and looked both ways. She always imagined stepping off the elevator into a hallway and into the midst of a hoard of zombies. She even imagined stepping off the elevator and seeing the bloody and skinless Doberman pinschers from the *Resident Evil* movies.

Monica walked off the elevator and slowly made her way down the hall in search of her room, fumbling to balance the files she carried and the small suitcase with the unsteady wheels. Once she reached her room, she stepped inside and tossed the plastic evidence bag and the files onto her bed. Monica started the shower and then went back into her room to rummage through her suitcase for clothes. She was exhausted but motivated. She'd had her fill of psychos with Jasmine and Kochese, and this case was all too reminiscent of those two.

She sighed heavily as she shed her clothes and headed to the shower. Monica stopped in front of the mirror and stared at her profile. She placed her hands over her stomach and imagined being pregnant. *You gotta get some dick to get pregnant, boo,* she thought. She had known girls growing up that slept with whoever the baller of the week was and thought that having babies would keep them by their sides . . . only to be disappointed to find out that they were pregnant at the same time as two or three of his other baby mamas. Monica, on the other hand, was just the opposite. She'd kept her sexual experiences to a minimum because of her grandfather's teachings.

Pop Pop had taken her to Cold Stone Creamery on her fifteenth birthday and given her the Birds and the Bees speech. His conversation was deep and managed to touch Monica more than she'd realized. He'd sat her down at the ice cream parlor and looked deep into her eyes.

"Monica, are you sexually active yet?" he'd asked.

Monica's face flushed red as she answered with a coy, "No, Pop Pop."

"Listen, baby, I'm not going to bore you with the common sex talk that most parents give their children. I want to be as real and as candid as possible. Throughout your life, dear heart, you will meet some young men who say all the right things and make all the right moves. It will be your choice whether you want to meet your soul mate whole or incomplete," he'd said.

"What do you mean whole or incomplete, Pop Pop?"

He zeroed in on his granddaughter, knowing full well that he now had her attention. "I mean that most people go through life searching for that perfect person with whom they might make a life. Instead, they drift from person to person, giving bits and pieces of themselves, sharing their hopes and dreams, their fears and ambitions, with the wrong ones so that by the time they meet the man or woman that God has ordained for them, they are incomplete because they've given so much of themselves to the wrong person. To be whole when you meet the person you've fought through this darkness to meet, baby girl, you must maintain control of your goodies. There's a power within you, baby, that only you and God can control. I'm not talking about having

*power in sex, but power in knowing—knowing that you
don't have to lie down with a man to see into his heart
and soul, knowing that you were born attached to your
soul mate by God's umbilical cord. And when you meet
that person, the spark will be so amazing, so undeniable,
that you'll call it love at first sight. You'll see this person
and believe that you've met before. You'll see him in
your dreams and smell him in passing. You'll crave him
because this will be the man that has been sent to you.
Guard your power, baby; guard it with your life."*

Monica was stunned. She knew about sex, but at 15, she
was still a virgin and had no plans of changing it anytime
soon. His words had been so eloquent, so touching, that
Monica had remained a virgin until her senior year in
college. Many boys and men alike had tried, but Monica
had never wavered.

And now, it seemed as if life had passed her by, and
she would never give birth to a child of her own. And why
should she want to? After what she had witnessed in that
motel room, this was no world she wanted to bring a baby
into.

Monica stepped into the hot shower and let the water
run over her silky locs. She bathed quickly, anxious to
speak with Porscha and Millie. She didn't even dry off.
She simply lay across her bed, allowing her body to air
dry. She dialed her home number, and Porscha answered
on the first ring.

"Hello?" she screamed into the phone.

"Porscha, why are you answering my phone like that?"

"Oh, hey, Miss Deitrich. I thought you were whoever's
been playing on the phone. They've been calling for a few
days," Porscha said.

"What have they said? Is Millie okay?"

"Yes, she's fine. She's sitting here in her jumper playing. Whoever it is that's been calling are just being assholes, excuse my language. Like one call, they'll just breathe on the phone, then the next call, they'll threaten me and the baby. I called the police, but they were being stupid, talking about it. Unless I knew who was making the calls, there was nothing that they could do."

"Shit, okay. Hopefully, I'll be home in a few days. I'll take care of it when I get there," Monica said.

"Okay, but listen, Millie is almost out of Pampers, and I'm afraid to leave the house with her. She misses you, Miss Deitrich. She's been fussy."

"Awww, I miss my Millie Bean too. Put me on speakerphone so that she can hear my voice."

"Okay, Miss Deitrich, you're on speakerphone."

"Hey, Millie Bean. Hey, Mama's baby, what you doing, huh? What's that baby doing? I loooove you, honey bunny," Monica said.

In the background, she heard Millie coo and giggle, and then she heard the familiar sound of Noisy Boy's yelp. "What's Noisy Boy been doing, Porscha?"

"Believe it or not, he won't let me or Millie out of his sight. It's strange. Like he never leaves her side, and when I'm occupied with her, he sits next to the window and watches the street. He's very, very protective of her. It's cute," she said, giggling.

"Good, good, that's exactly what I expect him to do. Okay, girl, I'll call you tomorrow to check on the baby. Give her kisses for me, please."

Before Monica could finish her call, she heard a knock on the door.

"Who is it?" Monica yelled.

"It's me, D'Angelo."

"Porscha, if you have DoorDash on your phone, you can have the pampers delivered and left at the front door. I'll call tomorrow. Gotta go," Monica said.

Then Monica moved to the door and cracked it slightly, meeting D'Angelo's gaze. "I'm still naked. Can you give me another half hour?" she asked.

"I can either give you half an hour or come in and help you get dressed. It's your choice."

Monica stepped to the side and flung the door open, revealing her symmetrically curvy body. D'Angelo reached for her, but she smacked his hand away. "What makes you think you deserve to touch me?" she asked with a knowing smirk.

"Because I brought this with me," he said as he stepped out of his slacks and boxers. His penis jutted forward, erect, bouncing, throbbing. It was nothing spectacular, but Monica had long since stopped comparing D'Angelo's average-sized penis to Kochese's magnificence.

"If you want to impress me, Agent, it will take more than that. Don't get me wrong. That's cool, but you're in the doghouse, mister. Convince me that you're worthy," Monica said. She stepped back and lifted her foot to the bed, exposing her pink moisture.

D'Angelo dropped to his knees and ripped off his shirt quickly. He cupped Monica's ample ass and lapped her pussy eagerly. He was into it, moaning, stroking his manhood, licking and slurping, attempting to make up for lost time.

Monica pushed his head away and dropped her leg. "You like the way that tastes?" she asked.

"Yes, ma'am, I do."

"Beg me to eat this pussy, D'Angelo. Beg me, and I *may* let you have another taste," she scolded.

This was their game. D'Angelo was a freak for Monica Deitrich—well, D'Angelo was a freak for anyone who would show him attention. But Monica had that unique blend of dominance and submissiveness that he craved. She choked him, she slapped him, and she made him beg, and he, in turn, loved every minute of it. When it was his turn, though, he did his best to crawl inside of her. She was insatiable, and he couldn't get enough. He wanted her every day, but Monica wasn't trying to take it there for whatever reason.

"Please, Monica, please, let me taste you. I've missed you. I just want to fuck you with my tongue. I want to show you how much I've missed you."

Monica didn't utter a word. She plopped down on the bed, opened her legs wide, and lay back. She closed her eyes and waited. Any second, D'Angelo would enter her with his sliver of pink heaven. His head was decidedly incredible, almost addictive. She felt it, his syrupy tongue circling her clit slowly. His hand reached her nipple and circled it gently, then cupped it. Monica moaned and gyrated; she bucked and thrashed against his slivery goodness. She was so turned on that it was unbelievable, partly because of the things that he was doing to her body and partly because every time she closed her eyes, she'd see Kochese's face. D'Angelo inserted two of his fingers into her honeypot and reached her G-spot, that ribbed area about two inches into her vagina that controlled the gusher brewing inside of her. She wanted to scream and shout to the heavens how much she still loved Kochese Mills.

"Oh my God, K-K-K-D'Angelo!" she screamed. She'd nearly screamed Kochese's name in the heat of the moment. Monica pushed his head away and stared at him.

"What's wrong? Are you okay?" he asked.

"I'm fine. I just can't believe that a human can eat my pussy like this. I had to see your face," Monica said, giggling.

"You ain't seen shit yet. Watch this."

D'Angelo flipped her over and lifted her tummy off the bed. He buried his face in her ass, probing her pussy with his tongue as he teased her clit with his thumb. "You ever had your pussy eaten from the back like this?" he asked between breaths.

"Fuck me, please! Put it in, baby, please!"

D'Angelo pushed her head into the pillow and inserted the head of his penis into her. She stirred, trying to push back onto it so that she could feel all of it, but D'Angelo was methodical with his stroke game. When Monica pushed back, he thrust deep, filling her up with his man meat. Monica squealed in ecstasy, trying to run from the carnal thrashing. Her insides were on fire. D'Angelo was the only man besides King who could make her squirt. As much as she wanted to control it, it was coming. She shuddered and bucked, thrashed and grinded, until finally, she could no longer hold it. Her wetness came bursting through and coated D'Angelo's pelvis with her moisture.

Finally, Monica collapsed onto the bed on her back and stared at the ceiling. "You're gonna have to stop doing me like that," she said.

"What do you mean? I just want you to be satisfied, that's all."

"Yeah, I hear you."

"You hear me, huh? Can I ask you a serious question?" he asked.

"Sure, what's up?"

"We have some crazy sexual chemistry, and I know people need more than sex to make a relationship work, but why can't we give it a try?" he asked.

"Do you want the truth, or do you just want an answer to make you feel better?"

"No, I would appreciate the truth. What is it?"

"You're a great guy, D, except when you're being an asshole at work. And I like you, but I'm not in love with or even love you. What we have is volatile and borderline toxic, and I'm not going to bring that around my daughter. Let's just keep things the way they are for now, okay? Who knows what the future holds," she said, stroking his cheek.

"Don't do that."

"Do what?" Monica asked.

"Don't try to finesse me with that 'who knows what the future holds' shit. I respect that, and I'm willing to go with the flow. How old is she?"

"She's almost 1 year old, and I'm not trying to finesse you. I'm just saying," Monica said.

"What? When? Is she mine?" D'Angelo said, sitting straight up in bed.

"Noooo." She laughed, then added, "Remember the King Kochese case that I worked on before I came to the FBI?" she asked.

"Yeah."

"Well, one of the keys to that case was an informant named Calvin Bircher, but everybody called him Bird. While we were working that case, we became very close and—"

"Wait, you had a baby by an informant?" D'Angelo cut in.

"No. Shut up, D'Angelo. Do the math. If she's almost a year old, I would have had to be pregnant in your course. No, I was close to Bird and his child's mother. When she was murdered, they were able to save Millie, the baby. Bird was a heartbroken mess, but he loved that baby. He made me promise that if anything happened to him, I'd take care of her like he knew something was coming. So, when King murdered him, I adopted his baby."

D'Angelo didn't say anything. He just lay there staring at the ceiling. This was a part of Monica that he had never known. Then again, he had his own secrets, his own skeletons. He stood and started to dress.

"Say something, D'Angelo."

"There is nothing to say. I respect that. Like you said, who knows what the future holds? Now, if you don't mind, I need to make a phone call. I'll meet you downstairs."

Chapter 25

Fire and Brimstone

Cyril Griffin knew that he had mental problems because his father had told him so. He'd endured torture
at the hands of his father since the death of his mother
when he was 7 years old. Life before age seven had
been nice. He could remember going to church revivals
with his mother and father and sitting underneath the
giant circus tent. He was made to listen intently as the
reverend spouted words of repentance and redemption.
He warned the congregation of God's impending fury,
especially for the unforgivable sin of race mixing. Mixing
with the mongrels, as he called them, was contrary to
God's law. Whites were superior in every way, and they
were God's chosen people. As an example, he'd say that
niggers loved to hoot and holler about being Egyptians,
and if that was true, then we need only look at how
the Egyptians treated the Hebrews. He'd scream in his
high-pitched southern drawl that it was a simple case of
what goes around comes around. If the Egyptians had
held the Hebrews in bondage, then it was only fitting that
the Hebrews returned the favor. Slavery, in God's eyes,
therefore, had been justified. He'd go on and on about
the differences between Blacks and whites until it was
ingrained in his young, impressionable head, and to seal
the deal, the entire congregation would gather around a

bonfire and burn the cross, a ritual that he thought was religious, *not* racial.

Yeah, he remembered it all. He remembered how his father had blamed him for his mother's death, saying that she couldn't bear to live knowing that she had given birth to such a little shit. He could still see his mother's sweet face lying in the hospital bed, unresponsive to his pleas for her to come home. Years later, as his father lay in the same hospital dying, he would learn that his mother had died of walking pneumonia. Even after her death, Cyril had found himself waiting for her every day after school. It was his no-good father who had made him call his mind back and realize that his mother was never coming home.

He'd left home wearing his favorite *Dukes of Hazzard* T-shirt, holding his *Happy Days* lunchbox. After school, he'd waited well into the night for his mother to arrive. Much to his dismay, it was his father who finally pulled up in front of the school in their rusty Chevelle, reeking of cheap rotgut liquor. The car sputtered and clunked, expelling thick white smoke as his father threw the car into Park and jumped out.

"You should've been home hours ago, you little shit. Let's go," he shouted.

"I'm waiting for Mommy."

"You got a long wait, boy. Your ma ain't coming." He spat a thick glob of brown spit and wiped his mouth with the back of his hand. Then he snatched the boy up by his shirt, yanked the passenger-side door open, and said, "Now get in the fucking car. I got company coming." He shoved Cyril inside as hard as he could and slammed the door.

And that's when the beatings started, gradually at first, and then more frequently until the abuse was daily.

He and his father were the epitome of a stereotypical trailer-park trash family. The dirty, single-wide trailer with its moldy siding and littered lot sat in the middle of Paradise Cove Mobile Home Park. There was, however, nothing "paradise" about it. A more befitting name might have been Parasite Cove. Their home had always been kept rather nice by his mother, but after her death, a beer can in the yard had slowly turned into dozens of beer cans, empty milk cartons, and old Busch Light beer boxes. They were there for life, as his father had said, partly because of price but mostly for convenience. The trailer was located near several meth labs, and his father loved meth more than he loved his own son.

Dingy rebel flags hung from nearly every dilapidated trailer in the compound except for one. It belonged to Peggy Evans and her family. They were the only Black family in Paradise Cove, and the whites there never let them forget it. Willie Evans was a short, slender, hardworking man who, according to the legend that he'd created for himself, was as strong as an ox. Cyril didn't find that hard to believe because his wife, Tanya Evans, was as big as an ox. She was as dark as the day was long, but she was pretty and a hard worker—at least from Cyril's viewpoint. The extent of Cyril's knowledge in dealing with Black people came from television, but his interaction with the Evans family gave him a newfound respect for Black people. They didn't make fun of him the way that the white people did.

Much to his chagrin, the family, especially Tanya, was very kind to him. They fed him and sheltered him when his father would beat him, shoot the grocery money into his veins, or fall asleep drunk and refuse to unlock the door. Cyril and Peggy walked to and from school every day, and by the end of their third-grade year, Cyril Griffin was in love. As he lay across his bed scrawling "Cyril loves

Peggy" across a tattered notebook, his father stumbled into his room, full of drunken belligerence.

"You a nigger lover, boy? You wanna mate with that little coon beast you always sniffing behind?" he slurred.

"She's nice, Poppa, and Miss Tanya is nice too."

"Only reason they're nice to you is because they want something from you, boy. Now, I'm warning you, nigger lover: either stay away from that little girl, or something really bad might end up happening," he threatened.

Cyril ignored his father's wishes. After all, what did he know? All he did was drink, shoot drugs, and work on cars all day. No, he wouldn't stop walking to school with Peggy, he wouldn't stop having dinner with the Evans family, and he wouldn't stop playing with his Black friends at school.

It wasn't until the middle of their fourth-grade year that his father's threat manifested. Fatty McMillan had come down with chickenpox, and instead of his parents keeping him at home, they'd sent him to school with it because they couldn't afford to take off work with him. By the time the school realized the outbreak's source, nearly half the third- and fourth-grade classes had come down with it. Only a select unlucky few escaped the chickenpox and were still made to go to school.

Peggy Evans was one of those few. She'd rush home to call Cyril every day after school and share stories with him of the day's school yard festivities. Except one day, her call never came. No, it never came, and on top of that, it wouldn't stop raining. It had already rained three days straight, and Peggy hadn't called on either day. Frantic, Cyril had run full speed to their small trailer, only to be greeted by police lights and a distraught Mr. and Mrs. Evans. Mrs. Evans's eyes burned through him as if he'd done something wrong. Peggy had been beaten and hanged, and her naked body had been left inside the dank, abandoned airplane hangar at the end of Red Hawk Road. Everyone in town knew that Tucker Griffin was responsible, but no one was going to be the cause of a white man losing his freedom for taking the life of a Black person, regardless of whether it was a child.

Cyril was grief-stricken, and life just didn't seem the same without Peggy. He regressed and drifted further and further into his fantasies. In those fantasies, every animal that he encountered was his father. He'd started with bugs at first, burning and torturing them with an old magnifying glass that he'd found on his way home from school one day. Slowly, he graduated to bigger animals like dogs and cats. He'd catch them, mostly strays, and torture them to death. He'd found a certain amount of pleasure in watching the small animals squirm in pain until he grew bored. He wanted something bigger, something that would fight back . . . like a human. They would be the perfect prey.

His first victim had been Becky Ann Mumford, the wholesome, blond-haired, blue-eyed Sunday school teacher who had a crush on the withdrawn 17-year-old bookworm. She was everything his father loved and everything he'd subsequently grown to hate. Murdering her had been his greatest pleasure. As she sat with him on a blanket in Shaker's Park, expounding on the wonders of God's gracious love, he let his hand slip underneath her dress and finger fucked her like the slut that he knew she was. He had to kill her because she'd lied. She'd made him believe that she was pure, that she was untainted. He would help her make it to heaven through cleansing her by way of death. He mounted her, pumping like a madman as she moaned from their carnal escapade, and at the height of his arousal, just before he climaxed, he slipped his hands around her throat and squeezed. She resisted and struggled, but he tightened his grip. Her eyes bulged, and her body seized, and he kept tightening his grip until he felt her body go limp.

Yes, Becky Ann had been his first, the first in a long line of white women, women his father would have loved to have as his own or to have seen his son with. He'd left Becky's body there in the park, half-naked, with her milky white breasts and pink nipples exposed for the world to see. He'd carved a cross on her chest as a reminder that she was his sacrifice to God almighty, his God, and before his days were done, he'd give others unto God who didn't cherish His grace and mercy nearly as much as Cyril Griffin did.

Chapter 26

Unified

King Kochese stood on the tarmac of a private airstrip in Costa Rica with nearly his whole staff. He wanted Jasmine to have the warmest welcome possible, and everyone present anxiously awaited her arrival. King stood next to Manny and his wife, who was all smiles. King was sure that Manny hadn't discussed his demotion with his wife because she was overly excited.

"I can't wait to meet your wife, El Rey. There is so much to discuss. I know we will be very good friends," she said.

Blah, blah, blah . . . Kochese knew Jasmine better than anyone, and he knew that Manny's wife, Cecilia, smiled too much. Jasmine didn't trust anyone who smiled for no reason. She said that smiles were masks that confuse and disarm their prey, and Kochese agreed. He hadn't smiled, really smiled, since he and Jasmine had been separated. As much as he adored his children, with their mother away from the family, he felt it hard to muster a smile for them.

Kochese's maid, Lucinda, and her daughter were tending the twins, and each soldier in the camp held thirteen jasmine flowers, petals perfectly pristine. None of the soldiers had brought their families—none of them except Manny. He'd brought his wife and their twin girls, Martina and Helena. They were typical 15-year-old girls who happened to have well-to-do parents. They suffered from entitlement syndrome and felt that the world owed them a debt. In their young, delusional minds, their father's supposed wealth and pseudo-power were theirs as well. They were the heirs to a fortune that only existed in show. The twins went to the finest prep school in Costa Rica, and, unfortunately for Manny, his heartstrings, his princesses, were two of the biggest freaks on campus. Manny's biggest fear, like that of many other men across the world, was that his son would grow up gay or that his daughters would grow up to be sluts, and his fear had been actualized. King wondered how that had happened because his girls looked more like Manny than anything. They were, however, known as an easy lay around town, and many men had fallen victim to the hellish ménage à trois, perhaps from the sheer fantasy of being with two young girls at the same time or perhaps from the allure of getting their hands on the millions that Manny didn't have. Whatever the case, if Manny caught wind of any men, or boys, for that matter, fucking his underage daughters, he had them murdered.

His son Mateo was two years older than the girls and was everything they weren't. He was 17 and extremely bookish. He hated his father and everything that he stood for. He refused to take money from Manny, although he did allow him to pay for his education. As Mateo saw it, it was a father's duty to ensure his sons were educated.

King could see the jet approaching in the distance and felt instant anxiety, a nervous churning in the pit of his stomach. No woman had ever made him nervous, not even Monica's ratchet ass. Thoughts of Monica angered him because he had allowed her to get close to him, to infiltrate his very soul, but those feelings dissipated as the jet bounced and skidded to a stop on the runway, only yards from the crowd.

The Phenom 100 skipped and slid to a halt not one hundred feet from where the small crowd had gathered. The jet's engine sounded like a swarm of angry hornets, and Fuego waved to the crowd from the cockpit just before he cut the engines. The silence was deafening, and even though King tried to hide his excitement, his giddiness showed in his stride toward the plane. There was so much to share with his Jasmine, so much that he wanted to discuss, and missing her was an understatement. The exit of the plane opened, and Fuego exited first, with his gun drawn.

"King, what's good, my dude?"

"Chillin', bruh, any problems?" Kochese asked, embracing the rail-thin man.

"Nah, homie. Once we got in the air, it was smooth sailing. Thought them Feds was gonna get our asses for a second, but your boy E is nice with that heat, you feel me?" Fuego said. He turned and waved toward the plane, and Jasmine and Ernest exited.

Jasmine stood at the top of the stairs and tried to smooth out her hair. She looked rough and knew it, but she didn't care. This was a homecoming, not a fashion show. Ernest stood behind her. "You look great, JD," he said.

"Thanks, E. Let's meet our audience, shall we?"

The sun beamed magnificently. Rays of light danced on the concrete runway as Jasmine and Ernest descended the steps of the private plane. Jasmine saw the twins first. Angel and Apache, her babies and her lifesavers, were playing with each other, oblivious to their surroundings, until Jasmine knelt before them. They stared at her, and then both of their toothless faces spread into broad smiles, cooing and reaching for her with outstretched arms, wiggling their tiny, fragile fingers as if summoning their mother. She was at eye level with her precious babies as they rested in their double stroller. She kissed them repeatedly, roaming from one face to the next.

"Oh my God, I missed you two so much," she gushed as she kissed them repeatedly.

Jasmine had her hand on the children's legs when a feeling she couldn't explain gripped her. Her head snapped up toward the crowd to find a curvy, young Spanish girl staring down at her with a smirk on her face. They locked eyes, and in that brief second, Jasmine felt challenged, envied . . . hated.

Jasmine's features quickly softened as she looked back at her babies. She pinched their cheeks gently, stood, and surveyed the crowd in search of her husband. Near the nose of the plane stood a tall, dark-skinned man talking to the pilot, Fuego. His chocolate skin glistened and almost glowed against the radiant sunlight. Two distinctive features caused him to stand out. First was the long scar that stretched from his earlobe to damn near the corner of his mouth. Second were his icy blue eyes.

King shook Fuego's hand and handed him a bag of money. "I appreciate you coming through for me on such short notice, dawg. I don't know how I woulda got my baby up outta there if it wasn't for you and buddy. So, you say he's a shooter, huh?" Kochese asked, eyeing Ernest, who was still standing by the plane's steps.

"Yeah, brother, like bull's-eye accurate, sharpshooter-type shit."

"Good to know. Call me if you need me, mi *hermano*." He dapped Fuego and then walked with him back to the entrance.

"What's up, bruh? I'm Kochese; you must be E?"

"Yeah, I'm E. Nice to meet you."

"I wanna thank you for everything you did for my wife. If it hadn't been for you, she'd probably still be in that bitch."

"No thanks needed. JD didn't deserve to be in a place like that. I think she would've still found a way back to you all, though. I was just an instrument in her plan." Ernest shrugged.

"Yeah, I can believe that. If Jasmine sets her mind to something, no matter what it is, she will come out on top."

Jasmine could see Kochese and Ernest talking, smiling, and shaking hands. She pushed the children in the stroller toward the duo, and as soon as she made it to King, she threw her arms around his neck and kissed him deeply, letting her tongue swirl around his, jockeying for position like two snakes mating.

He pulled back from her, held her at arm's length, and looked into her eyes. "Now, how did you know that it was me? What if you'd been kissing some random nigga?" King Kochese asked.

"First of all, baby boy, nobody, and I mean *nobody,* has your swag. Second, third, fourth, and fifth, daddy, you can put on a choir robe, cowboy boots, a floppy wig, sunglasses, and a fake mustache, and I can still pick you out in a crowd," Jasmine teased.

King laughed, but Jasmine was serious. She had studied King, taught him, and learned from him, so she knew him. She knew him from the top of his head to the curve in his dick, and she'd be damned if some young, hot, twat chick with the IQ of a boiled turnip came between her and her love. She turned and stared at the girl, letting her green laser beam eyes burn through her as she pulled Kochese's face back to hers and kissed him again. The little bitch was playing a game that Jasmine was sure she wasn't ready or equipped to play. Only King Kochese knew that Jasmine felt no guilt and offered no apologies for her penchant for murder. She returned the same evil smirk that the girl had given her earlier.

Lucinda tugged at her daughter's arm, trying to break her frozen gaze with their boss's wife. *"¿Quieres que nos despidan, nena? Tienes que jugar bien con ella, ahora es nuestra jefa. El rey Kochese lo ha dejado perfectamente claro. Así que tienes que recomponerte,"* Lucinda said through clenched teeth.

"No, I don't want to be fired, Mamita. She's beautiful, and I am just admiring her beauty," the girl said, but her eyes were still locked on the family.

"Then look away, *Mija*, look away," her mother pleaded.

Lucinda stepped to Jasmine to apologize to her on Consuela's behalf, but Jasmine ignored her and turned her attention to the young girl.

"What's your name, sweetie?" Jasmine asked.

She smirked again and shifted her body with an air of superiority. "My name is Consuela."

Jasmine gave a smug "Humph" in her direction, pushed past her, took the handles of the twins' stroller, and made her way toward the limousine. She looked back at Kochese as if to say, "Nigga, if you don't get yo' ass in this car . . ."

Chapter 27

Little Rock

Cyril Griffin drove the deserted stretch of I-40 just north of Little Rock, Arkansas, thinking of the conversation he'd just finished. The man he knew as King had berated him on the phone. He'd been chastised for the elaborate staging of the murders he'd committed. King said he was drawing too much attention to himself with the over-the-top scenes, but Cyril had countered by saying that King himself had instructed him to make the murders as memorable as possible to shake up the FBI.

"Man, just do what the fuck I tell you to do. Agent Deitrich is no joke, bruh. You keep doing this goofy religious shit that you're doing, and you're going to lead her to you before it's time. Stick to the fucking plan. Move the way I tell you to move, when I tell you to move, and where I tell you to move. You feeling me? I'm not the type of man you want to annoy," King Kochese said. His voice was calm and smooth, unbothered almost.

"Maybe I should just kill the bitch to get her out of the way and be done with it."

"Maybe you *shouldn't,*" Kochese said.

"Why not? If you're worried about her catching up to me, then it's probably better if I wait for her to find me and dispose of the little cunt."

"Cyril, do I sound worried? I will tell you this, though. If you harm one hair on Special Agent Monica Deitrich's pretty little head before I give you the go-ahead, I will teach you the meaning of pain. I will personally splay your torso with a dull, jagged knife, muh'fucka. Just do what the fuck I say, get your money, and disappear. Simple," King said.

Before Cyril could speak, their call was disconnected. He was fuming. Who the fuck did he think he was, talking to him like that? He should kill Monica Deitrich out of spite. No one had spoken to him that way since his father, and it drudged up old, bitter memories. Yes, he would kill her, and after he received his money from King, he would reveal to him the wonders of fucking with the mentally unstable.

Cyril drove in silence, brooding. He looked at his gas gauge and noticed his needle was well below the quarter tank mark, so he drifted into a small gas station. The gas station looked deserted, save for a lone flickering light just above a wooden, weather-beaten sign that read: *Last Stop Before Big City Gas Prices*. Cyril looked toward the dirty windows of the gas station and saw a young white man, maybe 25 years old, sitting behind the counter, picking his nose. He rolled the wet booger between his fingers, then let his hand fall below Cyril's line of sight. *Nasty fucker,* Cyril thought.

He looked up from his phone as if he could feel Cyril's murderous gaze on him and waved. Cyril frowned at him, remembering his booger-rolling episode. He waved back while his eyes darted up and down the desolate highway, searching for oncoming traffic, but there was none. Only darkness and the moonlight shone brightly against the reflector on a green sign that said, *Little Rock Next 4 Exits*.

Cyril slipped his hands inside his pockets and shuffled to the front door, but a car's headlights caught his attention. With its music blaring, the car pulled into the gas station and slid to a stop in front of the door. A petite blonde stepped out of the vehicle, and Cyril pulled the door open for her, trying to be the gentleman that he knew his mother had raised him to be, but little Miss Rich Bitch took her time as if *his* time were less important than hers.

As they entered the store, the clerk stood and tried to smooth out the wrinkles in his shirt. "May I help you folks?" he asked.

The blonde looked at Cyril, turned up her nose, and rolled her eyes. "Oh my God, as if we're together," she snorted.

Her words sliced through Cyril like a straight razor, and he bristled under her harsh words. He locked eyes with the clerk and noticed a smirk spread across his face. His look made Cyril feel that the clerk approved of the woman's snotty behavior. Cyril wiped his brow but there was no sweat, only the feeling of his own heat. He looked around the store at the eclectic mixture of things that they had to offer and disappeared down a nearby aisle. The store resembled the type he'd only seen in movies—the old general stores with everything from dried goods to hardware.

Cyril perused the aisles, keeping his eye on the girl over the top of the shelves. He grabbed a few things along the way . . . a hammer, a box of thick, tenpenny nails, a crowbar, a section of barbed wire, and a roll of duct tape. Cyril placed all of it on the counter, went back into the aisle, and almost collided with the young lady. "Excuse me," he said as he passed her. She had the audacity to cringe when he passed as if he were some sort of hideous creature that reeked of hot piss with unbearable features.

Cyril brought his hand up to his face and stared at himself in the mirror above the beer cooler. He thought he was a very handsome man—except for the scar. His old face *was* hideous, with its pocked skin, stringy hair, and jagged teeth. This face, King's face, was a welcome sight to even his own eyes, so the bitch obviously didn't have good taste in men. *If I was a bitch, I'd fuck me,* he thought. Cyril grabbed a couple of bags of Ruffles chips, a jar of Picante sauce, and a few Slim Jims. He placed them on the counter and waited patiently for the disheveled clerk to finish gawking at the young socialite behind him.

"Will this be all for you, sir?" he asked.

"No, I need a fill-up on pump two also."

Behind him, the young lady huffed and puffed while conversing with a friend named Jenny on her overpriced, gold-toned cellular phone. Jenny was probably bred from the same selfish piece-of-shit stock that Miss High and Mighty was bred from. "Ugh, Jenny, hopefully, I'll make it to the party before Nelson leaves. Yeah, I'm trying to get gas, but this idiot in front of me is taking forever to pay for his shit," she hissed.

Cyril's head snapped back, and he stared at her. She was rude, like his father. They were the type of people who thought they had the right to say and do whatever they wanted. He smiled at her and winked. "I'm sorry, ma'am. Please forgive me. Would you like to go ahead of me? I would hate to hold you up, little lady," Cyril said, stepping back, clearing a path for her to get to the counter.

She eagerly took the opportunity to skip ahead of him with not so much as a "thank you" for his troubles. "Jenny, I'll call you back when I'm on the road again," she said, disconnecting her call.

The cashier was ringing up her Fiji water and sugar-free Mentos when Cyril struck her savagely across the back of the head with the claw hammer that he'd placed on the counter moments earlier.

"What the fuck!" the clerk shouted as he wiped her blood from his face.

"What the fuck, indeed. Why must people be so unkind? And to think you were encouraging this cunt."

"No, mister, she was an asshole. She deserved it." His voice trembled, and his body visibly shook.

"Who are you to determine who deserves what? No, no, no, don't reach like that," Cyril said, removing the pistol from his waistband. He waved the man around to his side of the counter with the barrel of his gun. "Bring your ass over here," he ordered.

The clerk raised his hands and did as instructed. As he made his way around the counter and saw the woman lying on the floor, bleeding from the large, gaping hole at the back of her head, he lost it. Cyril saw the wetness of the man's urinary expulsion and chuckled.

"Go to the beer cooler, pissy," Cyril ordered. Cyril pushed him into the glass of the cooler and threw the duct tape in his direction. "Tape your fucking hand to the handle," Cyril hissed.

"Listen, mister, I don't know nothing, and I ain't seen nothing. I swear if you let me go, I won't say a word."

"You promise?" Cyril asked.

"I promise I won't say a word."

"Shut your lying, filthy mouth and do what you're told, stupid," Cyril said as he slapped the man across his forehead with the barrel of his gun. After he'd taped his hand, Cyril taped his other hand to the handle on the opposite side of him. He was taped to the cooler with his arms outstretched as if he were being crucified.

"Please, mister, just let me go. Please, I'm begging you. Please don't kill me."

Cyril smiled. "I'm not going to kill you. You have to spread the word of the king." Cyril went to the front counter and scrawled *I am a king among peasants and a wolf among sheep on a paper bag*. He took a large hunting knife from the glass case near the back of the store.

"Awww, come on, man. You said you weren't gonna kill me."

"I'm not," Cyril said. He held the note up and plunged the hunting knife deep into the clerk's chest.

The clerk screamed. "Oh my God, oh my God, mister, please."

"Shhh, shhh, don't scream. If you preserve your strength, you might make it out of this alive."

"*911, what's your emergency?*" an operator said from the other end of the phone, but Cyril didn't speak. Instead, he placed the phone on the counter and left the store.

Chapter 28

Dirty Cop, Clean Conscience

Something about D'Angelo irked Monica, and she couldn't figure out what it was. She sat across from him, staring at him but not really listening. She'd nod occasionally just to keep him from asking if she was listening, but she hadn't heard a word he said.

"Monica?"

"Yes?"

"Are you ready to go? We were going to have the meeting in the trailer, but the Wichita office would be a more suitable place because, according to a phone call I got before I arrived, there have been new developments."

"What kind of developments?" she asked curiously.

"Your guess is as good as mine, but what I do know is that if we don't nip this shit in the bud quick and wrap up this case, heads are going to roll—and it won't be mine."

Monica let D'Angelo leave ahead of her. She didn't like people in her business, and the last thing she needed was for someone to see her and D'Angelo pulling up in the same car. Plus, she needed time to think. She knew what it was about D'Angelo that irked her nerves. He was *overly* ambitious . . . the kind of ambition that caused men to cut the throat of anyone who even remotely looked like they might stand in their way.

They'd had talks over dinner, over sex, and just about anywhere else where they happened to be together, and D'Angelo had always pictured himself as more than what he was. He wore the finest suits, ate at the fanciest restaurants, and drove one of the nicest cars in the bureau. He lived so lavishly that it was rumored that D'Angelo just might be dirty because he lived well above his means. Once over dinner, Monica had asked him why he was so flashy. He'd simply shrugged and said that he saw a rich man, not a nine-to-five working stiff, when he looked in the mirror.

"But how can you afford these things on your salary?" she'd asked.

"All men have sinned and fallen short of the glory of God, Monica."

"What? Wait. What does that even mean?" she asked.

"Kings, queens, rooks, bishops, knights, and pawns, Monica. I refuse to be a pawn."

"Then what are you? Because I think we are all pawns in somebody's game," she said reflectively.

"I'm the rook. I'm the closest thing to the king with a dick," he'd laughed.

She hadn't thought much about it then, but during their encounter earlier in the evening, he'd bragged about his new 5,000-square-foot, three-story house and how he could more than afford to care for her and Millie. That statement didn't sit well with Monica because she knew he didn't make that kind of money. As an FBI Special Agent, D'Angelo was making upward of $100,000 annually, plus another $40,000 as an adjunct professor of criminal studies. Even though a combined salary of $140,000 was, by no means, a peasant's pay, it was the veracity with which he'd made the statement that bothered Monica. If there was one thing that the agency had taught her, it was that she had to check everyone. D'Angelo was no different.

Her mind shifted to Bird—her friend, her brother. He'd thought enough of her to entrust his precious Millie to her, and before she took the plunge and brought any man around Millicent, he'd be checked out thoroughly. She didn't care who it was. Somehow, whenever she thought of Bird, her mind shifted to King Kochese. She had some serious issues when it came to him, and those issues were hindering her investigation. She loved him; she knew that much was true. But she hated him for making a life with her sister and stealing a life that should have belonged to her. Truth be told, Monica had had Jasmine committed because she wanted her out of the way—well, at least that's what she felt she was doing. It must have had some validity to it because it was pestering her. Considering the circumstances, she couldn't blame Kochese for hating her. And once King had laid eyes on Jasmine, Monica no longer mattered to him. She needed to capture him, not so much to bring him to justice, but to see his face.

Why should he give a flying fig what you think, Monica? After all, you were going to send the man to prison forever, she thought.

When she thought about the things that he'd done to her body and the conversations that they'd had, she felt a twinge in her clitoris. Ugh, she hated herself for thinking of him in that way, for thinking of his tongue between her legs, his tongue exploring the deepest recesses of her body. Monica leaned forward and placed her head on the steering wheel. From past experience, she knew that all eyes would be on her, so she most definitely had to get herself together.

Monica exited her car and cursed herself tersely as it dawned on her that she'd left her keys in the ignition and locked the door. *Oh well, at least it's not running,* she thought.

The moon fought to shine through the grayish white clouds that swirled above Monica's head. She could smell the sandy odor of the approaching rain and ran toward the building for cover. When she stepped through the glass doors of the nondescript brick building, she saw D'Angelo standing at the end of the hall and talking on his cellular phone. He turned and looked in her direction, and a look of terror spread across his face. His eyes never left Monica's as she moved down the hall toward him. The closer she got, the faster his mouth moved. She was within arm's length when D'Angelo muttered a quick "Yes, sir" and ended the call.

Monica and D'Angelo stepped into the compact conference room in silence. She wondered if it was possible that he'd strayed away from his sacred oath. She'd always had respect for D'Angelo, and even with his freaky ways, he was still one of the best agents she'd known.

As they entered, an eerie hush fell over the room, with all eyes falling on Monica. She took a seat amongst the assortment of agents in the room, waiting much like everyone else for the meeting to begin. However, they were staring at her, trying to read her, and it caused her to stir uncomfortably. A man that resembled the stereotypical FBI agent stood—navy-blue suit, white shirt, navy-blue power tie . . . the whole nine yards. He straightened his tie and addressed Monica directly.

"Agent Deitrich, first, I want to offer my condolences. Although we can sympathize with your loss, I'm sure every agent here shares my sentiment when I say we won't mourn the loss," he said.

"Condolences, sir? I'm not sure I follow," Monica said.

"Your sister and her accomplice were killed in a shootout with the Federal Marshals and were both confirmed dead. But not before taking four Marshals with them to the hereafter. Allow me to address the elephant in the room. You just happen to show up at the hospital when your sister is giving birth, and she's apprehended trying to escape. You also show up for a mystery visit, and she escapes. Now, she's dead, and I think this whole thing stinks to high heaven. Your lack of professionalism in this case is reprehensible, to say the least. You've yet to produce a viable suspect in this case. Effective immediately, you're being removed from this case. Please give D'Angelo your badge and gun," he said.

Monica looked at D'Angelo. The son of a bitch had walked her right into an ambush. Was *this* the development that he was speaking of? If so, he could have given her a heads-up or, at the very least, told her to prepare herself. Did he know that her sister was dead before they got there?

Monica opened her mouth to blast the grizzled old agent, but D'Angelo put his hand on hers and patted it lightly as if to say, *I got this; chill out.* But Monica snatched her hand away. She wouldn't allow anyone to speak to her in that manner. He looked important, authoritative, with that all-too-familiar air of superiority that white men carried who had no respect for women, but he had her fucked up.

"Wait a minute, Deputy Director Harden. Agent Deitrich is an integral part of this case. Before we jump to conclusions and demand her badge, let's hear what she has to say. After all, she's a profiler on this case, not the lead. I'm the lead agent in this case, and if anyone's head should roll, it should be mine."

"At this point, Agent D'Angelo, I don't give a fuck whose head rolls. The director is on *my* ass about Kochese Mills and Agent Deitrich's sister. The only saving grace is that I've reported that Jasmine Deitrich is now on ice, and we can focus on *one* fugitive. People are afraid that this is a repeat of those ungodly Monopoly killings. We must appease the public. People are dropping like flies, for God's sake, Agent. So, she'd better damn well tell me something, or the next move may not only be removal from the case, but we might also consider tampering charges," he shouted.

The tension in the room was thick, and everyone there was petrified with fear, afraid to utter a word . . . and glad that it wasn't their head on the chopping block.

Deputy Director Kenneth Harden was a hardnosed agent who had been in the bureau for over forty years and was as straight as they came. He'd been a beat cop in Boston and subsequently joined the FBI just in time for the great crackdown on organized crime. He earned his bones as one of the agents responsible for turning Whitey Bulger into a bureau informant. His philosophy was legendary: *If you don't do your fucking job, we'll find someone who will.*

Monica had heard tales of the man but never met him in person. Throughout her tutelage by Agent Muldoon, he'd shared stories with Monica concerning his mentor, Kenneth Harden. If he was, in fact, disappointed in her, then Monica felt that she was indeed letting Muldoon down. That still didn't give him cause to disrespect her in the presence of her fellow agents.

"If I may, I apologize if it seems as if I'm not moving in a timely enough manner, but the truth of the matter is, these killings are widespread, and they're mobile," Monica said, moving toward the map pinned to the wall at the head of the table. The agents present all leaned forward to get a better glimpse of Monica. She grabbed a handful of pushpins from a small box next to the map and began to tack different locations on the map while looking at a notepad.

"When I first started looking at the locations and the method of murder, I assumed that the killer or killers were patterning their killings after known serial killers, especially after the murders in Dallas and Savannah. The murder in Dallas followed the pattern of the Zodiac Killer. The murders in North Carolina were patterned after Jeffrey Dahmer. Hell, even the murders in Savannah followed the DC Sniper," Monica said.

"Copycat killings? C'mon, Agent Deitrich, this gets us no closer than we were before you started talking," Harden scoffed.

"As I said," Monica replied, ignoring his sarcasm, "I initially believed that we were dealing with a potential Leopold and Loeb—you know, killers that killed to show their intellectual superiority over the authorities while working in tandem with one another. I'm now convinced that these murderers, although tied together, are acting totally independent of each other," she said.

"You're talking in circles, Agent. And you're wasting my time and the time of everyone else in this room with this bullshit," Harden declared.

"Man, listen, I don't have to—" Monica started.

But she was cut off by a young, frumpy-looking agent. He was pudgy with curly red hair and freckles. He also wore large, thick-paned, horn-rimmed spectacles. He pushed his glasses from his eyes up off his nose nervously. Then he cleared his throat and began to speak in a nasal, Midwestern twang.

"Excuse me, sirs, ma'am. I think what Special Agent Deitrich is trying to say is that there is a definite pattern, but not as we'd originally thought. Under Agent Deitrich's direction, I've been able to come up with a theory that I believe will better depict how the suspect or suspects are moving," he said.

Monica looked on in bewildered amazement. She had never laid eyes on this kid until now, and she most certainly hadn't held a conversation with him. He looked at her with pleading eyes, silently begging her to hear him out.

"Go on," Harden said.

"Agent Deitrich's map . . . Look at it," he said, pointing to the map while moving in her direction. He took a couple of pushpins from the box and placed them on the map. "To the average person looking at the map, the murders would seem completely random and sporadic, right? Before we started the meeting, a call came in over the wire, announcing four more murders that were committed, which are the pushpins I just added."

"Okay, Agent Langdon, get to the point. I'm not here for theatrics," Harden said.

"Yes, sir. I figured out that they are acting under the guidance of a shot caller, a financial benefactor, and it has to be Kochese Mills," he said.

Both Monica and D'Angelo looked at each other and then back at the young agent. "What makes you think King is involved in these murders?" D'Angelo asked. He had his own theories, but outside of Monica, he hadn't shared his views.

"Initially, I thought that they were just some overzealous kill fans that admired King and Jasmine's murder spree, but if you look at the murders . . ." He removed a red marker from the box. Then he connected each pushpin from point to point, almost intersecting the lines of the additional points he'd added. He connected them in the order that the murders happened, and the light of realization hit them all simultaneously. It had been there in their faces the whole time, and none of them had seen it.

"As you can see, the murderers are doing this in the name of the 'king,' so to speak. The killings form a perfect crown. The only thing that's missing is the point of the crown. Considering the distance and frequency with which the murders are happening, I predict that their next target will be in Chicago, Illinois," Kirby Langdon said triumphantly, pinning a gold tack on Chicago. He stood back and surveyed his handiwork. Pleased, he turned to face his fellow agents.

Well, I'll be damned. This nigga King is playing games again. Having his murderers kill in the shape of a crown? Genius, Monica thought. She seized the opportunity to jump in and add to Agent Langdon's theory. "If we're right, this would explain the notes about being 'a king among peasants and a wolf among sheep,'" Monica said.

"This son of a bitch is playing another one of his sick games. The state of South Carolina wants us to impose a statewide curfew because they believe they have a serial killer trolling their streets. What's next, Agent Deitrich?" Harden asked. His entire demeanor toward Monica had instantly changed, but she wouldn't gloat in his defeat.

"If Agent Langdon is correct, then we need to mobilize a team to Chicago. We must remember that Kochese Mills, a.k.a. Khalil Cross, a.k.a. King Kochese, has unlimited resources. I believe Agent Langdon is correct in his assumption that Kochese will commit the final murder himself because not only is he an arrogant, sadistic piece of shit, but he's also very meticulous. He may not believe that these men can pull off his final coup de grâce," Monica said.

"Say no more. You have your team. I'll call the field office in Chicago and instruct them to give you their full cooperation and use of their resources. Let's nail these sons of bitches and move on," Harden said as he exited the room with the other agents in tow.

"Monica, excuse me. I need to make a phone call," D'Angelo said, leaving the room.

Once they were alone, Monica turned to Kirby Langdon. "That was a nice save. The question is, why did you do it?" she asked.

"I studied you when I was in the academy. You put yourself out there repeatedly, and I don't think the powers that be realize how much work you've put in. With all due respect, ma'am, I think you're kick ass, and it kind of . . . excuse my language, but it pissed me off when he was speaking to you that way. Sorry about your sister."

"Your admiration is greatly appreciated, Agent Langdon, and no need to be sorry. My sister played the game, and she lost. So, I guess my question to you is, are you willing to join this team?" she asked.

"It would be my privilege, ma'am. This is a dream come true, and I won't let you down, I promise."

"I don't need your promises, Agent. I need your vigilance, bravery, and intelligence. After all, I don't have the best luck regarding teammates. There's always the chance of death in dealing with me, Agent. I'm cursed. Haven't you heard?" Monica said.

Chapter 29

Feels Like Heaven

King Kochese had just spent the last hour rocking the twins to sleep. It hadn't been all that difficult, but they weren't on the same schedule for whatever reason. He'd managed to get Angel to doze off, only to have Apache scream and wake her up again, and vice versa. The twins had bustled and squirmed to their own beat until they'd finally decided that they'd made their father suffer quite enough. Slowly, after nearly an hour, they both drifted off into a sound and peaceful slumber.

He walked into his and Jasmine's massive bedroom, peeled out of his shirt, and tossed it to the floor. Since they'd been reunited, Jasmine had refused to let King do much. They'd play fight over who was going to care for the twins. It was a joy for him to watch her with the babies. She was so attentive, and her love was so genuine. He wondered if, at one point in his fucked-up existence, his mother had loved him that way. Jasmine's eyes sparkled when she mentioned the babies, and her demeanor when handling them was beyond gentle.

Jasmine stood with her back turned to King, looking out onto the dark beach below. Moonlight rode the waves, bouncing its radiance across the water, glittering like a billion diamonds, and for once, Jasmine felt peace. Without turning around, she said, "Are you naked yet?"

"Your sex drive is crazy, baby. What if I say I'm tired?" King asked playfully.

"Then I'd say you don't have to do anything. I'll do the work."

"Well, what if I just say no?" he asked.

"No? You'd tell me no? In that case, I'd have to take it from you," she said, turning to face him.

"Oh, take it, huh? That's illegal, you know?"

"I wouldn't be taking it because we're married. Besides, that's *my* dick, so I can do with it what I want. You need to get naked, or I might have to get aggressive with you," she said playfully.

"I don't want to, and besides, I'm tired. We've been doing it nonstop since you got here, baby."

Jasmine walked toward King seductively and, seemingly out of nowhere, produced a remote control to the stereo. She clicked it, and Jazmine Sullivan filled the room, crooning something about busting the windows out of her man's car in her luscious voice. Jasmine shimmied toward King, wiggling her hips like a belly dancer with her hands raised above her head. Her stomach rolled, and her hips swayed to the beat of the music. She stood in front of him and stared into his deep blue eyes. He was as handsome as the day that they'd met, and his new hue fit him. He looked powerful, more masculine, and it turned her on. She tiptoed over and kissed him on his lips, then reached down to cup his manhood.

"You sure you don't want to do it?" she asked seductively, rubbing his now-stiffening dick.

Kochese removed Jasmine's hand from his meat. "Yeah, I'm sure. No daddy dick for you," he said.

Jasmine grabbed his hand and put it on her breast above her heart, and then she took his other hand and put it between her legs. His fingers stroked her liquid heat as he bent to kiss her. "Are you absolutely *certain* that you want to say no, baby?" she asked.

"Yep, ain't nothin', shawt," he said stubbornly.

Jasmine tugged at the string holding King's linen shorts in place. She undid the bow, and his shorts slid to the floor, and so did she. She took him into her mouth, and he shivered with delight. Her mouth was magical, and he nearly lost it when she looked up at him with her green eyes. Between slurps on his erect dick, she moaned and fingered herself.

"I think he disagrees with your decision, baby," she said. Jasmine wrapped both of her hands around the shaft of King's erection and stroked it softly as she let his whole dick disappear into her mouth. She juggled his balls with one hand while continuously stroking his shaft with the other. "Whose dick is this, King?" she asked.

"Mine," he screamed.

"Stop playing with me, boy. Whose dick is this?"

"You want daddy's dick?" he asked.

"Nah, I don't even want it now. I only want what's *mine*," Jasmine said as she stood and turned her back to him.

King stepped out of his shorts and walked up behind Jasmine. He pressed his chest and manhood firmly against her soft and supple body. Then he reached around her body with his right hand and let his fingers slide into her wetness. With his other hand, he gently teased her nipple while kissing her neck. "You sure you don't want me to make love to you?" he asked.

"Yes, I'm certain that I don't want to make love to you. You know what I want?"

"Do tell, Mrs. Mills."

"I want you to fuck the shit out of me, King. I want you to ravage this pussy. We have our whole lives to make love, but tonight, I want you to fuck me. I want to be dirty. I want to be nasty with my husband." She grabbed his hand and thrust his fingers deeper inside of her.

King withdrew his hand and licked his fingers. He spun Jasmine around and kissed her deeply. He could feel her lips tremble as he kissed her, and his manhood throbbed against her stomach. He lifted Jasmine into the air, cradling her left leg in the crevice of his right arm and then her right leg in his left arm. With sheer strength and determination, he lifted her small frame until her beautifully bald love nest was even with his mouth. He made love to Jasmine's pussy with his tongue as he kept her body suspended midair, licking and darting his tongue in and out of her rapidly until he felt her body convulse. He sucked her clitoris gently as he walked her body to their bed. Before he could dismount her from his facial throne, he felt the stickiness of her orgasm.

"Ughhh, baby, I'm coming, King," she screamed.

"You ain't seen shit yet, shawt. Watch this."

Kochese tossed her from his grasp onto the bed, and she bounced playfully to the center. Jasmine clamped her legs shut and smiled devilishly. "I'm good now, daddy. You can go to sleep."

"Oh, it's like that? Oh, okay then," he said. King disappeared into the bathroom and returned seconds later with his hand cupped. He lay beside Jasmine and began to stroke his erect dick with the handful of baby oil that he'd retrieved from the bathroom.

"Ohhhh, baby, you're wrong for that shit," Jasmine pouted.

Kochese ignored her and stubbornly turned his back to her, continuing his deliberate masturbation.

"You can at least let me help."

"Nah, I'm good, shawty. Go on and get you some sleep, baby. I got this," he said, moaning playfully to make it seem more pleasurable than it actually was.

"Man, you think I won't take that dick, baby?" Jasmine asked.

"You said you were good. Besides, you ain't 'bout that life anyway, Jazz. Stop playin', mane."

Jasmine tried to reach around King to gain access to his man meat, but he moved quickly. "If you want this ding-a-ling, you're gonna hafta take it."

"That's okay; you don't have to give me any. Your ass is gonna wake up in the morning, and I'm going to be riding your fucking face. Are you absolutely sure you don't want this, daddy? Look."

Jasmine got onto all fours and buried her face in the down comforter. She reached between her legs and fingered herself with her perfectly manicured red nails. King tried to resist the temptation to look, but it was too much. He reached over and inserted one of his long fingers. In and out he went repeatedly, and with every insertion, Jasmine got wetter and wetter, moaning as if he'd already put his dick inside. He knelt behind her and pushed her stomach to the mattress, spreading her ass cheeks with the palms of his hands. He only inserted the head of his penis at first, barely pumping, until he felt her body relax, and then he thrust deep. Their bodies fit together perfectly, and as much as she tried, Jasmine could not take the entire length of King's dick. He loved that about her. She was indeed any man's dream: beautiful face, beyond smart, impressionable, feisty, and she had some good-ass pussy.

King pumped vigorously and slowly, alternating with long and short strokes, rolling his hips to the left, then right. He braced himself on his fists, stiffening his arms to give himself more leverage, then lifting his body so that he could drop his package deep and stiff inside of her. She squealed with delight, trying desperately to escape, scooting farther onto the bed, but King followed her and matched her every rhythm until she finally collapsed onto the bed. Before she could recuperate, he flipped her body over and hovered above her. Jasmine looked down the length of her body and saw King's monster pulsating above her, ready to devastate her insides. She'd asked for it, so she would wholeheartedly take it. She would enjoy all that he had to offer if she could. Jasmine lifted her legs and held them open with shaking hands.

"Oh, you gonna take it like a big girl, huh?" King asked.

Jasmine had meant to say *yes* but only managed to nod and whimper. King plunged into Jasmine's depths, trying to reach her soul, and she yelped. He wasn't sure whether it was from pain or pleasure, but at any rate, he only gave her three quick pumps before he pulled out. King lay on his stomach and spread Jasmine's southern lips with one hand while inserting a finger from the other hand inside of her. He let his tongue circle her clit until he felt her insides clench with spasms around his finger. She was close; he could feel it building. Her juices were flowing, and he meant to make her spill every ounce of orgasmic fluid that she had inside. Her innards quivered, and just as he felt the first signs of wetness, he withdrew his finger and mounted her, thrusting his dick into her as far as it would go. Kochese felt Jasmine's legs shaking, threatening to drop. He let her legs rest against his shoulders, and he rocked her body back until her butt was off the mattress and her shaven pussy was fully exposed. He leaned in and whispered in her ear while simultaneously grinding inside of her. He gyrated rhythmically, stroking to the left, stroking to the right, dipping in low, dipping in deep. Jasmine's floodgates opened, and she sprayed and squirted all over his pelvis. Her legs shook uncontrollably, and she screamed out in pure, unadulterated bliss.

"Ohhhh my God, baby, why? Why do you do me like this?" Jasmine asked between tears.

"That's my job, baby, to always make sure that you're happy and satisfied."

"Can I tell you something without you thinking I'm crazy?"

"I already know you're crazy, baby, but go ahead," Kochese laughed.

"Baby, that dick and that tongue are magical, for real, but you know if you ever give it to anybody else, I'm going to kill you and that bitch, right? I'm going to kill her first and make you watch, and then I'm going to kill you."

"That's not even a discussion we have to have, baby. I don't want anybody else but you, Jasmine. I have everything I've ever wanted: a beautiful wife, two beautiful children, a bunch of muh'fuckin' money, and real happiness. Why would I fuck that up for a random piece of pussy?" King asked.

"Yeah, I hear you."

"Yeah, you hear me, but you ain't listening, though. I'm all yours, baby, trust," King said as he kissed her lightly on the neck.

"We'll see about that," Jasmine said.

She pushed King off her onto his back and then straddled him. She reached down and grabbed his meat and stroked it until she felt it stiffen once more. She inserted it within the lips of her luscious snatch and wiggled onto it. Kochese moaned and grabbed Jasmine's waist. He watched, mesmerized, as she arched her back and rode him, sliding back and forth until she stopped and looked deep into his eyes.

"I love you, King Kochese, and I swear on all that is holy, I will watch the skin burn from your body before I let another woman have you. Tell all these little thirsty, groupie bitches that Mama's home, so they can stand down," Jasmine said.

It wasn't until King craned his neck that he noticed the steady stream of tears running down Jasmine's cheeks and over the icepick pressed firmly against his neck.

Chapter 30

We Said 'til Death

Jasmine lay cradled in King's arms, staring at the ceiling. "Damn, that was intense, baby," she said.

"Yeah, it was, but, baby, what was with the icepick? You just gonna skip right over that shit, huh?"

"I was just making a point, that's all." She shrugged.

"If you want to make a point, baby, all you have to do is talk to me."

"I *was* talking to you, baby. I just have my own way of communicating, that's all," she said.

"You scare me sometimes, Jazz, for real. It's like I never know if I will wake up when I'm next to you."

"If you keep it real with me and keep your dick in your pants, then you don't have to worry about waking up," she scolded.

"See, that's the shit I mean. The old me would've had your fucking head cut off for saying some shit like that, but I love you, so I give you a pass."

"So, you would hurt me because I'm expressing my love for you? Because I'm telling you that if you give my dick and tongue away, I'll kill you?" she asked.

"No, I'll never hurt you. I'm just trying to get you to understand that there will never be another. What we have goes beyond sex. Nobody can come between us."

"So, why was that little bitch eyeballing me when I got off of the plane, Kochese?" Jasmine asked heatedly.

"Shit, I don't know. I have never said two words to ol' girl."

"Well, she was looking at me like she's been fucking you, and she was pissed because I came home."

"You're tripping, babe, for real. I don't want shawty. Trust me," he said.

"Oh, I *trust* you. It's that little bitch that I don't trust, Kochese. Men are blind to that type of shit, but a woman knows when another woman wants her man."

"It's too much shit going on for you to be tripping over the maid's daughter, Jasmine."

"Yeah, you're right, baby boy. I'll take care of it my way. Now, what's going on?" she asked.

"Remember the fat muh'fucka that was at the airport with his fat-ass wife and the twin girls?"

"Yeah, Danny or whatever his name was," she said.

"Yeah, Manny. That pussy-ass wetback gotta go bye-bye."

"Why? I thought you liked him."

King sat up in the bed with his back against the head-board. He let his fingers run through Jasmine's hair as he told her of Manny's treachery and deceit. He told her about how Chico had stepped up to the plate and came forward about how Manny really was. He also told her how Manny had overstepped his boundaries when he was trying to purchase the club. All of these things, King said, were red flags to him because Manny wanted his life.

"I just don't trust the fucker, you know? So, since I can't trust him, I'll have that fat bastard murdered. Probably have him murdered in his sleep and leave his body for his wife to find," Kochese mused.

"That's simple enough, baby."

"I did some sinister-ass shit, though, baby. It reminded me of the old days when I was running with Bird and Drak's bitch ass," Kochese said, shaking his head.

"Why do you look so sad, King?"

He dropped his head and took a deep breath before he spoke. "Let me ask you a question, baby, and be real with me."

"I'm always real with you, but okay."

"Thinking back, do you ever have any regrets about the murders and shit? I mean, are there any you wish you hadn't done?" he asked regretfully.

"Hell no. Let me tell you something: Every murder that I committed, that *we* committed, was necessary. Those bastards were evil and deserved what they got. Why would you ask me that?"

"Don't worry about it. Just forget I said anything," King replied.

"No, say what's on your mind, Kochese. Then I'll tell you what's on mine."

"It's just that Bird was like my brother, you feel me? My whole life, I didn't have anyone real in my life until you came along. With you, this shit is genuine, unconditional. Bird fooled me good, like even though I cut the nigga and refused to let him get out of the game, that nigga still held me down. Sometimes, I just feel like that shit could have been handled differently. Maybe I should've put some bread behind the nigga. Maybe I should have treated him more like a little brother instead of a worker. Then he probably wouldn't have turned on me," Kochese said.

"Look at me." Jasmine sat up next to Kochese and looked into his eyes. "Fuck Bird, fuck Drak, fuck Monica, and all the rest of those bastards. The hardest murder— not that I regret it—but the hardest murder that I had to commit was Muldoon. He reminded me of Pop Pop, and I murdered him—*we* murdered him. You know why?

Because he threatened our existence, baby. They didn't want to see us together because the selfish motherfuckers didn't understand what love was. They didn't understand what we had. No, I won't allow you to beat yourself up about that bullshit. Bird made his fucking decision, and he paid for it. Drak was a fucking Fed like Monica is a fucking Fed, so kill the regrets. You and our children are the only things in this world that matter to me. Do you know why I fell in love with you?" she asked.

"Because we're both crazy-ass muh'fuckas?" he laughed.

"That's part of it, but I fell in love with you because I could see you. I mean, really *see* you for who you were. Not what society made you, not for what people expected you to be, but I could see inside you, and I knew it was the same for you. Before you ever told me, I already knew that you were damaged. I knew that you could love me for me because we were the same person. I knew that you could feel and embrace my pain. Our love is a special kind that, if you're lucky, only comes once in a lifetime. This is that lifetime. When it comes to you, Kochese Mills, I will die to protect you and your heart, and I most certainly will kill for you with no hesitation."

"Man, I know Monica is pulling her fucking hair out trying to piece this one together. I should have just let the white boy kill her ass when he asked," Kochese laughed.

"Wait, who wants to kill her?"

"One of the white boys I hired. I was telling him to stop the bullshit and just do the murders because she was close to catching up to his ass."

"How do you know that, baby? How would you know how close she is? You still in contact with Monica? You still fucking her?" Jasmine asked.

Kochese laughed nervously. "Hell naw. I got somebody inside the bureau who keeps me updated."

But Jasmine didn't speak. She let her green eyes speak for her, searching Kochese for truth.

"How often do I need to tell you you're all I want?" Kochese offered, pulling Jasmine close to him.

"Until I don't ask you anymore, and when I stop asking, *that's* when you should be worried."

"I'm not finna argue with your little ass. Just know that all of this will be over soon. No more running, no more hiding . . . just living," Kochese said.

"We will have to hide forever. Monica will never let this go. She feels like she has something to prove, like she has to beat me. She's only doing this because of you, you know?"

"How you figure that?"

"Because she loves you. It was okay when she thought you were going to prison. She was even okay with it when she thought you were dead, but knowing that you're piping her little sister and that we have a family? She can't handle that, so she will search for us, trust me."

"Nah, the Feds think you're dead, my love. It'll take a miracle for Monica to escape with her life, let alone her career." Kochese pulled Jasmine close to him and kissed her softly. "All of this shit is going to end. You just let big daddy take care of this one, shawty. All I need you to do is raise these kids and spend this money."

Chapter 31

Best-Laid Plans

"Chico, where does your loyalty lie? Are you with us or that *pinché miaté* King?" Manny asked.

"My loyalty has always been with you, Manny. We are from the same place, amigo. Why would I side with an outsider?"

Manny looked around the room of the nearly twenty men assembled there and addressed them directly. "Listen, *compadres*, I happen to know that King Kochese— or El Rey, as some of you call him—is sitting on millions and millions of dollars. Besides the money, he has the club. He's an outsider, and we shouldn't have to answer to him. He thinks he's better than us, like we're beneath him and his precious family. I say we kill the pinché *rata* and take his money," Manny shouted.

A resounding yell of approval rippled through Manny's living room. He'd only invited the men that he felt that he could trust. He included Chico because he'd nearly raised the young man. He knew that Chico was money hungry, and whoever could offer him the best life, that's where his loyalty would lie. He would offer Chico a larger cut of King's fortune to keep him quiet, but he would, of course, keep the lion's share for himself.

"You *soldados* go home. Show up to work tomorrow like nothing has happened, and when the time is right,

we'll strike. Be careful not to look at him crossways because King is an expert in body language. If he suspects
anything, he'll act quickly and ruthlessly. When this is
over, whoever brings me King's fucking head will be
rewarded with his little sweet bitch wife as their own.
Salud!" Manny shouted.

Jasmine stood in front of the mirror naked, rubbing
lotion on her body. She couldn't believe that after the
night that she and King had had, she was horny again.
She rubbed her stomach. Three small stretch marks were
on her belly, and she considered herself lucky. When
she'd researched what the birth of the twins would do to
her, one of the first things that she'd seen were pictures
of stretch marks—not small, almost unnoticeable stretch
marks like hers, but marks so bad that it caused the
women in the pictures' stomachs to look like large,
oversized raisins. Next were the pictures of saggy breasts,
which had mortified her, but again, she'd been lucky
because her breasts were still perky.

She could hear King singing in his sultry baritone
from the shower. He actually had a nice voice to be such
a gangster; he just couldn't carry a tune very well. She
smiled at how cute he sounded, though, trying to sing
love songs off-key.

A light tap at the door drew Jasmine's attention. She
riffled through King's drawer and threw on one of his
T-shirts. It nearly draped to her knees, but her nipples
showed clearly through the thin material of the garment.
"Who is it?" she asked.

"It's Chico, Señora. Is Señor King awake? It's urgent."

Jasmine opened the door and ushered Chico inside.
"What's wrong, Chico? You sound shaken."

"I'd rather tell you both. That way—" Chico started.

But before he finished his sentence, King entered the room from the shower with a thick bath towel wrapped around his waist. "That way, what, Chico? What's up, amigo?"

"El Rey, please forgive me for this early-morning intrusion, but Manny is up to his old tricks again, Señor," Chico said, handing King Kochese a piece of paper.

Manny, Choco, Trooper, Smiley, Dreamer, Loco, Paco, Fredo, Luis, Flaco, Thumper, Maniac, Killer, Repo, Duster, Joker, Wedo, Gomez, Gordo, and Nacho.

"What's this list all about, Chico?" King asked.

"This is a list of all of the men in your organization that Manny has assembled that want to see you dead, Señor. He had a meeting last night and invited me," Chico said.

"Why would he invite you if he knows you're loyal to King?" Jasmine asked.

"Because he's an arrogant piece of shit who believes that his words are laced with gold. He raised me from a boy, but Manny is not a good person. We are all trying to eat, no? I believe in playing my position, Señora, and El Rey has been nothing but kind to me. I told him of my mother's illness in Mexico, and he spent his own *dinero* to hire her the best care. If that had been Manny, he would've made a lot of promises that he never intended to keep. I'm loyal to those who are loyal to me. He's promised that whatever man brings him your head, Señor, that man will be allowed to keep your wife as a trophy. It's disrespectful and blasphemous," Chico said.

"When is this supposed to take place, Chico?" Kochese asked.

"I'm not sure, Señor. He instructed us to act normal today and wait for his word. Knowing Manny, though, El Rey, it'll be soon because he's drooling over getting his hands on your money."

"It won't be soon enough. Thanks, Chico," King said. He turned his back to the young man and stared out his window toward the pool. He heard the door close, and then Jasmine's soft touch caressed his chest. She stood behind him and let her head rest on the bumpy muscles of his back.

"It's hard to find good help, huh, baby?" she asked.

"Yeah, but I got something real special planned for Manny's bitch ass. You would think as long as this nigga been knowing me that he wouldn't try me. Oh well, time to pull out the old me. Muh'fuckas ain't gonna show respect until I get disrespectful, so fuck it. Gear up," Kochese hissed.

Jasmine felt her pussy moisten because as much as it seemed wrong, she loved when his ruthless side came out. She let her hands drop to the towel and untied the knot holding it. She stroked his dick until she felt it stiffen and throb in her hand. She knew that he had a plan, but right now, he had work to put in on the home front.

Chapter 32

Anybody Killa

King couldn't rest until his Manny problem had been resolved, and he most certainly couldn't go back to the US and leave his family there, knowing that there was a bounty on his head. He knew the perfect place to dispose of Manny. He knew that Manny's wife was desperate to build a relationship with Jasmine, so he decided to use that to his advantage. If she went for it, then it would be easy to do Manny, but if she declined, King would know that Manny had told his wife of his plan. Most men didn't include their wives in plans involving taking another man's money because it made them look weak. Manny was egotistical and would need to maintain that façade in his wife's eyesight. Jasmine sat near him as he made the call.

"Hello, where's Manny?" he said.

"Hola, El Rey. I sent Manny to the market for some carne and leche. Would you like me to have him call you when he gets home?"

"No. I know you've been wanting to get to know Jasmine a little better, so I was thinking we could all go into the city for a day out. It'll allow you ladies to talk while the men discuss a little business. What do you think?" King asked.

"I think that is a wonderful idea, El Rey. No need for me to cook because they have some fantastic restaurants in town," she gushed.

I bet your fat ass knows every one of them by name too, he thought.

"Okay, it's a date then. Wait, hold on one second, please," King said. He muted the phone and turned to Jasmine, who'd been trying to get his attention. "Yes, baby?"

"Tell her to bring the whole family—you know, the kids too."

King nodded at her and unmuted his phone. "Hello? Hey, Jasmine said feel free to bring the entire family. Her treat," Kochese said.

"Wonderful. Let's say Los Tulipanes at two o'clock?"

"Sounds good. See you then," King said, disconnecting the call. He then dialed Chico's number. "Hey, Chico, I need you to gather two carloads of soldiers that you trust. Each man will make $10,000 US for their work today. All they have to do is work security. I need them to be heavily armed and ready to shoot," King said. He didn't bother waiting for Chico's reply because he knew he would handle his business.

"Well, I was going to wait to give you this, baby, but I guess now is as good a time as any," Kochese said. He walked to their closet and grabbed a beautifully carved, reddish-colored wooden case with a large bow on it. He handed it to Jasmine.

She studied it closely and felt tears well in her eyes. Carved into the box along the edges were beautiful jasmine flowers connected by what appeared to be vines. A tiny, childlike angel floated above another child seated on one of the jasmine flowers, and behind him in the distance sat a teepee. They both looked toward a tall, muscular Indian chief wearing a golden crown with four points. The two end points held their children's birth-stones, and the center points held Jasmine and King's birthstones. The vines of the jasmine flowers seemed to connect the entire family within the engraved scene. She could tell from looking at it that he'd put a lot of thought into it, and it touched her deeply.

Jasmine opened the box, and her eyes widened. Inside was a pair of dusted, pink, chrome .380-caliber pistols. The handles were pink pearl, and the gold inlay of each gun had an insignia. One read Angel, and the other read Apache. Between the guns was another wooden box, and etched into the wood were the words "*Until my last breath, I commit my life to thee.*" It was King's promise to her, and inside the box was a platinum wedding ring set. His was a simple platinum band with a few diamonds, but her set was 5.13 carats of heavenly bliss, a platinum engagement ring with a 4-carat, cushion-cut diamond fused to the wedding band that held the other 1.13 carats.

King stood behind her and extended his ring finger in front of her. "What God has brought together, let no man put asunder, baby. I'm with you until my last breath," he said.

Jasmine placed the ring on King's finger and held hers out in return. He put the rings on her finger and kissed her.

"Now, let's go show these muh'fuckas how the Mills clan gets down, shawt," Kochese said.

He dressed in a cream-colored linen shirt, slacks, and a peanut butter-colored belt with matching loafers. He strapped a chrome .45-caliber Desert Eagle pistol to his shoulder holster. He looked at his wife. She was even more beautiful now than when he'd first met her. She hadn't gotten fat, but the twins had most definitely filled her out. She wore a dress that seemed to accentuate her newly found curves. It was busier than the clothes that

Jasmine typically wore, but it made her eyes sparkle. It was white with red roses, but the dress was unique because the leaves and stems were the same shade of green as Jasmine's eyes. The green eel-skin heels with the red soles that she wore only highlighted her look even more.

King walked to the palatial room that housed his children and spoke to the guards. "If anybody, I mean *anybody*, outside of Consuela or her mother comes near this room, I want you to blow their fucking brains out, comprende?" King asked.

Both men nodded, and King walked away en route to meet Jasmine out front. When he stepped out into the sunlight, Chico was standing with Jasmine and ten of his most trusted comrades. The soldiers were all dressed in black combat gear, with automatic weapons at the ready. They were there for the money and the opportunity to prove their worth to El Rey.

"El Rey, I will drive you and your wife. There will be a car in front and one in back, so any attempt to get to you must go through them first. They have been instructed to shoot any threat on sight," Chico said.

"Good shit, Chico."

Lunch was torture for both King and Jasmine because they were forced to make small talk with the very man that they knew wanted them dead. Manny played nice with Kochese, but Kochese knew that if Manny got half the chance, he'd put a bullet in his head.

"Why so much security, El Rey? You're among friends here," Manny smiled.

"I'm out with my wife. I got a lot of money, and I'm in a foreign country. Why wouldn't I have security?"

"Understood. Where are those beautiful twins of yours?" he asked.

"They are safe at home, Manny. I see you brought your twins, but where is Mateo?"

"He's home. He doesn't like me much, so he doesn't care to participate in family-related functions," he said.

"Damn, that has to hurt a little, huh?"

"Yeah, a little bit. I mean, I wanted a son who would follow in his father's footsteps, but all he cares about is books and computers. The little shit has the nerve to call me a barbarian. Can you believe it?" Manny snapped.

In truth, it was the dumbest shit that Kochese had ever heard. What man would want his son to follow in his footsteps if he were a criminal? Kochese wanted nothing but the best for both Angel and Apache. No matter what path they chose to travel, he and Jasmine would back them wholeheartedly and nurture their passions. However, he could see why Mateo thought of Manny as a barbarian. The fat man had no class, no savvy.

Manny looked at the security detail lined up outside the restaurant with trepidation. It didn't sit well with him because King Kochese hadn't rolled that way since he came to Costa Rica.

"How about we walk off some of this food, Manny?" King asked, clapping the fat man on his shoulder.

"Sure, Kochese, sure," Manny said as he turned to his wife and daughters. His wife was busy yapping in Jasmine's ear about everything from parenthood to the best shopping spots in Costa Rica. His daughters, however, were totally detached from their surroundings. They both had their faces buried in their cell phones. "*Ojé,* get your pinché heads out of the phones before I take them. We're leaving. Let's go," Manny yelled.

The twins looked at each other and huffed. They didn't particularly care for their father—not to the extent of their brother's hatred for him, but the hatred one might have for a fruit fly. Even at their age, they were sexually active, and although their father kept a tight leash on them, they still found ways to slip below Manny's watchful gaze. The only time they were given any room to breathe was when their father was away on business, and they made sure to get loose when he was gone. On most weekends, he played poker with some of his high-roller friends, and that night was no different. They had overheard him talking about going to a poker game, so the girls had made their own plans. Rafael was the son of one of their father's henchmen, and they liked him. He was very generous with his money and drove a new car, plus he was muscular and cute, like a swimwear model. Yes, indeed, they would take turns with him and then together until he came, and they could share his taste. They were freaky as hell, thanks to Helena, who'd discovered her sexuality. She'd accidentally stumbled to her parents' door late one night to ask her mother a question and saw her lying across their bed with her legs spread wide as she pleasured herself. Her father had gone to Miami on a business trip, and her mother was alone—or so she'd thought—until she saw her father's most trusted lieutenant emerge from the shadows. Helena had tried to turn away, but her curiosity wouldn't allow her to avert her gaze. She watched as Fernando buried his head between her mother's legs, and her mother nearly went into a fit of convulsions. Her mother bucked and thrashed against the henchman's face, cursing and professing her love for him. Helena felt the moisture between her legs and touched herself where he kissed her mother. She was so into touching herself and watching her mother with her lover that she didn't realize how loud she'd gotten with her own pleasure. She heard voices and opened her eyes just in time to see her mother headed toward the door. She scurried to her room, hopped into the bed, and tried to play like she was asleep.

"Martina, Helena, I know that you're awake. Helena, Martina! Pinché, nosy *putas*!" Cecilia cursed. She stormed back to her room to recapture the orgasm that her daughters had interrupted.

Once she was sure that her mother had returned to her room, Helena eased into her sister's bed and roused her from her sleep.

"What do you want, Helena?" Martina asked.

"Mother is sleeping with Fernando. I saw him doing things to her."

"What things? Mother wouldn't do that to Papa," Martina said.

Helena had slowly climbed underneath the covers, and as they lay, she explained to her sister in graphic detail what she had witnessed. By the time Helena finished recounting her tale, Martina was ready to experience what her mother was jeopardizing their family for. That night opened them both up to an entirely new experience, and they vowed to share that experience with as many people as possible. They wanted El Rey, but he wasn't interested. He barely looked at them at all, let alone in a sexual way. True, their heads had been buried in their phones, but they'd been texting each other.

Oh my God, El Rey is so sexy.

I know. I want to taste him.

Me too, if his whore wife ever lets him breathe.

The women walked ahead of King and Manny as they strolled along the cobblestone road. Kochese made small talk with Manny, nothing major, but just enough to keep the fat man unbalanced. They walked onto the bridge that would allow them to cross the infamous Tarcoles River. Tourists would venture onto the bridge, most likely drunk, start showboating for their friends, playing around a little too much, and *whoops*—down they go. Some poor, heartbroken souls unable to live without the love of their lives might jump from the bridge, or, sometimes, a man may have crossed the wrong man and met his demise at the base of that bridge. No matter the circumstance, lives had been lost to the Tarcoles on many occasions. The river was home to the American crocodile, and *thousands* were waiting at the base of the bridge. It was said that before the unlucky drunks hit the water, their bodies were ripped to shreds by the starving monsters.

Ahead of the group, the first car stopped in the middle of the road, and its occupants emerged with guns drawn, refusing access to a group of approaching tourists and locals. Behind Kochese's and Manny's families, Chico's car stopped, blocking entry from their end of the bridge. Manny looked at Kochese with a nervous smile on his face. "Is everything okay, El Rey?"

"Of course, my friend, why wouldn't it be?" Kochese smiled, put his arm around Manny, and pulled the man close to him. He leaned close to his ear as they both watched their wives. "Would it be because a man I once called my friend plans to destroy what I'm building? Or is it because you plan to have me killed? To have my wife raped? What about my twins, Manny? What would become of their lives?" Kochese hissed.

Manny's pallor belied his Latino roots. His once-vibrant tan skin looked sullen and dull, and dread filled his massive gut. Manny had a two-inch grip on an eight-inch turd, and his bowels threatened to make a shitty situation even shittier. Kochese's grip tightened on his shoulder. "You okay, fat man? You seem a little shaky, but your wife looks happy, though. She and Jasmine seem to be getting along well."

His beautiful Cecilia was clueless. She was so wrapped up trying to impress Jasmine that she hadn't even noticed that Kochese's men had blocked the bridge.

"This is the famous Tarcoles Bridge, Jasmine. *Mira*, look," Cecilia said, pointing down to the bottom of the bridge—hundreds of sandy-colored crocodiles nested and sunbathed near the river's banks. Even more lurked just beneath the muddy water, teeth exposed, lying in wait.

"Yeah, they look hungry, don't they?" Jasmine asked.

Kochese walked to Jasmine and kissed her on the cheek, then turned to Manny, still standing where he had left him. "Manny, gather your family. Let me get a picture to remember you by," Kochese said.

To remember you by? Manny grabbed Cecilia's hand and pulled her close. He beckoned his daughters to join them. They both walked toward his voice but never looked up, their heads buried in their cell phones. King Kochese pulled out his own cell phone and snapped a picture of Manny and his family. In the photo, Cecilia smiled, oblivious to the tension and mounting danger around her. But there was no smile on Manny's face . . . only the look of a man who knew he had fucked up and overplayed his hand.

"Manny, Manny, Manny, you had to know that this was coming. You've known me long enough to know that if you cross me, I'll eventually find out. You also had to know that if I did find out, I was going to murk your bitch ass," Kochese spat.

Cecilia's smile evaporated, and the twins were glued to Kochese's every word.

"I-I-I-I don't know what you mean, El Rey," Manny stuttered. He felt his innards quiver and rattle from his fright, and he had to piss—badly.

"T-T-T-The fuck you stuttering for, muh'fucka? Could it be because you know you fucked up, you disloyal, lard-gut fuck boy? Money talks, Manny, and I got plenty of it. All of those muh'fuckas that you tried to hire to hit me are being murdered as we speak," Kochese said.

"This has all been one big misunderstanding, El Rey. I'm sure we can work this out."

Jasmine eased her twin pistols out of her purse and stepped in front of King, facing Manny and his family. "There's nothing to discuss or work out, fat man. My husband said it's over for you, and that's what that is. The only thing that needs to be discussed is who is going to die first: you, your slut daughters, or your talkative-ass wife," Jasmine said.

"El Rey, man—" Manny started.

But before he could finish his sentence. Jasmine slapped him across his temple with her pistol. He screamed as blood spurted from his head.

"His name is King Ko-motherfucking-Chese, *not* El Rey, asshole," Jasmine said.

Shock and panic spread across Cecilia's face as the realization that she might die dawned on her. "Please, Jasmine, Kochese, please don't kill us. We'll give you all of the money that we have. Just please let us go," Cecilia begged.

Jasmine backed up until her back was touching Kochese's chest. When she felt his arm encircle her waist, she smiled. She looked up and back, and Kochese kissed her lips. "Oh, I'm not going to kill you, and neither is Kochese," Jasmine smiled. Cecilia and Manny seemed to perk up slightly at the prospect of not dying and even managed a half smile. "Noooo, we're not going to kill you guys. We're going to allow you an option. Like a choice, you know?" Jasmine said.

"Yeah, Jazz, I like that. We'll give them a choice—a few choices, actually. Choice number one: who wants to die first?" Kochese said playfully.

Manny and his family all looked at one another warily, wondering if the two killers were actually serious.

"I think that Manny should go first, King. What do you think?" Jasmine asked.

"Nah, I think we should make him watch as his whole fucking family dies, knowing that it's his fault."

Both King and Jasmine laughed heartily, but Jasmine's laughter stopped abruptly. She cocked one of her pistols and stepped close to the twins. She pointed the pistol at Helena's head and began to chant. "Eeny, meeny, miny, moe, catch a young slut by the toe. If she hollers, let her go, eeny, meeny, miny, mo." Jasmine let her pistol come to rest on Martina's head. "Now, which one of you little bitches wants to die first?" she asked.

"Please, Jasmine, don't kill my girls. I'll do anything that you want," Cecilia pleaded.

"Jump."

"Excuse me?" Cecilia asked, puzzled.

"Jump. Let me show you. All you have to do is put both hands on the railing and throw yourself over. It's that simple," Jasmine said.

Cecilia hesitated but then turned to her daughters. They looked so small and innocent, like the first day she'd brought them home from the hospital. She grabbed them and hugged them tight. "I love you both. Don't ever forget that," she said. Then she added in a hushed whisper, "If this puta makes you jump, jump toward the bank. You may get lucky." With that, Cecilia turned and put her hands on the rails.

"What if I refuse to jump, you evil bitch?"

"Whoa, there is no need for name-calling, Cecilia. To answer your question, though, if you don't jump, I'll just put a bullet in your head and have one of these men dump your fat ass over the rails. Come here, though, let me show you something," Jasmine said, putting her arm around Cecilia's neck. She led her maybe forty feet away near the south end of the bridge where they'd come from.

"You see that? That's the least populated area of the bank. There's a possibility that if you make it there, then the crocs won't get you. Isn't that what you told your daughters? Yeah, bitch, I hear everything, even when you attempt to whisper. A little bit about me, though. I grow tired of games really quickly, so I'll tell you again: jump. Even if you make it onto the bank, I'll shoot you in your fucking spine to slow you down so that the gators can enjoy your greasy ass. If you want my advice, I'd dive headfirst. That way, maybe you'll break your fucking neck so that you don't endure the pain of broken bones and being torn apart by the crocs. Now, jump," Jasmine commanded.

Cecilia walked back to where the others waited and climbed over the rail. She stood on the ledge of the bridge and began to pray. She gripped the railing tightly and leaned back, willing herself to let go, but her fear would not allow it. She looked down to see if there were any crocodiles beneath her, but while she was looking, Jasmine grew impatient and shot her in the wrist.

Cecilia screamed and loosened her grip, falling more than a hundred feet toward the waiting water lizards. Her body crashed and crumpled onto a sandbar, stuck. She was dead as soon as she hit the hard surface. Her daughters screamed in horror as they watched the crocodiles drag their mother's body into deeper water before finally disappearing beneath the murky waters of the Tarcoles River.

Manny was visibly shaken as he ran to the railing and peered over the side, searching for his wife's corpse. He dropped to his knees and cried out, "King Kochese, please don't do this! I'm sorry. I swear on my dead mother that I'll leave, and you'll never hear from me again."

"Swearing won't do you any good, Manny. Prayer isn't a part of this equation. Did it work for your wife?" Jasmine teased.

"I'll jump, but my daughters are still babies. Please let them live, please."

"Manny, you can't be that blind. Babies? Your daughters are the biggest sluts in Costa. If they don't jump, at the rate that they are going, they'll die of AIDS in a few years anyway, but I'm going to save the world the trouble. Now, jump, fat man," Kochese barked.

"I won't do it! You'll have to fucking kill me and throw me over, you fucking piece of shit. I was loyal to you, baba. I can't believe you're doing this to me—to my family," Manny cried. He gurgled and blew snot bubbles, trying to regain his composure.

Kochese didn't argue with him. He simply whistled, drawing the attention of his soldiers. He beckoned to two of the bigger ones, and they trotted toward him.

"Yes, El Rey?" they said.

"Throw his ass over," Kochese ordered.

Before Manny could protest, the pair of henchmen were on him, holding him upside down over the rail. They could barely hold on to him because of his dead weight and his squirming.

"Can you hear me down there, fat man? I'm going to allow you the privilege of watching your children perish," Kochese said, turning to the twins. "Under any other circumstances, I would let you girls live, but yeah, that shit ain't happening today. You two little hoes need to jump," Kochese said.

He couldn't believe it. They didn't put up a fight, didn't beg, and didn't cry. They silently climbed up onto the railing, holding hands. Helena turned to Kochese with one tear streaming down her face and smiled.

"You know, you expected us to beg for our lives like our cowardly father, but we won't. You call us sluts and whores, but we think we're just curious. Maybe if the adults around us weren't so whorish, we wouldn't have turned out this way, but that's neither here nor there. What matters is that you won't get the satisfaction of making us beg." She looked down at her father and shook her head. "You're a piece of shit, Manny, and I hope you burn in hell for what you've done to our family," Helena said.

"I'm scared, Helly. I don't want to die," Martina sobbed.

"I know, Mar, me too," she said, squeezing her sister's hand. "Just close your eyes, and we'll jump on three."

They closed their eyes, counted to three, and jumped. As they fell, Helena grabbed Martina and flipped her body onto the top of hers so that her twin sister would land on top of her. They landed on the same sandbar where their mother had met her demise. Helena died instantly from the impact while the cushion of her sister's body had somewhat shielded Martina from the collision. Martina stared down into her sister's dead eyes and screamed. She managed to stagger up onto the rocky shore of the river. She was still stumbling, desperately trying to climb ashore, when the crackle of a slug from Jasmine's .380 struck her in the hip. The smell of fresh blood sent the crocodiles into a frenzy, first grabbing Helena's prone corpse and then ripping into Martina's injured flesh, dragging her to the water as she screamed. Kochese snapped his fingers, and the two men released Manny's body, sending him crashing headfirst onto the base of the bridge below. His body hit the footer of the bridge and bounced noisily into the water, where the crocs rolled and dragged his body, fighting for their share of the hefty meal.

Jasmine leaned over the railing, smiling as she dialed a number on her cell phone. Minutes later, Ernest walked through the barricade of armed guards and whispered something into Chico's ear. He nodded and opened the trunk. Curious, Kochese looked at Jasmine and then toward the car. Ernest pulled a gagged and bound Consuela from the trunk of the vehicle. Lucinda's daughter had crossed a line that would cost her life. Ernest nearly dragged the terrified girl to where Kochese and Jasmine waited. Jasmine ripped the gag from her mouth and stared into her eyes.

"Have you fucked my husband, bitch?" she asked.

"No."

"Do you *want* to fuck my husband?"

"No."

"Have you tried?"

"No."

"Why not? He's not good enough for you?" Jasmine asked.

Consuela wasn't sure how she should answer. Fear had gripped her and strangled the words from her throat. She wanted to tell her that she had dreams of fucking him and that she could see her lips wrapped around his dick. She wanted to tell her that before Jasmine came home, she fantasized about watching him shower, about being more than a nanny to his children. However, no words would come, though, only urine as her kidneys released and drenched her sandals with lemon-yellow piss.

"May I?" Ernest asked, holding out his hands. Jasmine handed him the .380, and he pushed Consuela toward the barrier of the bridge.

"Jasmine, what's up? We don't have to do this, baby," Kochese protested.

"You defending this bitch, Kochese? You don't want her to die? Your heart is tender for her? Nigga, you just—*we* just—killed a whole fucking family because Manny crossed you. Get your head out of your ass and get it in the game. It's us versus everybody, and anybody can fucking get it! If I can't trust this bitch, I don't need her around me. Ernest?" Jasmine shouted.

"Yes, JD?"

"Dead this bitch and make her gator bait. Nobody gets a pass," Jasmine screamed.

Chapter 33

Jacob and Esau

Cyril Griffin pulled into the parking lot of St. Mary's Catholic Church in Crown Point, Indiana, and parked. Church parishioners had started to file into the church, and he needed to hurry if he was going to catch the beginning of mass. The Eucharist would begin promptly at 5:30 p.m., and he wanted to blend into the crowd. He stepped out of his car and tucked his pistol deep into his waistband. Then he shoved his hands into his pocket, dropped his head, and tried to mesh with the crowd moving toward the door.

Once inside, Cyril sat in the back of the church near the door and inconspicuously thumbed through the pages of a hymn book. Bishop Anthony Ravenna began his homily by speaking from the book of Romans. His voice was soothing yet boring and only served to make Cyril sleepier than he already was. The quicker the bishop concluded his sermon, the quicker Cyril could finish his deed.

"Furthermore, just as they did not think it worthwhile to retain the knowledge of God, so God gave them over to a depraved mind so that they do what ought not to be done. They have become filled with every kind of wickedness, evil, greed, and depravity. They are full of envy, murder, strife, deceit, and malice," Bishop Ravenna preached.

Cyril sat mesmerized by the bishop's words. His speech and message were poignant yet unemotional and uninspired. Bishop Ravenna had been in the news for the molestation of more than thirty boys over his forty-year tenure at St. Mary's. He'd used his position in the church and his woeful sermons to give the impression of infallibility. He needed to be purged from God's house, and the Catholic Church refused to punish him.

Cyril watched thankfully as the churchgoers began leaving. Person by person, family by family, they filed out until there was no one left inside the hallowed halls except him and God. As he waited, the sun descended beneath the stained-glass windows of the church until the only light in the chapel was the flicker of candlelight from the altar beneath the feet of the statue of Jesus on the cross.

Cyril heard the large wooden doors behind him creak open. The magnificent weight of the wood dragged and screeched against the metal hinges, sounding more like the entrance to a haunted house than to the house of God. Cyril cupped his hands and bowed his head in prayer to avoid being identified, but he could hear the slow, methodical thump of footsteps headed his way. The footsteps stopped behind him, and he tensed, but the steps started again. He was afraid to look up. What if it was his victim? Bishops, reverends, and all manner of preachers were masters of manipulation, and the last thing that he needed was the priest trying to convince him of all the reasons why he deserved to live. However, the curiosity was killing Cyril. By the time he'd lifted his head, he could only see the stranger's back as he made his way toward the altar. The man seemed entranced as if he were being guided to the altar by some unseen force.

Cyril stood quietly and stepped out into the aisle. He looked back toward the front doors where the man had come from, but there was nothing except the faint glow of light from the outside floodlights shining through the stained-glass windows. He turned to make his way toward the stranger because whoever he was, he would die with the priest—for good measure, of course.

The stranger lit a few candles at the altar and kneeled. He'd taken something from his pocket just before kneeling, and it caused Cyril to stop. The flames flickered and crackled, sending tiny streams of smoke into the abyss. The glow of the candles made the large statue of Jesus Christ nailed to the cross look even more sinister and menacing than the act of crucifying the Savior itself. Cyril caught sight of a glimmer, an indistinct glint of something shiny to the man's left.

He let his eyes follow the flames to the brightest stained-glass windows. It was a depiction of Cain bashing the skull of his brother, Abel, with a stone. As he got closer, he saw that the man had placed a gun there. He wasn't sure of the caliber of the weapon, but it was big and chrome. If Cyril had his way, the man would never have a chance to reach his gun.

Chapter 34

Doppelgänger

Blaine could hear the footsteps of someone coming up behind him. Maybe it was King's contact. He'd been instructed to commit his final murder within the hallowed walls of St. Mary's. Blaine considered reaching for the pistol that he'd placed at his left side, but he didn't want to take the chance of spooking his intruder. It was probably just the parishioner that he'd passed in the pews when he'd first come into the church. At any rate, if that person got too close, he would have to reach for it, and he didn't want to. King had sent word for him to do a very special murder, and he would follow those instructions to the letter.

The man knelt next to him and bowed his head as if praying. He eyed his profile curiously, particularly the scar from the corner of his mouth to his earlobe. Blaine looked forward beyond the Jesus statue at the scene depicted in the stained-glass window. In the picture, Isaac stood holding Rebekah's hand as she gave birth to Jacob and Esau.

A shadow emerged from the back of the church and stood before him and the man who knelt beside him. "My sons, the Lord looks favorably upon twins. To have one that shares your soul is indeed a wondrous thing. God first revealed his magnificence with twins with the birth of Cain and Abel," the priest gushed.

Cyril looked up at the priest and smiled. "You pompous piece of shit. How can you claim to be a man of the cloth, a man of God, and not know His word?" Cyril hissed.

The priest opened his mouth to speak, but Blaine cut him off. "He's right, you know. You're giving the wrong information, Father. First, Cain and Abel weren't twins. They were brothers born of the same womb but not twins. The first set of twins was Jacob and Esau. Do you not remember in the very first book of the Bible, Genesis, where God spoke these words to Rebekah: *'Two nations are in your womb, and two peoples from within you will be separated; one people will be stronger than the other, and the older will serve the younger. When the time came for her to give birth, there were twin boys in her womb. The first to come out was red, and his whole body was like a hairy garment, so they named him Esau. After this, his brother came out, with his hand grasping Esau's heel, so he was named Jacob.'* Did you skip over *that* passage in the seminary, Father?" Blaine asked.

He gripped the handle of his pistol tightly, and then he heard it. The voice inside of his head spoke, threatening to rip apart the tiny shred of sanity that he had left. *Kill them, Blaine, kill them both!* it shouted.

Blaine shook his head violently, trying to expel the volatile echo.

Kill them, kill them now! the voice boomed.

Blaine stood, staring at the ground, tormented by the voice that seemed to fill his entire mind. He seethed with rage, gripping his pistol, tears streaming down his face. "You don't understand. You never have. You're inside; you're not out here with me. I have no one!" Blaine screamed.

"You have the Lord, my son. Put down the gun. Give your problems to the Lord," the priest pleaded.

"Don't you say that to me. Don't you *ever* say that to me. The Lord is a tool that you've used to control the masses. I'm *not* your fucking son. I'm *not* one of your sheep," Blaine said, shaking violently.

"We are wolf among sheep," Cyril said.

He stood and faced Blaine, and his entire identity was revealed to him. Their features were identical, from the icy blue color of their eyes to the jagged scars running along their cheeks. Cyril moved toward Blaine, who was still awestruck by their resemblance. King had most certainly created this man too, his living twin, his doppelgänger.

Blaine raised his pistol and pointed it at Cyril's head. "Who are you, and why do you have my face?" Blaine asked.

Cyril lifted his hands as a sign of trust and good faith. He understood the man's plight as if they were connected by more than just a face. He moved a step closer to Blaine. "I'm that voice in your head that won't go away. I'm the Esau to your Jacob. We are cosmic twins born of different seeds, but we share the same father. I can be the strength you need when you're weak, and you can be the calm to my raging storm. I can be your brother for life, and you'll never have to worry about being able to trust me," Cyril said. He reached out and gently removed the pistol from Blaine's hand.

"Thank the Lord. I was afraid that there would be violence. I thought surely that one of you young men would kill me. Riddle me this: how can you be identical twins if you're not related?" the priest asked.

They both looked at the slender, elderly priest.

"What makes you think there won't be violence, old man?" Blaine asked, menace and malice curled into his evil smile.

Chapter 35

Bathed in the Blood

Monica sat next to D'Angelo on American Airlines flight 1050 in silence. He had been texting nonstop since they departed, shielding his phone as if he had something to hide. She stood up and walked past him, leaving him in midsentence.

"I have to use the restroom. Excuse me," she said. She didn't really need to go; she just needed some peace and quiet. Between the constant chatter of the passengers and a crying baby three rows behind her, she was losing her mind.

Monica stepped into the lavatory, locked the door, and stared into the mirror. Maybe she was wrong. Maybe D'Angelo wasn't a dirty Fed. Maybe he'd come into some money that no one knew about. But she still couldn't shake the feeling that he was dirty.

Monica closed the lid to the toilet, sat down, and buried her head in her hands. She was nervous, a feeling she didn't get often, but the prospect of possibly seeing King face-to-face made her stomach quiver. The Monopoly murders had made her both famous and infamous simultaneously. She was exhausted, and her leg throbbed where Jasmine had stabbed her, causing her to curse her baby sister silently.

Monica dozed off quickly, letting the constant sway and the drone of the plane's engines lull her to sleep. In her dream, she was sitting ringside at a Floyd Mayweather Jr. fight, cheering for him to beat his opponent. She heard the bell as Mayweather walked to his corner, but when he got there, he didn't sit. Instead, he leaned over the ropes, looked her in her eyes, and yelled, "Monica, wake up!"

Tap, tap, tap came the sound from the other side of the bathroom door, startling Monica awake. She heard the faint, throaty hum of her own light snoring as the bell sounded again. It hadn't been a fight bell at all. It had been the bell on the plane instructing the passengers to buckle their seat belts and prepare for landing.

"Who is it?" Monica asked groggily.

"Are you okay, ma'am? Your husband seems worried about you. He says you've been here for nearly an hour," the stewardess said.

"Yes, I'm fine, and he's not my husband. I just had some bad egg salad, that's all," Monica lied as she exited the lavatory.

"Understood. Well, we're preparing to land, ma'am, so if you wouldn't mind taking a seat and fastening your seat belt . . ." She motioned toward Monica's seat.

Monica looked the woman up and down as if sizing her up. *If this fucking plane crashes, this fucking seat belt won't do shit, stupid,* she thought. She slid past D'Angelo and took her seat.

"Are you okay, Agent Deitrich? Were you in there taking a dump?" he laughed.

"I was in there not listening to you flap your gums," she snapped.

Ding, ding, ding.

"Ladies and Gentlemen, welcome to Chicago. Please prepare for landing. All lap tables need to be closed, and your seat should be in the upright position. The current temperature is a crisp 75 degrees, and the time is 7:15 p.m. We will be landing at Chicago O'Hare in approximately ten minutes. Thank you for flying American, and enjoy your stay in Chicago."

Once they were off the plane and had retrieved their bags, D'Angelo turned to Monica. "I'm going to get a separate rental and check a lead. I'll meet you later," he said.

"Where are you rushing off to so quickly? You've been acting really strange lately, D'Angelo, and I don't like it, but whatever."

"I just need to check a lead, Monica. Once I'm done, we can meet up, and I'll explain everything to you, I promise," D'Angelo said.

"If you're going to check a lead, shouldn't I be with you? You know what? Whatever."

Moments later, they were both in their respective cars heading toward downtown Chicago. As Monica drove along I-90 East, her phone rang. She fumbled for her purse while trying to keep her eyes on the road. When she finally reached her phone, whoever had been calling had already disconnected the call. She looked at her phone. It was Kirby Langdon. Monica called him back, and he answered on the first ring.

"Hello, Agent Deitrich. I've come across some new information I think you'll be interested in. I previously informed you that the target would be Chicago. However, after doing some statistical analysis of King Kochese's egotistical and often self-centered ways, I found that it's not Chicago. It is Crown Point, Indiana," he said.

"Where is that? What's my quickest route there?"

"Where are you now?" Agent Langdon asked.

"I'm traveling on I-90 East."

"If you continue on I-90 East, it'll dump you right into Crown Point. Take exit 249," he advised her.

"Where should I go when I exit?"

"I don't know. I haven't factored that into my equation yet," Langdon said.

Monica could hear him typing rapidly over the phone, perhaps searching for some overlooked algorithm in his analysis program.

"Come on, Kirby, I need that information," Monica shouted as she pressed the gas to the floor.

"I'm trying, ma'am. The program—" he started.

But Monica cut him off. "I don't need excuses, Agent. I need results, and I need them *now*. Just give me your best guess."

"Yes, ma'am. I-I-I-I, okay, okay, okay, if I had to guess, knowing King Kochese's penchant for opulence, I'd say go to the nearest and largest church in the area," Agent Langdon said.

"And what church would that be, Agent Langdon?"

"The largest church in Crown Point is St. Mary's Catholic Church," he said.

"Okay, I'll start there. While I'm en route, I need a favor, but I need you to keep it quiet. You think you can do that?" Monica asked.

"Yes, ma'am."

"I need you to do a silent probe into Agent D'Angelo's finances. Anything that doesn't look right or doesn't seem to be on the up-and-up, I need to know about it," she said.

"Will do, ma'am. I'll call you as soon as I have something."

D'Angelo pulled into the parking lot of St. Mary's Catholic Church and parked near the back entrance. He used a set of picks to go in through the rear, hoping to surprise the perpetrators without getting shot. D'Angelo drew his pistol and cursed himself. "Shit," he whispered as the door slammed shut behind him.

He eased his way down the dark hallway with his gun trained in front of him. D'Angelo was nobody's coward, but he wasn't especially brave either. The portraits on the wall gave him the chills, and he shuddered. There were pictures of priests and cardinals, all dressed in classic Catholic vestments. That's not what frightened D'Angelo, though. It was the vividly painted depictions of justified torture during the Spanish Inquisition that spooked him, those labeled as heretics being burned at the stake or drowned, all in the name of the Holy Trinity. They were on full display in the inner sanctum of St. Mary's.

D'Angelo pressed forward, going up the stairs just left of the sacristy. He climbed the steps of the bell tower quietly, careful to go undetected. He heard voices chanting, but he couldn't see who was talking because he was crouched low as he made his way through the upper nave. D'Angelo sat with his back against the railing, listening to the syncopated chant of the less-than-righteous.

"Our Father who art in heaven, hallowed be thy name.
Thy kingdom come, thy will be done, on earth as it is in heaven.
Give us this day our daily bread and forgive us our trespasses.
As we forgive those who trespass against us.
Lead us not into temptation, but deliver us from evil.
For thine is the kingdom, the power, and the glory.
Forever and ever,
Amen."

D'Angelo peeked over the railing and gasped in horror. An elderly white man was lying on top of the altar, bleeding from his head. His hands and feet had been bound with duct tape, and he had been castrated. His small, shriveled penis had been tossed aside as if it were merely a bag of giblets from a freshly defrosted chicken. The light from the candles in the sanctuary cast an evil glow onto the twin men who had been praying over the corpse. They smiled at each other as they waited for the last of his blood to be drained into two golden chalices. They both took a chalice into their hands, and one of them began to speak.

"Father God, we sacrifice your creation to you. We commit his soul to you, Lord, to do with as you please, but we condemn his body to hell, to rot amongst the maggots and grub worms. Amen."

They took the golden goblets, each dipping a finger into the old man's blood and drawing 6PCS on each other's foreheads. They then took the chalices and poured the blood over each other's heads. It was a macabre spectacle that D'Angelo had neither been prepared for nor that he cared to witness.

"With this blood, O Lord, we purify his soul to be sent to you, pure and everlasting forever and ever, amen."

The blood ran down over their low-cut, nearly bald heads, and as they smiled, the priest's blood ran into their mouths, framing their teeth in a crimson halo.

D'Angelo was petrified with fear, unable to move, unable to act or react, for that matter. As he stared down at them, one of the twins turned quickly and stared up at him, causing the other man to follow his gaze.

"Well, well, well, Agent D'Angelo, we've been expecting you," the man said.

D'Angelo slumped onto the floor quickly, trying to take back the fact that he'd been seen. His heart raced, and his underarms itched. He wasn't sure whether he was more frightened by the fact that he'd been seen or the fact that the man had called him by name.

"Agent D'Angelo, I'll give you until the count of three to come down before I come up to get you. One, two—" Cyril screamed.

"How do you know my fucking name?"

"I am a king among peasants and a wolf among sheep. Sound familiar? Our father, which art in heaven, King Kochese, wants your disloyal head on a silver fucking platter, Agent," Cyril said. He laughed, and his deep baritone voice bellowed throughout the empty sanctuary.

"That's funny because he sent me here to kill you both, so it looks like we've all been double-crossed," Antonio D'Angelo said. D'Angelo let his courage build and attempted to look over the railing, but as he lifted his head, he was blindsided by a staggering left jab from Blaine's fist.

"Liar!" Blaine screamed.

D'Angelo's pistol flew from his hand, skidding across the tile floor, coming to rest underneath a nearby pew. Blaine grabbed D'Angelo's gun and pointed it at his head.

"You should learn how to follow directions, Agent. My brother gave you until the count of three. It took me twelve seconds to climb these stairs to reach you. Now get the fuck downstairs," Blaine barked.

Chapter 36

The Truth Shall . . .

The floodlights nearly blinded Monica as she pulled up in front of St. Mary's Catholic Church. She caught sight of a shadowy figure moving quickly toward the rear of the church. She left the engine running and the door open while she went to the trunk to retrieve her weapon. Monica hated traveling on commercial airlines because she always had to pack her firearm in her checked luggage. She felt vulnerable without her gun, almost naked, and even though it was a well-known fact that there was always an Air Marshal aboard commercial flights, it never made her rest easier.

Monica rummaged through her suitcase until she found her .380 caliber and her belt holster. As she clipped the holster to her belt, she heard her agency cell phone ringing and vibrating against the armrest of her rental. She hurried to the front seat of her car before it stopped ringing. "Hello . . . Hello?" she said.

"Agent Deitrich, it's Langdon. Did I catch you at a bad time?"

Monica sat inside her car and closed the door. "I just pulled up in front of St. Mary's. What's up?" she asked nervously.

"I uncovered some very disparaging information about Agent D'Angelo. It appears for the past ten months or so, he's been holding a second job as a cybersecurity consultant for a company out of Dallas," he said.

"So, what's so disparaging about that?"

"A few things, actually, like, for starters, what company do you know that's going to pay $25,000 biweekly? Also, it must be fabricated because it shows D'Angelo working during times when he was clearly on assignment for the agency," Kirby Langdon said.

"Okay, but even if he's moonlighting for another company and lying about his schedule, that's not exactly a crime, Langdon."

"I wouldn't waste your time with trivial things, Agent Deitrich," Langdon said.

"What the hell does that even mean, Langdon? Get to the damned point."

"It may all be a coincidence, but after your sister's capture and Kochese's escape, that's when his 'salary' with the company began," Langdon said.

"Yeah, but that may be a coincidence like you said."

"Yeah, but here's the kicker: guess who's paying his salary and holds the deed to his brand-new house?" Kirby asked excitedly.

"Do tell."

"Cross-Tech Industries," Kirby said in his *a-ha* tone.

"What? Are you sure about that?"

"Yes, ma'am. Everything that he's acquired in the past few months was bought and paid for by Cross-Tech," he said.

"That slimy son of a bitch. Get me some backup here now, Kirby."

"Agent Deitrich, do you think—" he started.

But Monica had already ended the call and thrown her cell phone into the backseat. She eased into the church through the large wooden doors and stopped just inside the foyer. Monica cocked her pistol quietly and checked to make sure that it was off safety. She would shoot first and ask questions later. She could hear D'Angelo's voice as he conversed with someone. She wasn't sure who he was talking to, but it wasn't King Kochese. She had half a mind to burst through the doors with guns blazing and kill everyone inside, but D'Angelo would face justice—legal justice.

Her legs felt tingly, her heart raced, and from somewhere beyond her better judgment, her caution gave way to adrenaline, and Monica burst through the doors.

"Drop your weapons!" Monica screamed.

She couldn't believe her eyes. In front of her were mirror images of Kochese. Even through their blood-soaked façade, she could see King clearly in their features.

"Where is King Kochese?" she asked as she moved along the wall. She stood just off center from them so she could have a clear shot but still be covered by the pews if bullets began flying.

Cyril pointed his gun at Monica while Blaine kept his weapon trained on D'Angelo. "As you can see, we're not dropping shit. Now, drop yours, and you might save your partner's life," Cyril shouted.

"You think I give a fuck about a dirty Fed? Kill him if you want. But keep in mind that while you're shooting him, I'll be shooting you," Monica said.

"Well, I guess we'll all be some shot-up motherfuckers then, won't we?" Blaine said.

"I guess so. Now drop the motherfucking gun, asshole!" Monica shouted.

"Let's not be hasty, now. Monica, just drop your gun like the man said. Let's think rationally here. You don't want to die, and neither do I. Why don't you just let these guys walk out of here, and it's a win-win for everyone?" D'Angelo said anxiously.

The sight of D'Angelo on his knees, sniveling like a
frightened child, made Monica's stomach turn. Not only
was he a dirty cop, but he was also a coward to boot.

"Shut the fuck up, D'Angelo, before I put a bullet in you
myself. Listen, guys, King Kochese is playing you. That's
what he does. He manipulates people and uses them. He
makes you believe that he loves you, and when he sucks
you in, he snatches it all away. Do not sacrifice your life
for that piece of shit," Monica said somberly. Her tone
was low and withdrawn. It was almost as if she were
reminiscing versus trying to convince the killers to think.

"Okay, Agent D'Angelo, since we're in a Catholic church,
I think it's befitting that you make your last confession to
Agent Deitrich," Cyril said.

"O-o-okay, M-Monica, I betrayed you and the agency.
Every move that you made, that we made concerning this
case, I reported directly to King Kochese. Every detail
of your personal life, from your Social Security number,
credit card numbers, bank account information, email
passwords, and even your address, Monica, I sold to King
Kochese," D'Angelo whimpered.

Monica didn't care about any financial information
being leaked to him. It was the thought of him having her
address where her precious Millicent lay her head that
spooked her.

"You see, Monica? This is why your friend Agent
D'Angelo is going to die today—because he's disloyal,
he's a bitch, and because the king ordains it," Blaine
said. He cocked his .45 caliber, kicked a bullet into the
chamber, and removed the clip. He handed the gun to
D'Angelo and began to speak. "Since I'm in a generous
mood, I will allow you to pick your own fate. Your choice,
Agent. A) you can use the bullet in the chamber to kill
yourself; B) use that bullet and try your luck at killing
Agent Deitrich; or C) use that bullet to try to kill me, but

you're either going to leave in a body bag or the back of a fucking squad car. It's your choice, but choose wisely, and remember, you'll probably be in the Feds with some of the same people you locked up. Shit, I bet instead of D'Angelo, you'll be Angela before your first full night," Blaine said with a sinister chuckle.

D'Angelo was crying uncontrollably now, sniveling with snot and tears dripping from his chin. "I choose A."

"What's that? I didn't hear you, bitch boy," Cyril shouted, spittle escaping his lips.

"A . . . I choose A," D'Angelo repeated loudly.

"Get to it then," Blaine snapped.

D'Angelo's hand shook violently as he raised the gun to his temple. He looked straight ahead at Monica, his eyes pleading for a reprieve and a hint of forgiveness. There was still so much that he wanted to do. He had no children and still hadn't been to Italy, which was his life's dream. For that matter, he hadn't even thrown the housewarming party he dreamed of for the new house he'd bought with Kochese's blood money. He continued to stare at Monica, mouthing the words "I'm sorry" in her direction. "Long live King Kochese," he said and then pulled the trigger. His body slumped to the floor, convulsed, and then went limp.

Blaine knelt and felt D'Angelo's neck with two fingers. *Thump, thump, pause . . . thump, thump, pause.* He could feel his heart beating slightly, so he took the gun from D'Angelo's dead hands, replaced the clip, and pumped seven shots from the pistol into his side, neck, and face. Then he turned to Monica and smiled. "You see how easy that was for me? I didn't know him, I've never talked to him, and he never did me any harm, but if King—*the King*—says that he has to go, he has to go. That's called loyalty, you stupid bitch," Blaine spat, then added, "On another note, it's two against one now." He turned his pistol on Monica.

"You'll get the death penalty for killing a Fed. What's wrong with you? You can't be this stupid. Can't you see that he's using you? He—" Monica stopped talking and backed up toward the rear of the church. Both men were advancing on her from opposite directions, and she had no escape plan.

"He what, Agent Deitrich? Say it. He's playing us? He knows that we're willing to do whatever it takes to make this money, whether it be lying, stealing, cheating, killing—whatever. You, on the other hand, you have been a naughty girl, mind fucking anyone who will listen to the bullshit you spew," Blaine said. He let two shots ring out from his pistol, barely missing Monica, but it was close enough to send her diving for the pews.

"Don't do this. We can work this out. I don't want to hurt you," Monica said. Another four shots rang out, and Monica yelled again, "I'm warning you, drop the fucking gun."

"Fuck you, cunt. I'm going to fucking kill you and then go sit on the beach with loose women, get drunk, and fuck like a porn star," Blaine screamed.

Monica sprang from the floor, firing wildly in Blaine's direction, but he dropped out of sight beneath the pews. Monica peeked over the rail of the pews, but there was no sight of either men. It wasn't until she stepped out into the aisle that she saw him.

Cyril was slumped against the altar where the priest lay dead, barely breathing. She couldn't tell where he had been shot because he was covered in the priest's blood as well. Shallow wisps of air escaped his lips in short, strained clips. He stared at Monica, but all she saw was King. His chest moved quickly and labored as he attempted to speak. "Forgive me."

She took the gun from his hands and tucked it in her waistband. "You don't need my forgiveness. Was it worth it?" she asked.

"Damn, guess that means more money for me since church boy got capped," Blaine said, backing toward the door.

"Don't fucking move," she screamed.

In the distance, Blaine could hear approaching sirens. He looked at Monica one last time, and as they locked eyes, he smirked and raised his gun to aim, but he was too slow. Monica dropped to the ground next to Cyril and fired blindly in Blaine's direction. She heard a gunshot and then a dead weight hitting the floor. She shimmied toward the aisle on her stomach and peeked around the pew. There was blood and brain matter oozing down the wall near the door where Blaine had been standing. His body was slumped near the entrance, and his lifeless eyes stared at her.

Monica scrambled to her feet and went to Blaine's body. Blood fizzed out of the hole in his cheek just below his eye, and his jaw was swollen and deformed from the impact of the bullet. She kicked his gun away and turned back to Cyril, but he was gone. She went to D'Angelo and kneeled next to him. "What the fuck were you thinking, dude? I knew your ass wasn't right. Damn, D'Angelo."

Something didn't look right because the trail of blood looked more like Cyril had been dragged from where he was. But there were no bloody footprints and no blood droplets. Monica followed the blood trail from the altar through the sanctuary and down a long hall. The siren was getting louder, but it wasn't coming from outside. Monica kept her pistol extended in front of her as she traversed the hallway, careful not to walk in a straight line. It was dark, and she could no longer see the blood on the floor, but she was getting closer to the siren, and she could see a small light at the end of the hall. The next door she came to was an office, where she found the siren. She picked up the cell phone on the desk and pressed pause on the screen. A siren was looped and was being fed at a low volume to the exterior speakers.

Monica flopped down in the chair by the desk and tried to gather her thoughts. She had to piece together what had just happened. She pushed away from the desk and drew her pistol, "Come from under the goddamn desk, now," she barked.

A boy, who she guessed might have been 15, crawled from under the desk. "Please don't kill me. I swear to God I haven't seen anything. You will never have to worry about me telling, I promise," he cried.

"What the fuck are you doing here, kid? How long have you been here?" Monica asked, flashing her badge at him.

"Oh, thank God. I'm an altar boy and was here with the Father to help after mass. When the yelling started, I was going to see what it was about, but when I peeked into the sanctuary, the twin guys were beating the Father."

"Why didn't you call for help?" At this rate, Monica didn't know what to believe.

"I did, ma'am. I called 911, and they said they would send someone right over. He asked me if we had outside speakers and lights, and I said yes. He's the one who told me to put the siren on repeat so that the criminals would leave. I was just trying to help." The kid was still sobbing. "Is the Father okay, ma'am?"

"He? Who is he? And I'm afraid that your priest is dead. Let's get outside. I'll call for backup. What's the quickest way out of here?" Monica said, pushing the kid toward the door. There was no maternal instinct, no caring for this boy beyond removing him from a potentially harmful situation because, as far as she knew, he could be another one of King's plants.

"This way." He grabbed a candle from the table and led Monica down the hall toward the light. "This hall leads to the back parking lot." The flame flickered, and shadows danced on the walls, making the portraits of men and women look more like demons than saints. From the light of the candle, Monica could see smeared blood on the tile floor beneath them. They reached the exit door, and Monica pushed the kid behind her. "I'll go first. Stay behind me," she ordered.

Monica cracked open the heavy metal door and peeped through the narrow gap. "Shit," she cursed.

"What's wrong?" the boy asked. He had subconsciously grabbed the tail of Monica's shirt, and she swatted his hand away. "Sorry. I seek connection when I'm scared."

"Shut up. I can't see shit, and I don't want to stick my head out there and get it blown off and stop touching me."

"I'm scared," he whined.

"Me too, now hush." Monica opened the door just wide enough to see the thirty or so feet to the corner of the church. She eased the door open a little more and saw Cyril sitting in the front seat of an unmarked car with the door open. He was leaning against the steering wheel, and it looked like he was trying to start the vehicle. Monica pushed the door open and screamed to Cyril, "Let me see your fucking hands, asshole!" She stepped out into the night, gun aimed at Cyril. "I won't ask again. Show me your goddamn hands."

Cyril didn't lift his hands, but Monica heard a sharp whistle behind her. She turned to see where it came from, but before she could completely turn around, she was met with white light and the sound of deafening gunfire.

"Oh my God, you shot her, man; you shot her."

Monica could hear the boy screaming, but she couldn't see him, and then she heard another gunshot and another. She could hear the shuffle of feet and then something being dragged. Next, a car trunk closed, and then she faded into the darkness.

Kirby Langdon dragged Cyril's limp body from the front seat of his rental car and dumped him into the trunk. He took the gun that he had used to shoot Monica and the boy and planted it in Blaine's hand. He would leave the rest to a lackluster forensics team that liked their information spoon-fed to them rather than doing good old-fashioned police work. Once satisfied with his crime scene, he placed a call. "Yessir, it's done. Agent Dietrich is still alive, though. Should I kill her?"

"Nah, don't kill her. I want that evil bitch to lose everything, and you're going to make sure that she goes out in a blaze of disgraced glory, Agent Kirby," Kochese said and disconnected the call.

Kirby called 911.

"Help! Please help us. They're going to kill us all; they're killing us," he said and tossed the phone next to the boy's prone corpse. He knelt next to Monica and whispered in her ear. "I am a king amongst peasants and a wolf among sheep."

Chapter 37

Long Live the King

Kochese tossed his cell phone to his desk and cradled Apache close to his chest. He kissed the baby on the forehead with a tenderness he had never had for any of God's creatures, great or small. But here he was, holding his son, a picture of pure perfection created in his image. Kochese smiled at the infant as his tiny hand gripped his finger.

"What's going on, baby? You have happiness in your eyes, eyes twinkling and shit like we just won the lotto," Jasmine teased. She bounced Angel in her lap while the chubby, turquoise-eyed baby cooed between slurps of her pacifier.

"I haven't really given you the game on the pieces I put into motion since you've been home," Kochese said, walking to the bassinet and placing a now-sleeping Apache inside. Monkeys, giraffes, lions, and hippos danced to a magical tune as the mobile above the bassinet turned. Kochese let his fingertips rest on his son's chest, feeling his tiny but strong heartbeat pulse through his fingers.

"When I left you in that barn, I felt like my manhood had been stripped away from me, like I had failed you. It felt like God had reached inside of me and ripped out my heart with His bare hands. Me leaving you, not knowing what might happen to you or the twins, was hard for me. I need you to know that. I need you to know that you three," Kochese's voice cracked awkwardly, so he stopped talking. He was still learning how to process emotions, a task that he had come to find challenging for many years . . . until the twins were born. The thought of losing Jasmine or his children made him feel vulnerable, weak. But Jasmine loved him beyond words, had proven that she would give her life for him, and had given him two children at once. Tiny twin souls that he had helped to create, that trusted him completely, and whose love he could feel with every breath. Kochese walked to Jasmine, who was now breastfeeding Angel, and kissed her on the forehead, then his daughter's, before sitting on the floor Indian-style in front of them.

"Is everything okay, baby?" Jasmine asked, staring into his ocean-blue eyes.

"When I made it here, I had to put a plan into motion that would eventually bring you home to me. Kirby Langdon was an easy mark for me because his mother needed a kidney. Just the promise of a kidney, and that boy was ready to sell his soul. He's the one who brought the white boy Blaine in. Blaine's life as a kid was so fucked up that I almost felt guilty for fucking with his head. I had Kirby implant a neuromic in his head, so he was always hearing voices and shit, but it would be me." Kochese laughed, and his eyes excitedly beamed as he continued his tale. "Blaine damn near believed I was God, and I let him."

"Where did you get something like that, a neuromic?"

"They got all kinds of shit at Cross-Tech. I took what I could before your sister came around and fucked shit up. I asked Kirby who he thought was dirty enough to flush his career for cash, and he immediately said D'Angelo, so I sent bitches at him with an offer he couldn't refuse: help me and get paid or die, his choice. He's the one that found Cyril."

"Yeah, but how did you know that you could trust him, I mean Cyril?" Jasmine asked, handing Angel to Kochese.

He stood and placed her in the bassinet next to Apache's. He watched them sync their breathing to match each other's and smiled.

"I never trusted him, my love. He was a hardhead that D'Angelo had busted for stalking some congresswoman. He offered him a new life, somewhere else, to be someone else, and he went for it. What better way to disappear than by having an entirely different face and a pocket full of cash?"

"Yeah, but what if they had gotten caught?"

"Then they would have died before they ever made it to the station. I set out to confuse the FBI, and the shit worked almost too perfectly, too easy. Kirby and D'Angelo were always there to throw a stray bone to lead the case this way or that way, and I was trying to bide time until I could figure out where you were and how to get you out."

"I guess my mama shoulda named me Willamena," Jasmine smirked.

"Why Willamena?"

"Because they say where there's a will, there's a way. Well, I mean, I made a way out of that dungeon. Get it? Well, I mean, I made a way out," Jasmine laughed.

"Willamena. Your ass is corny as hell. Monica is no longer a factor. She's out of the game. Kirby made sure of it."

"Is she dead?"

Kochese studied her face. Jasmine was smiling like the news of her sister's death made her happy. She didn't have a stitch of love for her sister, and he admired that about her. She was stronger than he was in that regard. Even after his mother had told him that she wished he had never been born, he still loved her. Even after she chose death rather than be his mother, he still loved her. Kochese had always loved his mother and desperately wanted to prove that he was worthy of her love, but to no avail. She hated him; she had told him as much. Kochese had held the notion most of his life that love did not exist, that is, until he met Jasmine. The way that she loved him and made him feel proved that she was love manifested, that true love *did* exist, even for the wicked.

"She's not dead, but she's going to wish that she was by the time the Feds are finished with that ass. I got Kirby doing me one last solid, and then we're free," Kochese said. He took Jasmine's hand and led her to the balcony overlooking lush green grass and the dense jungles of the Costa Rican countryside.

Kochese stood behind Jasmine and wrapped his arms around her waist, letting his mind rest for the first time in months. He exhaled deeply and kissed her on her neck. "You know I love you, right?"

"I do," she said, turning to face Kochese. "Long live the King; long live my King."

Epilogue

Ain't No Redemption

Monica leaned against the hard pillows propped up behind her and winced from the excruciating pain pulsing in her head. She tried to concentrate on the barrage of questions being hurled at her, but the hospital bed was uncomfortable, and she found it difficult to focus her eyes. They wouldn't shut up about how things looked for the bureau, like she wasn't the one lying in the hospital bed.

"Do you have evidence to support your claims against Agent D'Angelo?" an agent asked.

Monica nodded.

"How do we know this wasn't a lover's spat gone wrong?" asked another.

"What the fuck is that supposed to mean?" she said. Every word was accentuated and slurred from the screws holding her jaw together.

"It means, maybe you went down there, you and D'Angelo, got into a heated lover's quarrel, and *bang,* or maybe D'Angelo and Kochese were both going to bang you since your sister is out of the picture—who knows," an agent named Guidry said.

"Fuck you, Guidry," Monica said.

"No, thanks, I heard it's tainted. Wouldn't want to soil my reputation," Guidry shot back.

"Okay, enough of the high school bullshit. The point is, you walked away from this with your life, Agent, and you should feel lucky. But the bureau feels that you failed to live up to the duties of your service. An agent is dead because of you, and a teenage boy is dead because of you. That whole 'working in tandem, dual suspect angle' was a farce. As far as the bureau is concerned, Jasmine and Kochese are dead, and this case is over. Effective immediately, we will accept your resignation, or the bureau is prepared to pursue criminal charges against you with expedience. We do not doubt that you and D'Angelo were in bed together, both physically and financially. We've learned you were on all his accounts as an authorized signer, with access to millions. Can you explain that? Doesn't seem like you're being forthcoming with information pertaining to your relationship with Kochese and D'Angelo," Director Harden said.

"With all due respect, sir, I've put my life on the line for two of this government's agencies. I'm unmarried, I've never had a social life, and my sister is dead. The one person in the world that I was supposed to go out with, get my nails done with, all that shit, is gone. I've sacrificed more for this job than I've cared to. I've lost everything for the sake of your corny-ass badge. I'm not being forthcoming? Look at my fucking face and tell me what the fuck being forthcoming ever did for me. Oh yeah, it got me shot in my goddamn face, I can't see out of my left eye, but I'm not being forthcoming? It may be because I'm tired of being crucified for doing my goddamned job, so forgive me if I don't seem fucking forthcoming," she screamed.

"I will take that as an admission of guilt and your subsequent resignation, Agent. Consider yourself lucky that Agent Langdon was able to talk the bureau out of pursuing charges against you," Harden said before exiting her hospital room, followed by his minions.

Her phone began to vibrate nonstop. She removed it from her pocket and gazed at it curiously. She didn't recognize the number, and no one ever called her on her personal number. "Hello, this is Monica," she said.

"How does it feel to have your life taken from you?" a voice asked somberly.

"Jasmine? Jasmine, is that you?" Monica asked, sitting up in bed.

"Yeah, it's me. You know, Monica, instead of hunting me and my husband like rabid dogs, you should have been here."

"I was doing my job, Jasmine. I don't understand. I should've been where? They told me you died trying to escape." Monica said.

"I am dead, Moni, dead to everyone that cares. You're always *doing* your job. Your job has always been more important than family, more important than me, Pop Pop, Kochese, Bird . . . more important than all of the people who loved you but that you failed to protect. Now, you're doing it again."

"Jasmine, you're talking in circles. Why don't you come to the hospital so we can talk about it?" Monica suggested.

"Why? So, you can prove to the bureau that you're not nuts, that you're not a criminal? Welcome to my world. But you should have been here."

"Been where, Jasmine? I should have been *where?*" Monica asked, swinging her legs off the side of the bed. The tile floor was cold against her bare feet as she attempted to stand.

"At home, silly, to protect Millicent with her cute little Hello Kitty jammies and rhinestone pacifier. I like what you did with her room—well, my old room." Jasmine giggled at first, and then her laughter turned shrill, much like one might imagine the laughter of the insane.

"Jasmine, you'd better not hurt her! She's just a baby. Hello? Hello? Jasmine, please." Monica screamed into the phone. Jasmine was still on the line. She knew it because the count clock on the phone was still going.

Traffic was clear except for a few stragglers on the road. They were probably regular people with regular lives and regular jobs, not filled with murder, mayhem, and plot twists. She had the needle of her Dodge Charger redlining as she weaved her way expertly through traffic. The more her adrenaline rushed, the more her face ached, but she kept pushing, skidding around corners, speeding through traffic. "Call Agent Tomlin," she shouted into the dash of her car.

"*Calling Agent Tomlin,*" a robotic voice said from the speakers.

"Tomlin here."

"I need your help," Monica said.

"Agent Deitrich, you're on the do-not-communicate list—incommunicado."

"Fuck that. I need a unit at my house now, please. It's urgent," she said.

"I'm not getting on the old man's bad side for you, no matter how hot you . . . *used* to be. I heard about the face thing."

"Fuck you, Ryan," Monica screamed and hit End Call. She could only see out of her right eye, and her head was pounding, but she kept driving. Monica swerved from lane to lane, head on a constant swivel, trying to best utilize her handicap as safely as possible.

She saw her house as she rounded the curb at the top of the hill on Miracle Lane. Her front door was open, and from the looks of it, only the kitchen light was on. Porscha's Mini Cooper was still in the driveway, parked too close to the road.

Monica pulled to the curb in front of her house, threw the car into Park, and jumped out, not bothering to turn it off. She took the steps two at a time and burst through the door with her gun drawn. She flicked on the light and froze in horror as the sight of what had happened there came into full view.

Porscha was stuck to the couch like a human pin cushion with more than a dozen knives protruding from her bloody body. A meat cleaver was buried in her skull, and her mouth was wide open with a butcher's knife lodged in her throat to pin her head to the wall behind her. Her eyes were wide open and frozen in terror as if she'd witnessed some gruesome spectacle. Monica followed Porscha's gaze and nearly fainted. Hanging from the upstairs banister was Noisy Boy. His leash had been tied to the railing, and he'd been tossed over. His blue eyes bulged, ready to pop out of his boxlike head. His tongue hung sloppily from his mouth, and his feet jutted downward as if he had been trying to stretch his legs to find footing on the ground below.

Monica pushed past Noisy Boy's dangling body as she ran to Millie's room. The wood of the banister creaked and crackled underneath Noisy Boy's weight, making the darkened house seem even creepier. She put her hand on the doorknob of the baby's room but then stopped. She tried to mentally prepare herself for what lay ahead. Monica took a deep breath. Tears welled in her eyes and threatened to break the floodgates at any moment.

She stepped into the room, turned on the lights, and immediately fell to her knees. She wept uncontrollably, sobs shaking her body. Millie lay in her crib, breathing peacefully, unaware of the atrocities that had taken place in their home. Monica shook with joy as she watched her baby girl sleep. Millie lay on her side with her hands cupped underneath her chin like a sleeping angel. Her hair was matted to her head in large black ringlets, and a slight, barely visible smile was spread across her tiny face.

A cell phone lay on top of a note in the far corner of Millie's crib. In the opposite corner was a teddy bear with a bloody butcher's knife buried in its chest. The note had been crudely made with letters cut from magazines and circular fliers that read: *I Am a King Amongst Peasants and a Wolf Among Sheep. Long Live the King.*